Shakespeare's Will

Meredith Whitford

Copyright © Meredith Whitford 2010, 2018

Published by Bewrite Books (UK) 2010
E-book published by Endeavour Media Ltd (UK)

Published by Vivid Publishing (2018)
P.O. Box 948, Fremantle
Western Australia 6959
www.vividpublishing.com.au

National Library of Australia Cataloguing-in-Publication data:
Author: Whitford, Meredith, author.
Title: Shakespeare's Will / Meredith Whitford.
ISBN: 978-1-925681-88-8 (paperback)
Subjects: Australian fiction.
Dewey Number: A823.4

Also by Meredith Whitford

Treason

Churchill's Rebels: Jessica Mitford & Esmond Romilly

Missing Christina

All books published as e-books by Endeavour Media Ltd, UK.
Paperback versions are available from Amazon and other online
book stores, and selected retailers.

Except for the Dark Lady, the boy Nol and Anne's old cousin, everyone in this novel actually existed. Although the author followed historical data, their characters, emotions and actions are her own invention and any resemblance to any real living person is entirely coincidental.

***

The only spelling of his name that Shakespeare never used was 'Shakespeare'. His extant signatures, and the way his name was spelt in official records ('Shagsper', 'Shaxberd') suggest that in his time his name was pronounced with a short 'a' in the first syllable, and an unstressed second syllable. His actual last will and testament, dated in 1660, was headed 'Shackspeare' and signed 'Shakespere'. Only in print was he, for technical reasons, 'Shakespeare'. In this novel I've used 'Shakspere' as a half-and-half measure.

'Wriothesley' is pronounced 'Rizley'. 'Henry' was always pronounced 'Harry'.

Many biographies of Shakespeare use a multiplier of 500 to convert money in his time to ours. Other sources use a multiplier of 100. A mark was worth two-thirds of a pound.

Dedication

For my family and friends, and in memory of my birth mother.
In addition, I thank the late Neil Marr for loving this book and
being the first to publish it.

.

Portia: "… Am I yourself
But, as it were, in sort or limitation,
To keep with you at meals, comfort your bed,
And talk to you sometimes? Dwell I but in the suburbs
Of your good pleasure? If it be no more,
Portia is Brutus' harlot, not his wife."

Julius Caesar, Act 2, Scene 1.

Part One

1582

1.

The clock's gilded hand jerked forward. Another minute gone. Another thirty and the bell would ring for end of market, eleven o'clock and home for dinner. The crowds were thinning; most people shopped earlier in the day, when it was cooler. Other stalls were closing up, packing away their goods. He dared not follow suit, for his father was strict and every penny counted, dare not miss a sale. But under the counter, propped open, Ovid took him far from Stratford's Thursday market, took him, as he stroked the leather binding, back to Lancashire and earnings to buy books, then as he sank into the words, into the world he wanted to be his.

But into that world came duty, trade, a woman saying, "...in fact *selling* gloves?"

He looked up, the vendor's patter ready on his tongue. Saw grey eyes, dark hair under a straw hat, an amused smile. A familiar face.

"Anne. Mistress Hathaway."

"I wondered if you would remember me."

"Of course, why should I not? I've not been away that long. Two years."

"I had heard you were back. You should have come to call on us."

"My father keeps me busy. As you see."

"Yet somehow I forced my way through the eager crowds."

"You're right, trade is poor today. But just the same..."

"Well, cheer up, it's about to improve a little, for although I am glad to see you again, I really do need to buy gloves."

"Mistress, you shall have gloves; the finest in all England, the finest in the known world. Cheveril? Deerskin? Pigskin? Your

1

size, madam, and the colour you prefer? For everyday or something finer?"

"Brisk and business-like; that's the way. The finest in Stratford will do. I don't know my size, and I want the gloves for best. When did you return?"

"Last week."

"And bored already?"

"And bored already. Give me your hand."

She had already taken off her own gloves. He took her hand, stroking her fingers straight, the finger and thumb of his right hand encircling her wrist. When they were children he had often clasped her hand to gain her attention for his chatter or to keep up with her as they walked. This, now, was a different touch. She was a farmer's daughter, a country woman, but hers was no housewife's hand, red and scarred and rough from work. Of course, the Hathaways were well-to-do. Their daughters didn't labour in the fields and Anne could afford the rosewater he smelt on her skin. He liked the trusting way her small, sun-browned hand lay in his.

She was looking at him oddly, the beginning of a frown pulling her dark brows together. Quickly he smoothed a glove onto her hand.

"See how sweetly it fits, how smoothly, how…"

"Fittingly?" That made him laugh. "You are very poetic for a glover."

"But 'glover' is very close to 'lover', and must a lover not be poetic, Mistress?"

"You may well be a lover, sir, but to me you are a glover."

"I would be both, lady."

"Maybe, but I am in the market for gloves, not love."

"Give me first refusal when you do shop for love, Mistress."

"But I do not look to *purchase* love."

"Nay, I give it freely."

"So if 'love' is close to 'glove', you must give me the gloves freely – which is just as well, for I do not require crimson gloves, and nor can I afford them."

"But the crimson becomes you. With your hair, your eyes. Yes, crimson. Try the other glove, if you will not try my love."

Resistless, laughing, she tried the other glove. Cheveril was the most expensive leather, and *crimson* gloves… "Your father knows

2

his business when he leaves you in charge. I will take them. But I must have some plainer ones as well. Yes, those."

"Will you have them sent? May I bear them like a gift to you?"

"No, *I* will bear them: or at least I'll wear them. Best wrap up the crimson ones." As he did so and she thrust them deep into her basket, she said, "Where is it you've been, William? In the north, wasn't it?"

"Yes. Lancashire."

"Beautiful?"

"If you like moss. No – it has its own kind of beauty, much wilder than here. Fewer people."

"At least you've travelled. I've been no more than five miles from Stratford all my life."

"And would you like to?"

"Very much. Doubt I ever will, though; ordinary women like me don't. I would like to see London."

"Tell you a secret – and it really is a secret – I was supposed to come straight home from Lancashire but I told some lies, fudged the time I was to leave, and I went to London. I had a whole week there."

"Oh," she sighed, "and is it marvellous? Beautiful?"

"Full of marvels, and beautiful in lots of ways. Also crowded, dirty, noisy. And I loved it."

As if by way of punctuation the bell rang for the close of market. And, prompt as conscience, came the voice of Anne's stepmother at her shoulder.

"So there you are! I've been looking everywhere for you, we'll be late home. Have you bought the cascara for Tom's constipation?"

"Yes, Mother."

"And the flannel?"

"Yes, Mother."

"Then come along."

"I must pay for my gloves. I'll catch you up." Putting the money on the counter she said quickly, softly to William, "Will you come to visit us? You're always welcome. Please do."

"I would like that. I haven't forgotten the way."

"Good." Mrs Hathaway was waiting, staring back at her. "I must go."

"Yes. Goodbye."

They were barely out of earshot when Anne's stepmother said, "You'll get yourself a name as a trollop, flirting and giggling with shopkeepers' apprentices like that."

"I wasn't flirting, I was buying gloves. Though I may have laughed once or twice. And he's no apprentice, he's Mr Shakspere's eldest son."

"Oh!" You could tell Joan Hathaway's mood by the way she walked. Now she twitched her bum like a cross cat. "And of course you and the Shakspere's are on such *close* terms."

"Father was friendly with Mr Shakspere, as you know. He came to Father's funeral."

"But wouldn't stay for so much as the usual drink."

Anne said nothing. The fact was that in marrying Anne's father, Joan Hathaway had risen a little above her station in life. Her father had been a hired man on one of the Earl of Warwick's estates, so a prosperous widower of some standing, whose family had for many years farmed ninety leasehold acres, was quite a catch for her. Of course her own people were respectable, but they had no position, no roots going generations-deep into the life and management of Warwickshire's community.

These things counted in the country, and people like the Shakspere's, the mercantile class that ran the towns and inherited their land, were courteous to her as Mrs Richard Hathaway, but no more. Even after thirteen years she didn't quite speak the language, as it were, she didn't know her way through the web of relationships and feuds and alliances. Anne's own mother had called Mrs Shakspere 'Mary' and talked of childhood days at Wilmcote and traced connections through third cousins who had married second cousins' in-laws; Joan Hathaway curtseyed when they met and called her Mrs Shakspere.

After a few more steps: "Not that the Shakspere's are so grand these days." Twitch, twitch. "They say he's losing money hand over fist... Still... Large family, isn't it?"

"Five children."

"How old?"

"William would be eighteen now, Gilbert sixteen or so. Joan's about thirteen, Richard a few years younger. Then there is the little boy, Edmund; he's two." Well used to her stepmother's mental processes, such as they were, Anne knew she was matching these ages with those of her own four children. John

4

Shakspere might be having money troubles now, but things could change, and he had been an alderman and Bailiff of Stratford, he owned that big house on Henley Street besides other land, he had a finger in many pies, and his wife had been an Arden. A Shakspere son of ten, a Hathaway daughter of eight. Come to that, a Shakspere son of two, a Hathaway daughter of six... It was never too soon to plan.

"Didn't they have to send that William boy away?"

"Someone found him work in the country, tutoring a gentleman's sons."

"Hmm. Well, if he's only eighteen there's no use your flirting with him. Not at your age."

"No, Mother." What had happened to change this woman from a kind stepmother, a friend, into this carping, sour-tempered nag? Well, grief, of course, the uncertain future as a widow... and yet... That night last year when Anne's father had drawn his last breath, and they'd known it for the last, Anne and her stepmother had turned instinctively into each other's arms for comfort, united as if they were truly mother and daughter. They'd wept together, and could begin the business of death only because they had each other.

Then, next day, it was as if they were barely acquainted. Anne suspected, and disliked herself for the suspicion, that this first storm of emotion had been only shock, that her stepmother had felt no more than a workaday fondness for her husband, and resented others' real grief, or took it as a reproach.

Whatever the cause, within three months Anne's brother Bartholomew had married and moved twenty miles away, her sister Catherine had married the first man who asked her, and Anne was trapped with a woman who valued her only as child-minder, maid, housekeeper. A woman who seemed to dislike her. A woman who was inclining more and more to Puritanism. And no doubt that was Anne's present offence: that she'd laughed and enjoyed herself with the glover's son. Remembering their silly banter, she almost laughed aloud; just in time she turned it into a cough and a murmur about the dusty road.

And if the glover's son remembers, Anne thought, and if he comes to visit Grafton, I might have someone I can talk to.

By the time William closed up the market stall, returned the goods to the shop and put the meagre takings into his father's strongbox, it was midday. He was hungry; breakfast, at five had been only the heel of a loaf and some argumentative cheese. As he went from the grubby, dusty hall to the empty dining parlour, then to the kitchen, he allowed himself a memory of this house before he'd gone away. Then, he would have come home to the smells of cleanliness and good food cooking, to the cheerful sounds of a family gathering for dinner. The table would have been laid, the silver and pewter would have gleamed, there would have been flowers in every room. His mother would have come to meet him with a smile and a glad but casual kiss.

Now, nothing. No one about. In the kitchen there were no signs of dinner, or not unless you counted a bowl of apple slices in water and a dubious piece of cooked beef on the table. He looked at this, and realised it was crawling with maggots. Feeling sick, he took it on the tip of his knife and went to the back yard to throw it to the dog.

"Oh, William, you're back."

Comfortable in the sunshine, where rosebushes surrounded a tended patch of grass, his mother sat sprawled in a cushioned chair, suckling the two-year-old Edmund. The dreaming adoration with which she watched the child faded to indifference as she glanced up at her eldest son.

"Yes, I'm –"

"Good takings today?"

"Not bad."

Edmund was trying to wriggle away from his mother. A sweet-natured child for all his mother's spoiling, Edmund had been enchanted, not alarmed, to have an unknown brother come into his life. Perhaps it was only the charm of novelty, but William was his favourite person. "Will. See Will."

"No, my pet…"

"See *Will*." He battered at his mother's clutching hands.

"He's growing spoilt, Mother," said William, wishing she would fasten her dress.

"You are jealous."

"No." As flatly as she had spoken, he repudiated the statement. Two when his brother Gilbert was born, William could not remember the halcyon time when he had been the only child and longed-for son, all the more precious because two earlier children had died. After Gilbert, baby had followed baby at a steady pace, and only when Anne, the short-lived Anne, was born had William noticed that with each birth the present children ceased to matter to their mother. Perhaps he had been jealous of Gilbert; of the others, no, because he loved his siblings and even a toddler knew that babies must take up a lot of time. But after Richard, born when William was eight, there had been no more babies, and once he was breeched the four children had basked equally in their parents' attention.

Then, after eight years, there had been Edmund, or at least the announcement of another baby, and once more Mrs Shakspere forgot her other children and decided to resent her eldest son. Suddenly he must leave school, forget university, go out to work. Younger, he might have blamed and envied the new child, but at sixteen he knew about his father's money troubles, had even been consulted; he could accept his duty.

Now, returned after two years as an adult, he saw that his mother valued her children only for their dependence upon her; she existed to be needed as a source of food and bodily intimacy, to fill her babies' world. As grown or growing people, they held little interest for her. She was over forty now, and coldly William wondered if she realised there would be no more babies and that Edmund wanted to chase after his brothers and play with other children. Already he was pushing away her proffered breast, was impatient with cuddles and being held upon her lap.

As now. Escaping his mother, Edmund ran to William, clamouring to be picked up. William swung him up onto his shoulders, laughing as the infant grabbed his hair, then saw the flash of malice in his mother's eyes and felt as if the sun had gone behind a cloud.

"Mother…"

"I have all the work of him all day then you come home and play with him until he's overexcited and crying. Your father is the same."

"Perhaps we simply love him."

That was trespassing too far on her preserves. "Loving a child takes more than half an hour at noon or evening when all is done for you. Give him to me."

"Edmund stay with Will," the child announced.

"Mother," William tried again, "it is dinner time, I've worked hard, there is no dinner ready, the maid's not here …"

"Where is your sister?"

He sighed. "I don't know."

"She is thirteen. I look to her to help me."

"And so she does. Mother, can we not afford another maid? Can't we hire a girl to do the rough work?"

She gave a harsh, ironic laugh. "Ask your father why we cannot afford another maid – two, three, and a cook, as we used to have." Slowly, reluctantly, she fastened her dress. "I married a well-to-do man who could afford a proper living. Now I have to send my children out to work. Gilbert is to leave school at the end of the month and be apprenticed to a haberdasher. And you, my boy, are to take work as an usher at the grammar school."

"Truly?"

"Yes. Then your father can take on another apprentice; we need the indenture money."

The hand with which she laced her bodice still bore its jewelled gold rings and, much as he knew they were the last, cherished symbols of the wealthy Arden lady and Alderman's wife she had once been, William often longed to point out that just one of them would buy the services of a cook and several maids. Or would have paid for his three years at university.

"I shan't mind working at the grammar school, although I could do better. Is it certain? It's been arranged?"

"When we knew you were coming home."

"Thanks for telling me."

"Don't speak to me like that, William. Turn your clever tongue on your father. It was his idea. You'll start next quarter-day."

"I shan't mind," he repeated. "But I am eighteen, Mother, too old to have decisions made for me willy-nilly. And if it's only a matter of money, then let me go to London, I've told you I could earn more there."

"Being a common theatre player! A mummer!"

"Why not? The theatre is in fashion in London and –"

"In fashion it may be; respectable it will never be. We may not be noble people but you are an Arden and a Shakspere, you come of old families with some position and standing. The Ardens – "

"I know. Are the oldest family in Warwickshire. We have noble kinsmen. I am well aware of it."

"And think it a matter for mockery, I see."

"Not at all. But must we never do anything new?"

"Not if it means something like the theatre."

Unwisely, desperately, he persisted. "It's not as if I have no experience, I —"

"What 'experience', pray?"

"Mother, please listen! For Sir Alexander de Hoghton, then for Sir Thomas Hesketh."

"But you went to Lancashire as a tutor. Teaching schoolboys. Not to strut around in fancy dress."

"Parliament passed an act against unlicensed schoolmasters. It was safer and easier to keep me on as one of his private troupe of players and musicians. So you see, Mother…"

But she turned it against him, mocking, "Much ice a few private mummings would cut in London. What'll you do, boy, go to some lord whose players have performed for the Queen and whine, 'Please, sir, I once entertained some country people in the north'?"

"I'm a little better than that. There could be money in it."

"Ha!"

"And I think I could write for the theatre, I wrote a play —"

"You! No, you'll work at the grammar school and that's flat."

"When I'm of age…"

"Oh, no doubt you'll do what you like then. No doubt you'll turn your back on your dull and humble parents and your dull and humble country town and get yourself appointed Master of the Queen's Revels." She reached up for Edmund who, bored because William showed no sign of playing any of his usual games, went happily into her arms. Over his head she stared up at William, her face icy. "Do what you like when you are twenty-one, but until then you will do what your parents tell you."

2.

Another morning in the workshop, stitching gloves until his eyes ached, then an afternoon spent making deliveries and running errands for his father. "Take the horse," his father said, "and wear your best clothes. Be polite and make a good impression."

At least it got him out of house and shop, into the summer countryside, and there was no limit set on the time of his return. Out of anyone's sight, in the country roads, he dawdled, free for once to think and daydream without interruption. At home there was always noise, some demand.

Late in the afternoon he realised he should have planned his round more carefully, for he was riding west, into the sun. It was a hot day and he was thirsty. He pulled his hat lower over his eyes, remembering with pleasure that going west would take him past Shottery, where the Hathaways lived. He had one last delivery to make, then on his way home he could stop at Hewlands Farm and beg a drink. Maybe Anne would be there. He had liked her that day at market. She was the only person he had met since he came home who didn't meet his jokes with a blank stare.

Then, as if his thoughts had conjured her up, he saw her. He recognised her at once, even though she was hopping and stumbling down the road. For an instant he wondered if she was drunk or suffered from the falling sickness, then as he drew closer he saw she was merely favouring her right foot.

"Madam! Anne! What's wrong? Can I help?" He reined in, and swung down from the saddle.

"Oh, William. What are you doing out here?"

He held out his arm for her hand, letting her lean on him. "Deliveries for my father. Sprained your ankle?"

"Turned it," she said through clenched teeth. "I climbed a gate instead of opening it. I jumped down and fell awkwardly. It's nothing much, but it does hurt."

"Are you on your way home?"

"Yes, from Temple Grafton. It's only another half mile."

"I know. I'll take you home. You can ride up in front of me on the horse."

"I'd be grateful," she said. "Thank you. If it's not taking you too far out of your way?"

"Not at all. It will hurt your ankle somewhat, getting up, but there's no help for it, I'm afraid." Wincing, she put her weight on her right foot. He took her left in his hands and tossed her up. She had to scramble to get her seat, clutching the horse's mane, then she nodded and he put his foot in the stirrup and mounted up behind her. The horse had stood patiently, and now walked on when he shook the reins.

After a moment he said, "It will be easier if you lean back against me. I'm afraid you'll have to take off your hat."

She did so, holding it rolled against her knee. Her hair was a pretty shade of dark brown, shot through with autumn-leaf colours. She must have washed it not long since, for over the dust of the road and her fresh sweat, he could smell soap and rosemary. She was a slender woman and not tall; she fitted nicely into the curve of his arm, against his shoulder. He had never held a woman so closely before, even in all innocence like this. Before he went to Lancashire he'd taken little interest in girls, and, there, he had been closely supervised. One of the maidservants had kissed him at Christmas and made it plain he need not stop at kissing, but she had been a loose and reechy girl, as repellent as attractive, and he had taken fright. The gentle swell of Anne's breast was pressing against his arm. Nothing he could do about that, even had he wanted to.

As if conscious of the same thing, she shifted a little to sit more upright. "Are you still bored with Stratford?" she asked, making conversation.

"Yes." He saw her eyebrows lift and realised how short he had sounded. "Sorry. But yes, I am bored. I can't help it. Aren't you ever bored with your life?'

"Often. Not much I can do about it, though. I suppose it is worse for you, having been away, having experienced other things and places, I mean."

"It's partly that. And… well, my parents won't listen. They want the best for me, I suppose, but it's the same old things, same old ideas as if I were still a child. I'm to work at the grammar school, usher to the little boys."

"And you don't want that?"

"It's not what I would choose but I don't mind it. I quite liked being a tutor, although that was in a private house. But – if I tell you, you won't laugh?"

"Of course not," she said gently.

"I told you at market last week that I had gone to London. Well, while I was there I went to the playhouses, all of them, and I saw every play I could. And that is what I want to do. To be a player. To join one of the theatre companies. My parents won't hear of it, of course."

"Perhaps they think you're too young yet."

"It's not only that. They say it's not respectable, but what they mean is that no one in our family has ever done anything like that before, therefore no one ever shall. *I* shall not."

"You're the eldest son. Your father must want you to take over his business."

"Perhaps he does, eventually, but for now it's the grammar school. I have to earn. My brother Gilbert, too. I'm to be an usher, Gilbert a haberdasher, probably Richard's to work for Father in a year or two. Meanwhile Father kills two birds with one stone – sends us out to work and gets the indenture from the apprentices he takes on in the business. Not that I'll earn much as a junior usher. It's not as if I have a university degree. I could probably make more as a player but of course they won't hear of it."

"Perhaps they just don't want you to go away. Their eldest son must be special to them."

"They sent me away before when I was only sixteen, and sent me much further than to London."

"You resent that?"

It was the first time he had thought of it in just those terms. "I think I do, a little. I did miss my home and family, at least at first. But I enjoyed those two years. I wanted to stay on in the north, but my employer died and there were other difficulties. Catholic sympathies."

"Ah."

Her eyes were grey, a soft clear colour emphasised by the darkness of her brows and lashes. She was not quite pretty, but she had something; any man would call her attractive. He tried to remember how old she was, how much older than he. Certainly old enough to have been trusted to mind him and his brother when they were children.

Not knowing why he said something so dangerous, except that he liked her eyes and she was the only person who had ever listened to him, he said, "My father too. Catholic sympathies. He conforms, of course, and I've not seen him do anything open, but it's – well, it's one of those things that are known within a family. I hope it's no more than sympathies." Belatedly, more boyishly than he realised, he added, "You won't repeat that to anyone, will you?"

"Of course not. For one thing, you told me in confidence; for another, your father was my father's friend. Plenty of Catholic sympathisers around here, too."

"But not you?"

"No. My stepmother and brother incline to Puritanism, but my father was staunchly Church of England. I do what is lawful."

"Me too," he said, and laughed. "And sometimes I do what is right."

"Often not the same thing, I agree."

"No. But, to be both right and lawful, I shall stay here obeying my parents until I'm of age. Three years."

"And then?"

"I shall do what I want. Go to London. Try to join one of the playing companies. And – this is what I meant before when I hoped you wouldn't laugh. I know how it sounds, but…"

"Tell. I shan't laugh."

"Well then, I think I could write."

She didn't laugh. She said, puzzled, "Write? Books?"

"I meant plays. Poetry too, perhaps. I am sure I could. Always I have such ideas; words, tales and legends. I wrote, well, helped with, a masque for Lord Stanley when I was in the north, and I know I could write." He caught her eye. "I suppose I only mean I want to."

"I've never known anyone who even thought of such things, but I'm sure you could. Have you ever tried? Writing a play, I mean."

"Er, no, not really."

"And your experience is limited to the plays you saw during your week in London?"

"There is no need," he said stiffly, "to make fun of me."

"I wasn't. But I do think that perhaps you're not yet quite equipped to take London by storm. And making plays might be harder than you think. If your parents won't let you go away, you've got three years. You might as well make use of the time.

Look, I know it's not exactly London, but my cousin Frances married Mr Davy Jones in Stratford and he has a little troupe of mummers. He sometimes puts on a play."

"I don't know him."

"I could introduce you. You could ask him if you could write something for his players. Perhaps you could take part. It's a start. You could write something and next time one of the touring companies is in town, you could show it to them; get a professional opinion."

"That's good sense. Would you really introduce me to Mr Jones?"

"Nothing simpler."

"Thank you. And, if I wrote something, would you... I mean... could I show it to you? Read it to you?"

"Oh, William, I'm no judge. I'd have no idea."

"Why not? You've seen plays. And you're a clever woman."

"You'd better stop."

"I didn't mean to sound impertinent."

"No, I meant you're about to go past our gate."

"Oh." He had been so swept up in his grievances that he had forgotten she was more than a chance-come-by and welcome listener. "I'm sorry, I forgot. Is your ankle very bad?"

"Better for not walking on it. If you could set me down now..."

"Oh no, I'll see you inside, help you. Is there someone at home to care for you?" Earnestly he said, "You should soak your foot in cold water, then bandage it up." Leaning down, he unhooked the gate and kicked it open. The horse seemed to remember it had been here before, and approved, for it walked contentedly into the farmyard behind the house.

"My stepmother's probably at home. The maids will be."

"I'll help you in," he insisted. She began to demur, but when he dismounted and lifted her down and she put weight on her damaged foot, she gasped and he saw her turn pale. Quickly he put his arm around her. Then, with a better idea, he simply lifted her up in his arms and carried her into the house.

Anne's home was a large, handsome house, built on a slope running down to a brook. To one side was an orchard, to the other a spreading kitchen garden. The kitchen into which William carried Anne was broad and low-ceilinged, spotless, and full of good cooking smells. Two maidservants, three children and a little, round, fair-haired woman all turned to stare at Anne in a strange man's arms.

"Mother," she said hastily, "I turned my ankle – nothing too bad – and very luckily William Shakspere found me on the way and gave me a ride home. William, you remember my stepmother, Mrs Hathaway."

"Of course. Good afternoon, madam."

"Good day to you." Mrs Hathaway dried her hands on her apron, looking William over. "It's very kind of you, Master William."

"Not at all. Mistress Anne should soak her ankle in cold water. Could I fetch water from the well?"

"Tom will do it," said Anne. The stout boy, about ten, didn't move. "Please, Thomas."

When he still didn't move William said easily, "It would be too heavy for him. Let me fetch it. Can I set you down somewhere?"

"It's not too heavy for me!"

"Well, if you're sure."

"Clever," Anne whispered as the child shot out the door. Aloud she added, "Mother, I shan't be in your way; William, if you don't mind taking me to the dining parlour. You remember where it is?"

"Of course." And he carried her through the connecting door. Here too everything was very clean and tidy. There were excellent pewter and brass pieces on the mantel and sideboard, handsome furniture, three painted hangings. The air smelt of lavender, beeswax polish and the flowers that stood in an earthenware jug. The table, covered with a crimson cloth, had chairs and benches arranged around it. William deposited Anne in one of these and knelt to undo her boot.

"You needn't."

"Sorry." Awkwardly he stood up.

"No, I'm sorry, I didn't mean to sound offended. It's just that I'm not used to people helping me."

"Then let me."

He knelt down again as she leaned forward. Their heads cracked painfully together.

"Sorry!"

"No, my fault." Feeling stupid, he whisked the boot undone.

One of the little girls from the kitchen came in, very carefully clutching a tray on which stood two pewter tankards. "Please, sir, Mother says you're to have a cup of ale for your kindness to Anne."

"Thanks." He grabbed the tankards before they could spill.

"One's for Anne. And Mother says you must stay to supper."

"How very kind of her. But I am afraid I cannot." He handed Anne her drink.

"Oh."

"Another time, perhaps?" Anne said, then blushed.

"I'd like that. Er – excellent ale."

"Anne brewed it," said the little girl. "She's good at that."

"She is indeed. What's your name?"

"Frances. What's yours?"

"William."

"My little brother's name is William."

"There are a lot of us about. Frances is a pretty name."

"I know. Anne has a cousin Frances."

"Yes I have," she said quickly. "But I haven't seen her lately. Frances, ask mother for some bandages for my ankle, please." When the child had gone she said quietly, "Don't mention what we were talking about to my stepmother, please. I'll arrange it, but she… Well, best not to mention it."

"All right. The children are your stepmother's?"

"Yes, my half-brothers and sisters. Four of them; Frances, Margaret, Thomas and William. My own brother and sister – you'll remember Bartholomew and Catherine – are both married now and moved away."

"I see. Should I go to help Thomas with the water?"

"Yes. Oh – no."

Heaving and staggering under the weight, slopping water everywhere, the child dumped the bucket down in front of Anne. "Does it hurt a lot?"

"If I stand on it."

"Don't stand on it, then," he said with a smirk William would have enjoyed smacking off his face. Instead, he gave the brat the look that worked on his own younger brothers, and Thomas fled. Affecting great interest in the proverb on one of the painted hangings, William turned away so Anne could in modesty take her stocking off; also he didn't want to discover she had ugly legs.

When he heard the rustle of skirts again he turned back. Grimacing, she was dipping her toes into the water. She had pretty ankles. Very pretty.

"All the way in," he said too loudly. "Plunge it in. Your foot. Into the water."

"I know, but it's straight from the well, and cold."

"That's the idea. Go on, screw up your courage to the sticking point." She did so. "And keep it in. All the way in. Until the water's no longer cold. Then bandage it." He finished his ale and put the tankard down, too sharply. "I had better go."

"If you must. But if you would like to come again? For supper?"

"Please."

"Good. Although... no, that's all right... I may be going to stop with an elderly cousin of mine over at Temple Grafton, it's she I was visiting today. I, er, I..."

Gently, remembering something she had said, drawing a conclusion from her family's unconcern today, he said, half under his breath, "I'm not the only one unhappy at home."

"Quite right," she answered as softly. "Useful to have an elderly cousin whose daughter is going away. But I'll see you next market day. Thursday. Could you be free for dinner? I'll arrange it with my cousin Frances."

"Thank you. But don't mention what we talked about to my parents, please."

"Of course not. William, thank you for helping me today. I'm sure I've held you up; please explain to your father and give him my apologies and thanks."

"I shall. I hope your ankle mends soon. Well, goodbye."

"Goodbye."

"Good manners, that boy," Mrs Hathaway said when she came to remove the bucket.

"Yes, he's a very pleasant lad."

"Good looking, too."

Bent over to bandage her ankle, Anne didn't have to meet the other woman's eye. "I suppose so," she said indifferently. "Takes after his father. His mother's much lighter in colouring. By the way, Mother, my cousin's daughter said that if you can spare me she would like to go away on Monday. She wants to see her new grandchild in Bristol."

"I can spare you."

"Then I'll send word that I'll be at Temple Grafton on Monday."

"Very well. Don't encourage that Shakspere boy to hang around you. Hè's far too young, but people will still talk."

"Oh, Mother," said Anne, "don't be so ridiculous."

3.

"Summer's lease has all too short a date," said William.

"Quite right," said Anne. "Pass the wine."

Instead, he took her cup and refilled it. Putting the cup into her hand, folding her fingers around it, he said, "That was rather well put, don't you think? The summer's lease bit?"

Half asleep from wine and sun Anne said, "Very well put. Poetical. But what do you know about leases?"

"Quite a lot now from tending Father's business matters for him and clerking for the local lawyer. Writing letters, doing accounts, juggling mortgages, avoiding creditors. Mind you, it's better than making gloves. I might work that summer's lease bit into the play. Tactfully."

The note in his voice made her open her eyes and smile at him. "They're really not very good, are they, the local mummers."

"Better than nothing, though."

"Poor Will."

"It'd be Poor Will and no mistake if I hadn't you to talk to."

"And to introduce you to Davy Jones's players, despite their shabby standard."

"Not only for that."

"Because I read what you write?"

And he *could* write. All summer he'd been bringing Anne bits of plays and even poems. Laughing, she had protested that she was no judge. She could read and write a little, because her father had admired the learned Queen Elizabeth and thought that in changing times it did no harm for all his children to have some literacy (her stepmother disagreed, to the point where Anne's two books had to be hidden, smuggled out of the house when she came to tend her ancient cousin) and she had seen some plays, by those troupes William's father and the Stratford council had paid, but that was all. Surely, she had said, he could find someone more fit to read his efforts? No he couldn't, he said, and continued to bring her whatever he wrote.

Now he said, with an odd intensity, "It's not only because you introduced me to Davy Jones, or read my work. I like you, Anne, I like your company."

"But one day you'll go away to London."

"Years from now. I was to have gone to university, Anne. Both my parents wanted it. But Father's had such money troubles it's impossible."

"I'm sorry. But at least you can plan such a future. For me, a woman, it's marriage or helping rear my half-brothers and half-sisters and dwindling into an old maid who's never been five miles from where she was born. Or an old housewife who's never been away."

"Why aren't you married? Are all the local men blind? Or stupid?"

Anne knew she should have told him he was impertinent, or that she was unimpressed by boyish flattery, but he'd spoken so matter-of-factly. And she *was* flattered.

"I've had offers, but none of them appealed. My father was a little choosy on my behalf; he died only last year, you see. My stepmother had one of her Puritan friends lined up for me, a pig-farmer, and I refused. That's why she's angry with me."

She glanced across at the old lady sleeping so peacefully in her cushioned chair in the sun. "I let my stepmother think I don't like being here, that it's close to a penance, but I love my cousin and no one could be less demanding, so it's a holiday for me here." One old lady, even a half-crippled and frail one, and a three-room cottage, after a big house, three maids, a stepmother, four children under twelve, five farmhands, harvest, all the work of a busy household and a farm… "A holiday," she repeated.

"Holiday for me too, coming here." William grinned and poured them both another glass of wine.

"But summer's lease, as you just said… Autumn soon, then winter, and I'll have to go home when my cousin's daughter returns."

"Something will turn up." He leaned back comfortably against her bench, his head close to her knees. Roses surrounded this tiny garden, their scent heavy as smoke on the air. All the other flowers of summer, the lazy humming of bees, the occasional chatter of birds, the purling of the stream not far away, an azure sky with lambs-tails of clouds, a sun so hot William was in his shirtsleeves and Anne had taken off her shoes and stockings and her cap, and had pinned her hair high up on her head.

Nights so hot Anne slept naked in her bed, and woke from dreams of wantonness. Dreams which, rather too often, featured this charming hazel-eyed boy. *Boy.* Eighteen was a man's age, but eighteen against her own twenty-five. It was ludicrous. She should go home, make peace with her stepmother and marry the pig-farmer. When she needed gloves she'd buy them from the Shakspere shop and ask William if he ever remembered the days when he'd wanted to be an actor. Perhaps one of her children would marry one of William's. He'd have pretty children, because he'd marry a golden-haired, blue-eyed girl with big breasts.

"Ouch!"

"What's the matter?"

"You kicked me." He looked at her reproachfully.

"Cramp. Sorry."

Perhaps it was William's exclamation that woke Anne's cousin, for the old lady stirred, blinking, and struggled up against her cushions. Glad of the excuse, Anne rose and went over to her.

"Is there anything you want, cousin? Are you too hot?"

"No, I like the sun. Oh, lovey, I've been asleep, haven't I."

"Just for a little. Would you like a drink?"

"Some more of that wine. And the rest of the story." Her faded eyes twinkled at William. She liked his visits, for himself and for his endless fund of stories. She would have stared in puzzlement had she known she was hearing classical works that university men and great ladies knew: Homer, Ovid, Aesop. Chaucer she had heard of, and adored, for she liked a risqué story. When she'd nodded off they'd been in the middle of the Miller's Tale. She never tired of that one. So Anne poured her another cup of wine and William took up effortlessly from where he'd left off.

William stayed to supper, and when the old lady had been put to bed, Anne lit a candle and said, "Go on with the play."

"You really don't mind?"

"Not in the slightest. It interests me. I've seen some plays acted, of course, but never one being made."

"Mended, not made," he said glumly.

"Improved. I'm sure you'll make one of your own some day."

"I will, you know."

"I just said so."

"You were humouring me. Speaking as you would to a child. 'What a lovely toy horse, dear. You'll have a real horsie one day when you're grown.'"

"Have it your own way."

That broke his sudden mood and made him laugh. For a boy just growing into manhood he was remarkably able to laugh at himself. "Know what I really want to do? To be?"

"You've told me – a theatre player. One who can write plays."

"Oh, that," he said with a quick, dismissive gesture. "That, yes, but I'd like to write things that would be valued by literary men, things that would be remembered. Poetry, in fact. But I don't suppose I ever shall because only university men, gentlemen, can write that sort of thing and be taken seriously. Even if I ever do get to London and work in a playhouse, I'd be nothing but a country boy, a jobbing actor who could patch up old plays and at best write a few decent passages of new stuff."

"You don't know that."

"I do know that."

"William, a week in London does not make you an expert."

"Nor did I say it does. But I've a little more than that. In Lancashire I lived with gentlemen, and I was good enough to be an entertainer, a mummer and musician, but that's all. I know how people like that think and what they believe. I was on quite friendly terms with Ferdinando Strange, Lord Strange, you know; the Earl of Derby's son. But when I say 'on friendly terms' I mean that he was kind to a grammar school boy who was tutor to his father's friend's children and not bad at music or playing a part when the gentry wanted entertainment. If I'd told him I wanted to make poetry or plays he would have laughed."

He lifted his cup and swilled the last of his wine in one fast, angry gesture. "That's all I am or ever will be, you see. An uneducated country man, a glover's son, fit for nothing but patching up old Italian plays for a group of country-town mummers, with no one to talk to, no one who can know or understand the sort of things I love, surrounded by illiterate yokels and tradesmen."

"And farmers' daughters."

"Yes."

The silence hummed like the tension left in the air when the plucked string of a lute ends its note.

"I'm sorry," William said helplessly. "I did not mean that."

"Of course you did, and of course you are quite right. That is what I am. A yokel's daughter who can barely read. How boring for you."

"I've hurt you."

"Of course not," said Anne, so hurt she didn't know whether to hit him or weep.

"Of course I have. And I am sorry. But, honestly, I didn't mean what I said in the way you took it."

"How else could I take it? At least I never pretended to be what I am not – your equal."

To her surprise and indignation William looked at her for a moment then swept her up in his arms, kissed her on the mouth, set her down, and shook her. "Now will you listen?"

"You have my attention."

"Good."

"But I don't think you should have kissed me. Or shaken me like that."

"But it got me your attention. If I want to spend an hour of hurt feelings and apologies and being told how cruel and heartless I am, I'll stay at home. Plenty of that there, along with old saws about learning to cut my coat according to my cloth. Listen, Anne, and heed me. I am miserable at home, in Stratford. I want a life I can't have, or at least not for years to come. No one at home has ever read a book, except by way of school work. Nor have most of my friends. I do have friends, of course. I spend most of every day with people who've shot their intellectual bolt when they've talked about the harvest or juicy local gossip.

"You're not learned, but you are clever and interested and quick, and you don't laugh at me because I want things few boys like me want. And I am afraid that when you said that about spending time with a farmer's daughter and I said yes, I was trying to be funny; ironic. So I'm not as clever as I often think. And I hurt your feelings. I insulted a friend. If I hadn't you to talk to, I'd run mad. Oh and don't dare say you're not my equal. In everything but book-learning you are infinitely above me, and my store of learning is small enough. So please forgive me, Anne."

"Are you really that unhappy?"

William took a breath and looked at her warily. "If I say yes, will you think I only mean so unhappy I have to come and pass the time with a farm girl?"

"Not unless it's the truth."

"It's not. I come because I like you and I enjoy myself with you. But yes, I really am unhappy."

Anne rose up, intending to fill their glasses, but there was no wine left. "Ale?"

"Thank you."

"Why are you so unhappy? Apart from what you've just told me."

William drank some ale then sat, turning the cup between his fingers. "You know my family so I don't feel disloyal talking of them. Sometimes I think that if I'd never gone away I would have been perfectly happy with my lot, for I would have known no better. Or perhaps I'm simply at an age to be impatient with them and find them lacking.

"My father has money troubles and my mother can't forgive him that she's no longer a wealthy woman with a houseful of servants and everything her heart desires. She takes no interest in any of us children except the baby. Joan, my sister, is growing up without a mother's care, and she's trying to manage the household with no help or thanks. My brothers are aimless. I'm the eldest so I have to hear everyone's troubles and try to mend them."

"But you don't do too badly," Anne felt obliged to point out. "Your father still has position in Stratford. He's been Bailiff for years, after all. And he has a good business and a very fine house. And a certain amount of money, at least." She touched the sleeve of his doublet. John Shakspere might restrict his son's activities, but he didn't stint on money for clothes. In the last few years London fashions had reached the country, and William wasn't the only young man laughing at out-dated sumptuary laws and going about in embroidered Holland shirts, the best woollen cloth, even velvet and silk. His father dealt in wool and leather, so probably his elegant boots had cost nothing, or had been paid for in trade, but it was doubtful that he wore his best to visit Anne, yet that doublet was the sort of subtle green you didn't buy in a country town's market.

"I bought my clothes out of my Lancashire wages. But of course you are right; many people are much worse off." He took another swig of ale. "Perhaps you are."

"Most people would say I too have little to complain of. But consider my life, William. My father died last year and my family seemed to fall apart. My stepmother and I are barely on speaking terms. Bartholomew and Catherine both married as fast as they could, to get away. The four little children, my father's second family, are dears but they are much younger than me. My stepmother is an excellent housewife and taught me to be the same, but she sincerely believes that's all a woman can want or should expect in life; marry a man with a good house and a little money, have children, run the house and the farm.

"Nothing wrong with that. Except that I am twenty-five and bored. Lonely, too. Bart and Kate gone, my stepmother preaching Puritanism at me and sure that books are the Devil's work. Perhaps they are; perhaps I only prove her point. What makes me different from any other woman? – Nothing except that I've turned my brain with book-reading. I'm not even sure I want anything different. I'll marry one day, probably soon. I've a little money that my father left me. I'm a good catch. I would like children. It's just that I love going to plays and having pretty clothes and reading books and listening to you talking about that sort of thing. All the people I know talk about the harvest, too. And cooking. Worthy, ordinary, and dull."

"You a good cook?"

"Not bad. You a good glover?"

"Not bad. But Anne, you have friends like Davy Jones and his mummers; his wife your cousin."

"So do you."

"True. So you're bored and I am caged. What's to do?"

"Nothing, probably. I do realise that most of my troubles are not troubles at all and it is just that too many things have happened too quickly in my life. A year ago I wasn't discontented. Perhaps in another year I shan't be. Time cures most things."

"And in a little less than three years I will be twenty-one and can kiss Stratford and the glover's shop goodbye. But in three years I probably won't want to. I'll be reconciled to my lot. Resigned, at least."

"Who knows. And you're lucky, you can go away if you want to, do what you like. I can't. Anyway, could your father actually stop you if you left? Could he bring you back?"

"In law I think he could. And somehow I can't quite bring myself just to leave. For all my complaints, I love my family. My father is proud of me and glad I am here to help him. He knows, dimly, that I am not happy, and he often curses himself that he was foolish with money and I can't go to university. It is very hard to walk out on a well-meaning, kind man who blames himself that he cannot make you happy."

The silence stretched, but more comfortably now. At last Anne said, "This isn't getting that play improved for Davy Jones."

"No." But he made no move to take up the papers or his pen. "I've no money," he said sadly.

"I could lend you a little."

"No! No no no no no. I didn't mean that. That's one thing I've learnt from Dad's troubles: don't borrow, don't lend. Especially don't lend. He ran himself into trouble by lending money; usury's illegal, and he was charging high interest on his loans. I'm going to make money, though, one day. No, all I meant was that I don't have enough money to buy the books I want."

"Surely there are sometimes books sold at market? Davy Jones has some. There are rich men around Stratford, men educated enough to have books. Make some friends, go cap in hand to the gentry and ask."

"Perhaps." Now he did take up his pen, a rather fine goose quill that Anne had obtained on a visit home. He spent a moment scanning over his papers and then began to write.

When the candle had marked two hours' passing he sat back, yawning and stretching. "That will have to do for now. Would you care to read it over when you have time? Try to picture it being acted out upon the stage."

"Very well. Though I really am no judge, Will."

"You've seen plays. It's the audience's opinion that counts. I wonder how much a London company would pay for a play. As much as a pound, do you think?"

"Surely not a pound! Perhaps you could find out."

"Yes, perhaps. Anne, it's late and I must go."

"Very well." Much as she enjoyed his company, Anne was sleepy. Like most women, her day began at dawn and she would have to get up to her cousin at least once in the night. "When will you come again?"

"Not sure. My parents are complaining I spend too much time away from home. My father is finding an extraordinary amount of business for me in the evenings."

"Oh."

"I think they suspect I have a girl somewhere."

"Oh," said Anne, dying to ask if he had.

"But I could come next Saturday. Or, no – I thought that on Saturday I might go and look over what costumes and stage things Mr Jones has."

"Saturday is my birthday," Anne said.

William smiled, but she could tell his mind was elsewhere. "Does your family make anything of birthdays?"

"No." But her father had. A little gift, a sweetmeat or a ribbon bought from a pedlar, and something special to eat at dinner. Nothing much, but enough to note the day. Her stepmother disapproved of such frivolity. Of anything that cost money.

"I wish I could give you something," William said earnestly. "I cannot even ask you to dine with my family or anything like that. Well, I could, but it would be no pleasure for you."

Anne laughed, wondering what he would do if she said 'give me another kiss'. "You needn't. I don't know why I even told you. Write me a poem for my birthday."

She was joking, but he nodded and said, "Very well. And I'll come on Saturday."

"No no, you want to go and look at Davy's stage things."

"I could do both. That's if you're interested. Come with me and look at the costumes."

About to say no, Anne realised that he was offering her something he considered a treat. "All right. I can get a village woman to sit with my cousin for an hour or two."

"Then I shall see you on Saturday."

4.

Davy Jones had hopes of the Stratford council sponsoring his little group of mummers. They paid touring companies, he argued, so why not their own? So far the answer had been: because the touring companies are professionals who play in London and have their name-lord behind them. Local men, artisans and mechanicals might do their best, but it is hardly the same. People pay for a touch of London glamour, they pay to see actors who have played for the Queen and court, not to see John Smith from the next street in a wig. Besides, if the touring companies come here it means Stratford is an important town. Jones countered with: but the London companies come perhaps twice a year at most, are Stratford people meant to be content with that? Would, say, ten shillings break the council's budget?

The council hemmed and hawed, but Davy Jones pressed on. He had his little group, he would put on plays regardless, and he would play the political game and work on the men who would be elected to next year's council. Meanwhile, he kept his small stock of costumes and properties in a tiny room at the back of the Guildhall and advertised his performances by word of mouth.

"What's that?" asked Anne, looking at a painted backcloth tacked roughly along the wall, and wishing she had brought a duster.

"A hell's-mouth," said William. "Light a candle, would you please?" He was on his knees prying at the hasp of a trunk. The lock yielded and the lid flew up. He sighed in delight and began to lift the things out.

Anne prowled the little room, touching the strings of a lute, rapping her knuckles on a cauldron, studying something that proved to be a hobby-horse.

"I'm a king," said William, and she turned around and almost cried out.

A long crimson velvet cloak swept from his shoulders to the floor, its ermine bands falling around him. On his head was a golden crown studded with jewels the size of a man's thumb. He held a golden sceptre, and a jewelled gold chain spread across his breast; a sword hung at his side.

He looked taller, older, altogether different. Magnificent. The illusion was complete. He had become a king, and Anne understood.

"Now I see."

"Do you?"

"Yes."

He stared at her, his eyes darker in the candlelight. "Be a queen. Queen Anne."

"I couldn't."

"You could. You can."

He reached out and undid the strings of her cap, threw it aside. A swirl of colour, and a matching cloak fell around her. Gently, and as earnestly as if she were indeed a queen at her coronation, he put a crown on her head.

"Let your hair down."

Even his voice had changed. As shocked as if he had told her to take off her clothes, and as unable to resist as if it were truly a king's command, she pulled the pins and combs from her hair and ran her fingers through the plait as it tumbled down. She only ever trimmed the ends of her hair when they split and grew ragged. It fell past her waist, a shining dark-brown mass, clean and scented because she had taken a bath the day before.

"A queen," he said, and put the crown upon her head. "Jewels for a queen." A rope of pearls for her neck, diamond and ruby rings for her fingers.

It didn't matter that the velvet of the cloaks was worn and rubbed, the ermine only dyed lambs' wool, that the pearls were made of fish scales and glue, the jewels were glass. The crowns and sword were painted wood and tin. But the world of illusion was a double one where falseness was transmuted and seductive. The tiny looking-glass on the wall showed a king and queen, not a woman and a boy in makeshift costumes in a country town.

"King William and Queen Anne."

"They never ruled together."

"Here they do."

In the glass she saw the king bend and kiss the queen. She saw the queen tip her head back so that her veil of hair echoed the fall of the crimson cloak, and accept the kiss as her due.

It was play-acting, of course; playing at playing. A king kissed a queen on their coronation day.

More than that. He kissed her again. She should reprove him, move away, tell him to go. Not just stand here clad in silly clothes, leaning against him, breathing in his warm male smell, letting him play with her hair. But when he closed his arms around her and kissed her again, and harder, she could only say, "Will." And the protest was lost in his mouth. *She* was lost.

Whether he meant anything more than a brotherly, friendly kiss she never knew, because when his mouth touched hers something happened that was quite outside her experience. Just a kiss, an everyday thing – but it was as if lightning leapt between them and set them both afire. Each saw the other's eyes ablaze with swift desire, their bodies seemed to melt together. Helplessly Anne wound her arms around his neck and let his tongue meet hers, drenching her in sweetness. His hands slid up to frame her face, holding her still for his kiss, his lips moved to the corner of her mouth, her eyes, her brow, her throat.

And now it was she who held his face and looked into his eyes and brought her mouth to his, she who held him, caressed him, and made no more resistance when he lifted her up his arms and kissed her in earnest. No bed but the velvet cloaks. Enough.

So this was what all the ado was about. A boy's lean body, a man's hard prick, a poet's tongue, all on a summer's night. Hot breath, hot flesh, hands following mouths, soft endearments, then lovely completion.

Afterwards, he held her sweetly against his heart, stroking her sweat-stuck hair. With her fingertips she traced the line of his lips and, daring, kissed his nipple.

"Did I please you?" he whispered.

"Yes. It was sweet, Will. Sweet William."

"And your first time."

"Yes."

"Mine too." Astonished, she craned up to look at him. He smiled, his brows lifting. "Truly, it was. And I had no idea what a woman's body would be like. So beautiful, Anne."

She had thought all men wanted women with breasts like udders, plump hips, golden hair. What could be beautiful about her narrow body with its small breasts? But she *felt* beautiful, she felt old and alone no longer. In the distance lightning cracked. Anne counted, waiting for the thunder.

"Six miles away."

"Mmm." He moved her closer to him, drawing her head down on his breast, stroking her hair. A moment later he was asleep, and while he slept Anne could hold him, touch him, love him as she would.

Thunder growled again, closer. William murmured in his sleep, his arm clutching her closer. Lightning, again, and more thunder, and William woke.

"The storm's breaking. There will be rain in a moment."

"So if we go out we'll get wet."

"Clever of you."

"I mean we had better stay here till the rain ends."

She would have moved back into his embrace, but he sat up and, naked, reached into the costume trunk again. A flurry of orange satin, then blue wool. Women's dresses. A tin breastplate; for a Roman, William said. Another sword. Two doublets, a black lawyer's gown. A long blonde wig. More pearls. Face paints, lead paste to whiten the skin, kohl for the eyes, rouge for cheeks and lips.

"At Sir Thomas Hesketh's house and once at the Earl of Derby's, I played a girl. I made a very pretty girl."

"I prefer you as a man."

"I think I do too." Putting down the armful of costumes he swivelled around on his knees and held out his arms. They kissed, he touched her in some remarkable ways, then he was inside her again, to the accompaniment of thunder to muffle the sounds they made together, lightning, at last the rain.

It was only a brief summer storm, soon over.

Soon over. Summer's lease.

The jewels were paste, the ermine lamb's wool, the silks and velvets tawdry and smelling of other people's sweat.

Anne braided and pinned up her hair again. Dressed. Tidied herself. Watched William doing the same.

Her voice sounded harsh when she said, "Will the costumes do for Davy Jones's mummers?"

"Oh yes. As my patched-up play will do."

"Good enough for a country town."

"The costumes and the play are. You are infinitely better."

"I doubt it. Will, I must go."

"And so must I."

Well, what else had she expected?

31

"Anne."

"What?"

"Your poem."

"Poem? Oh." She took the folded paper he held out to her. "Thank you."

"It's a sonnet," he said hopefully.

"What's that?"

"Oh … eight lines, then six; proposition and answer. I hope you like it."

"I'm sure I shall. I must go."

"I'll see you home."

"Thank you."

They put the costumes and properties neatly away and latched the door behind them. In silence they walked back towards Temple Grafton, then halfway there William took Anne's hand and kissed her again, and she found the courage to say, "Did you take me there to play with the costumes in the hope of what we did?"

"No. I never thought of it. But you looked so beautiful."

"Ha!"

"You did."

"I'm not beautiful, not even pretty. I'm a farmer's daughter. I'm brown from the sun, I'm skinny."

"You made a beautiful queen."

"In borrowed finery. Cheap stuff."

"You looked beautiful. Desirable. Whatever I say here will be wrong, won't it."

"Probably."

"As a matter of fact I think you are pretty. You've glorious hair, and I like grey eyes with black brows and lashes. I've always thought you a pretty woman. That poem I wrote for you, shall I recite it?"

"Yes please," said Anne, who didn't care, unless it was a declaration of undying love.

He took a deep breath and began.

> "Those lips that Love's own hand did make,
> Breath'd forth the sound that said 'I hate',
> To me that languished for her sake:
> But when she saw my woeful state,
> Straight in her heart did mercy come;

Chiding that tongue that ever sweet,
Was used in giving gentle doom:
And taught it thus anew to greet:
'I hate' she altered with an end,
That followed it as gentle day,
Doth follow night who like a fiend,
From heaven to hell is flown away.
'I hate', from hate away she threw,
And saved my life saying, 'not you'."

They walked on for a while.

"You noted the pun on 'Hathaway', didn't you? Hate away –
Hathaway."

"Yes, I noted it."

They walked on for a while.

"Don't you like it?"

"I like it," said Anne, who thought that as a poet he made a
good glover. "I'm not sure I understood it."

They walked on for a while.

"Shall I say it to you again?"

"Yes please."

He did so.

They walked on for a while.

"I like it very much," said Anne. "But isn't it a poem about a
lover languishing because the woman he loves doesn't love him?"

"It's just a poem. Playing with words. Following a style, a
fashion."

They walked on for a while.

"I've never had a poem written for me before. Doubt I ever
shall again."

"You might. Shall I write you another?"

"Yes please."

"Good."

They were at Temple Grafton. Anne's cousin's cottage was on
this nearer side of the village. It was too late for the old lady still
to be up. At the gate Anne turned to William. "I must go in now.
Will you come again, as you used to?"

"If I may," he said stiffly.

"My cousin likes your stories."

"I'm glad. Anne."

Startled, she looked up, and he kissed her. "I hope you liked your birthday. I certainly did."

"I did. I did, Will, I did."

"Then don't be cold to me, don't turn me away."

"I'm not, I won't. But now I must go in and you must get home before it rains again. Goodnight, my dear."

"Goodnight, Anne."

5.

William didn't care for the glover's trade, but he did like his father's workshop. His earliest memories of beauty were, equally, of spring flowers and of the colours and textures piled high in the shop. Leather of all kinds, soft and subtle as a whisper, or tough and no-nonsense. The satins, silks, taffetas for linings in colours that improved on nature. Gold and silver wires and threads, pearls and beads and sequins. Herbs, sweet wood and spices to perfume the finished gloves. Even the knives and shears and needles, the patterns and stretchers, held their own fascination.

At one time John Shakspere had employed another master cutter and six stitchers, and a clerk to write his letters and keep his accounts. In those days he had been a wool dealer and a money-lender, and those things absorbed his time and interest more than the glove shop. They had also been his downfall, those illegal and costly dealings. Now he did all the cutting and fine embroidery and had but two apprentices. William, and Gilbert when he wasn't fast enough to escape, clerked for him. Richard did the unskilled work.

One night they were working late, the older man doing the close work on a pair of gloves for a special order, the younger trying to make sense of the accounts. John Shakspere had a habit of whistling under his breath as he concentrated. It annoyed William and grated on his nerves until he lost track of the numbers he was trying to tally and he turned and snapped at his father to stop it. Like most boys of his class he had been bred to treat his parents with courtesy and he was astonished when there was no rebuke. Instead his father had put down his work and asked if he wanted a drink.

"Yes," said William, puzzled.

"I keep a bottle in here. No need to tell your mother."

"I shan't, sir."

"Oh, sir, sir, sir. Let's have a little less sirring and a bit more talk, as men. The cups are behind that roll of taffeta."

It was French brandy, and from the quality he was used to in the north William recognized it as rather fine. Expensive.

"Talk of what?"

"Anything. Chat. Tell a joke. Because, boy, I have enough of glum faces and cold silences and being reminded I'm a failure." He tossed off his brandy and poured another.

"Not a failure."

"But nothing worked out the way I planned it. Most of my money is gone and I spend my time hiding from my creditors. Your mother reproaches me, my friends make excuses for me and I do not like my life. So talk to me. With me."

"Well then… why did you give up being a farmer? Why move into Stratford and take up the glover's trade, and all the rest?"

"I thought I could better myself. And for a long time I did. Your mother was a pretty girl with a little money, my father's landlord's daughter, a little above me, and I wanted to give her everything. I liked making things. I liked doing something I am good at. I enjoyed the dealing and taking chances. Never gamble, son."

"I don't. I think I've no taste for it."

"Just as well. Some people will bet on a game of cards or a football match, or two raindrops running down a window. Others, like me, enjoy the risk of investing money, going a little outside the law, playing both ends against the middle. And see where it gets you. Never gamble, and don't lend money. If your debtors don't get you, the law will. Another drink?"

William had never had more than one brandy at a time, but recklessly he held out his cup for more.

"Good lad. What's all this your mother tells me about you wanting to go to London?"

"I don't know what she has told you but it's what I would like to do."

"Why? All this play-acting nonsense?"

"Perhaps. Yes."

"Any money in it?"

"I'm not sure, Father. Well, players are paid, of course. And if I could sometimes write material for them – plays – there would be money in that."

"Is it a matter of an apprenticeship? To one of these playing companies?"

"Well, yes, I think so."

"But I suppose they don't take just anyone."

"I suppose not."

"Your mother said you spoke to her of having done something of this kind at Sir Alexander's house. Apparently you told her you'd met people who could be of use to you."

"One or two, perhaps."

Pushing away his work, his father refilled his cup and sat back, his legs stretched out. "We feel it, you know, that we couldn't send you to university. That schoolmaster you had, Whatisname, said you were one of his cleverest pupils and could have a great future. The law, perhaps. Or some government position. But it wasn't to be. Money is all, and I hadn't enough. But none of your brothers shows much promise in that sort of way, although I admit it's too soon to tell about the little boy. But Richard just plods through his school work and Gilbert's lazy and too keen on girls. By the way, have you got any particular girl?"

Wherever William's acting talent came from, it wasn't from his father. He had never seen a worse pretence of casualness.

"No, Father."

"Just as well, you're too young yet. But you see rather a lot of Mistress Hathaway?"

"We're friends, yes."

"She's a good woman from a good family. A very suitable *friend.*"

"Yes, Father."

"But if, and, mind, I only say *if*, this playing company business seemed to have money in it..."

"Yes?"

"I suppose it wouldn't hurt to make some enquiries. Your friend Dick Field, now, he's in London, apprentice to a printer. He would know his way around London a little."

"I'm sure he would." William felt breathless.

"Not that I am entirely without friends, useful people, even now. Look, son, don't tell your mother but I've a little put away that she doesn't know about; a few pounds only."

"Sir Alexander left me a tiny annuity in his will, and I've some savings." *O please, O please...*

"Suppose we let you go to London." Quickly, as William began to speak, he held up his hand. "Only to *ask*, for now. To make enquiries. You could lodge with Dick Field and make some enquiries. There's a Mr Burbage, who owns the Theatre." He saw his son's face, and laughed. "I'm not entirely ignorant, and not quite as stupid as you think."

"Of course I don't..."

"Well, well... and the other one, the play-house, called The Curtain I believe. If you went to these people, asked about being apprenticed, found out what sort of costs are involved, well, then we could think again. After all, if it's a paying business, you might as well do something you're good at and enjoy."

"Like you with the glove shop and the wool dealing."

"Just so. I couldn't wait to leave the farm and I see the same impatience in you to be done with all this. So I'll go this far: you may go to London for, say, a month, to make sensible enquiries about work and lodgings and pay. If necessary you can lay down indenture money. But be sure you speak to a lawyer first. I'm no admirer of lawyers but they have their uses, I suppose."

"Father, thank you! Thank you. But what about Mother?"

"I'll deal with your mother." He took another drink. "I am," he said, "still master in my own household."

Anne was hanging out washing when someone behind her coughed and spoke her name. A young girl stood there, shifting from foot to foot. She had russet hair and hazel eyes.

"Mistress Hathaway?"

"Yes. And you're Joan, William's sister. You're very like him."

"Everyone says that. Will asked me to bring you a message."

"Oh?" said Anne, annoyed to find that her first reaction had been delight. It was a week since she had seen him. Then she realized that Joan was holding out a folded paper. Anne wiped her hands on her apron, and took the letter gingerly. It was sealed, and she could see the clear imprint of his thumb in the wax. She hesitated then flicked it open.

She could read print well enough but had had little practice with hand-writing. Still, he wrote clearly, with care. She had no trouble making out what he had to tell her.

...my father has given his permission... to London at once... dare not hope for too much but... nothing decided yet... no time to visit you before I went... always remember your kindness...

"Joan, come inside, let me give you something to drink." Chattering away, fetching the ale jug from where it hung in the well to keep cold, serving out the honey cakes she had made that morning, until at last she could say with seeming unconcern, "So your brother has gone to London?"

"Mmm." Joan's mouth was full. "I was supposed to bring the letter yesterday but…"

"But?"

"Oh, well, it has been rather difficult at home. Mother didn't want Will to go but Father insisted. They've been arguing. Mother's made herself ill with it."

"A sudden decision, was it not? I thought your parents were against him going away?"

"So we thought, but it seems it was Mother, not Father. And Mother was so upset that Father told Will to go at once, before it could be any worse. So he did."

"When?"

"Thursday."

"And did he send any other message, anything more than the letter?"

"No," said Joan, looking puzzled. "It's not for ever, of course," she added. "He's only to go and find out if he can be apprenticed. Although I suppose that if they said yes, he would stay there. He said it takes four days to get to London, so I don't suppose he will come back unless he has to."

She left soon after, saying her mother would worry if she was away too long.

Well, thought Anne. Just like that. He is gone. Half a page of glib remarks that could have been addressed to his maiden aunt or, come to that, to Davy Jones. *I will always remember your kindness.* She had listened to his dreams and his ambitions and made love to him seven times. Once for every year in the difference between their ages. She had been his first. Or so he had said. He had been hers. Now he had gone and he hadn't even said goodbye.

When she told her cousin, the old lady said, "At least he wrote you a letter. It's more than most men would do."

6.

Every country area had a woman like this. Wise woman; meddling old crone; daft old besom; witch; all according to your way of looking – or your need. Learned in the ways of herbal cures and the old lore of the Egyptians, with a deft touch for a sick animal or child. Yes, you would go to her, perhaps sneaking in the night, if you wanted warts charmed away or a potion to bind your beloved to you, if you couldn't conceive or conceived unwillingly. Openly, by day, you'd give at least a nod of respect, a friendly greeting, you'd take her a gift when you killed a pig or put up fruit. Just in case.

The cottage was ancient, a hovel whose walls stayed up only for lack of the energy to fall down. Inside it was surprisingly clean and orderly, but stank of unwashed old woman, herbs, the dog's farts, the midden by the door, wood smoke and something else, indefinable but which always made Anne's spine prickle.

"So. Mistress Anne."

"Good-day to you." Anne could hardly see the old woman through the smoky haze, and she nearly fell over the dog. "I baked today and thought to bring you a gift." Briskly, although her hands shook, she unloaded her basket onto the table. A pie, two loaves, a cheese, a pot of honey, apples, a pair of thick, warm stockings. And two silver coins.

"Generous o' you." The old woman's chair squeaked as she rocked. "What do you want? Sit down where I can see you." Anne obeyed, and for a moment the old woman leaned forward to peer at her. "So y're in trouble."

"Yes. They say you can help. *Please.*"

"Whyn't marry the man?"

"I cannot."

"Got a wife already, 'as 'e?"

"No."

"Spread y'r legs for some nobleman bored wi' summer in country, did you, an' now 'e's off back to London an' laughs when you say y'r carryin' 'is child?"

"No. It is nothing like that. But I cannot marry him."

"An' does 'e know? Did 'e send thee to me?"

"No."

"Aye. Women bear their troubles alone. An' their babes, when the man's long gone. Tell 'im and mak 'im wed thee. Pride's cold comfort." The rocking of her chair was a rhythm that seemed to numb Anne's mind. She felt queasy.

"I cannot," she whispered. "Please. They say you've helped other women. A potion. Pills. Anything."

"'Ow far gone is thee?"

"My... my last flux was at the start of August."

The wise-woman laughed, and Anne wondered if she practised that witchy cackle to awe the credulous. "Left it late, din you. Nigh on three months."

"I was not quite sure. My flux is not always on time. And my cousin has been very ill."

"Aye, so I've 'eard. An' you waited for y'r man to speak of love an' marriage."

"Yes," Anne whispered, feeling tears prickling her eyes. "But he did not, and I am in trouble. So please, we cannot marry and our families are respectable. Please help me."

"I can," the other woman said slowly, "but three months is late... Gi' me y'r 'and."

William had said that, in such different circumstances. Afraid, Anne laid her clean, shapely hand palm-up in the old woman's filthy, hook-nailed one. The silence held and stretched until, at last, the wise-woman stirred and said, "Three children. Marriage. Deaths and journeyings. Great want, then money. A man you'll love, who'll break y'r 'eart; but bide an' 'e'll come back to you and love you at the end. Another love. Rivals. A golden man; a woman dark as night."

For the first time her voice lost its drone, and with it the rustic blur. She sounded puzzled. "I see kings and queens and lovers dying. And your name will never die." Abruptly she folded Anne's fingers back against her palm and tossed the hand back in her lap.

Is that all? The common fortune she probably tells everyone? Money, love, a journey. A few vague warnings. Your name will never die — such stuff for fools! Not much for my silver coins. She must do a brisk trade with country simpletons, no wonder they say she has money put away.

Then the old woman said, still in that new voice, "Marry your boy, Anne Hathaway. Marry him, comfort him, let him go when it's time. He'll always come back to you."

"I..."

"And don't whine at me that you cannot. But if you *will* not, you can try this." She stood up and went to the shelves that crowded one wall. Word was that the village carpenter had built those shelves for her, in exchange for – what? In her chair the old woman seemed all warts and knobs, her body twisted as an ancient tree. Standing, she was revealed as tall and straight and lithe of movement. Anne wondered how old she really was.

Almost contemptuously she dropped a screw of paper into Anne's lap. "Pills. Put 'em up y'r cunny, one at nightfall, one at dawn, for three days. And drink this each mornin', twelve drops in wine." A tiny stoppered bottle followed the paper.

"Will they work?"

"I make you no promises. If they do it will 'urt, but not as bad as child-bed. You can pass it off as a bad flux. But y'r a fool, Anne 'Athaway. Y'r boy will love the child and 'e has need of you."

"Love the child – perhaps. Need of me – I doubt that. Thank you, ma'am." She bobbed a polite curtsy and took her basket. "Good-day to you."

She was at the door when the wise-woman said, "'E's an 'andsome boy, William Shakspere."

Anne whirled about, her spine prickling again. "How did you know? Did you *see* it? In my hand? In a glass?"

The other woman laughed; not the witch's cackle but a clear, ordinary, almost girlish laugh. "No, but I guessed and you just told me. I seen 'im. Comin' and goin' to Temple Grafton, eager in goin', grinnin' and whistlin' in comin' away again. You pleased 'im in bed, you know."

Anne could have smacked her grinning chops. "So all that nonsense you pretended to see in my hand was simply that – nonsense. If you know of Will, you know of his ambitions, and you made it all up."

"No. I saw true. Not all was clear, but I told you true." Then, laughing again, she lapsed back into her crone's manner. "If them pills and the nostrum doan work by the end o' this week, you'll no get rid of that child. It's a girl, if you care. Marry young William." The cottage door slammed shut. She was still laughing.

Perhaps it was too late. Perhaps the wise-woman had cheated her. The pills and potion did nothing except to make Anne rackingly sick. In fact, the child seemed to flourish on the witch's brew, for in that week Anne's body suddenly burgeoned. Her waist spread, her breasts swelled, her belly rounded. And with these changes she became weepy and tired. Soon there would be no disguising her condition.

Her cousin noticed, of course, and in the course of one chilly evening she had the whole story out of Anne.

"He must marry you."

"But..."

"But nothing. Do you want your child born a bastard?"

"No."

"Probably neither does he. He need not live with you, but marry you he must. He's a decent boy from a good family. He'll want to do what is right."

"But he is only eighteen."

"Old enough to play the man in bed. Old enough to know that you pay for your pleasure. Why should you be the only one who pays?"

"True. But he's in London."

"Then go and see his parents, tell them to fetch him home. Or... can you write?"

"A little. Enough, I daresay. But how do I send a letter to London?"

"That's easy. Ask someone who's going there; a carter taking goods, someone visiting. Pay them to take a letter. Or simply hire a man to go, someone from the livery stables." She reached over and took Anne's hand. "Don't think of going there yourself," she said quietly. "It's too far for a woman in your condition and in this weather. And if the news of the child doesn't bring him home, then your pleading with him yourself won't do it either. In that case, better no father at all. And if worst comes to worst you can live with me here."

Yes, then, she would write. But, another problem; her cousin could neither read nor write and had no ink or paper. Nor would she find such things at home, any more than she would find any sympathy for her plight.

She went to her other cousin, to Frances Jones, Davy's wife. They were astonished, shocked and disapproving, but they gave her paper, ink, pen and sealing wax, and Davy knew someone who would take the letter to London. He also knew, on the

Stratford grapevine, where William was staying with his friend Dick Field. Anne paid two shillings for her letter's carriage.

Then all she could do was wait. It was November, she was nearly three months pregnant, and marriages were forbidden after Advent.

7.

He came. Ten days after she had given the letter to Davy Jones, he knocked on her cousin's door and walked straight into the kitchen. Anne, who was sitting at the table tiredly stuffing a rabbit for supper, simply stared at him.

"Your letter reached me. As you see."

"Will... I... I'm sorry."

He shrugged. "It takes two."

"Yes, it does. Won't you sit down? Would you like some ale?"

"Thank you."

She tossed the rabbit into a pan, then rose and washed and dried her hands. She poured the ale and sat down again. Across the table they looked at each other. She knew what he was seeing: a plump, untidy housewife whose hair needed washing and whose condition unbecomingly showed in the way her dress strained across her breasts and waist. He, on the other hand, looked suave and elegant in a new dark green doublet. He'd had his hair cut and a small line of paler skin showed at the back of his neck.

"How was London?" she asked inanely.

"Enjoyable. I went to a lot of plays. No one was in any hurry to take me on as a player."

"I see."

"Which is just as well, isn't it."

"I suppose it is, but still I'm sorry you didn't find your dream. Or will you go back and try again?"

"How can I? You are having my child and we must be married."

She had a brief thought of what it must be like to tell a beloved husband you were carrying his child; to see his joy, to be kissed and congratulated, to go together to tell your families.

"Yes, I think we must. It *is* yours, you know."

For the first time he smiled. "I know. I've no doubt about that. And although I had no idea of getting married, there's no one I'd rather marry."

"Kind of you to say so."

He leapt up and took three fast, striding paces up and down the room. "It is not particularly kind of me. I wanted to stay in

London, for I think I could have made my way there, there are all sorts of things I could have done."

"And perhaps still can," she cut in.

"What?"

"You have to marry me for the child's sake, but you don't have to stay here. I can live at home or here with my cousin. You can return to London or do what you like."

His turn to stare blankly at her. "Is that what you want?"

"No. God, Will, of course it's not."

"Well, there's no need to cry about it."

"So you say."

"I do." He knelt down beside her and took her hand. Smiling, he kissed the corner of her mouth. "Will you marry me, dear Anne?"

"I will. But I am not… your dear Anne, am I."

"Yes you are. Quite dear enough. We'll be married and we'll have our child." He drew her head down onto his shoulder and patted her until she stopped weeping. "It's Advent soon, and we can't marry in Advent. So I'd best get busy. I need my parents' consent because I'm under-age, then I think it's a matter of obtaining a special licence from the Bishop. But it will be done and we can be married in a week. Good God in heaven, woman, did you think I'd abandon you?"

"But…" Married at eighteen, a father at nineteen, tied to a wife seven years his elder, scandal and talk and the loss of all his dreams. A Stratford glover or schoolmaster forever. "No, I never thought that. But will your parents give consent? Do they know?"

"I told them."

"I suppose they were shocked."

"Not quite the right word. But they have given their consent. They will welcome you as their daughter-in-law and give us a room of our own. It has a bed."

"A bed would be useful."

"And will see some use." He laughed. "But all I meant is that I've little enough to offer you, but… the room has that much furniture."

"I can do a little better than that, Will. I've bride-goods, you know, all manner of household stuff. Furniture, blankets, rugs, hangings. And my dowry. My father left me ten marks."

"Excellent! I would like to say very grandly that I am above needing my wife's money, but one never knows."

"No, one doesn't. How will we manage for money? Why not go back to London if you think you could do something there?"

"Later, perhaps. For now I'll do what my parents planned for me, I'll take a job as usher at the grammar school in Stratford. We'll manage. But first I have to arrange the licence. Now cheer up, we'll be married soon and... I should have said this at once: I am very happy about the baby. Are you?"

Putting away the memory of her visit to the wise woman Anne said, "Yes. I am now I am used to the idea. Yes."

"Good." He kissed her again, and stood up. "Anne Shakspere has a ring to it, doesn't it? Speaking of rings, I'd best buy one. Now I must go. I've to arrange about the licence. Oh and Mother bids you come to dinner the day after tomorrow."

They went together to tell Mrs Hathaway, and because William was there she had to mind her tongue. She was visibly impressed and a little awed by him, and because he flattered and deferred to her, she offered to hold the wedding breakfast at Hewlands Farm, less out of Christian charity than in a spirit of stopping people gossiping.

Two friends of Anne's father stood surety to the sum of forty pounds for the marriage licence bond, required because William was under-age. The Bishop granted the licence. The marriage bond was signed and witnessed. The banns would be called the once that time allowed, the next Sunday. They would marry on the Monday.

And Anne dined formally with the Shaksperes. The house was immaculate and the best pewter and glass had been brought out for the occasion. Mr Shakspere did his best to make conversation, referring often to his friendship with Anne's father. The children were quiet and respectful. Mrs Shakspere was ominously friendly.

Anne discovered why when, after the meal, the older woman made an excuse to take her aside. "Well, of course this is hardly what we would want for our son, but least said, soonest mended, and at least you are a respectable woman of a family known to us."

"Thank you, ma'am."

"And of course, once he is married there will be no more talk of going off to London. He'll stay here and forget all this playhouse business."

Anne looked at her. It was from her that William had his oval face and his hazel eyes. In the course of that one polite meal Anne had come to realize that his friendly, open nature, and his sensuality, were from his father and his intelligence and air of breeding from this woman who clutched her sleeve and peered at her with sly satisfaction. A possessive woman for all that she was openly critical of her children.

Instead of answering in words, Anne curtsied. Let Mary Shakspere make of that what she would.

She could feel the woman's eyes on her as she went upstairs with William to see the room that would be theirs.

William closed the door and pulled Anne into his arms. "Give me a kiss." Anne felt her starved body respond. She couldn't stop herself twining her arms around his neck and opening her mouth under his. Against his chest her nipples hardened, wanting his touch. Pregnancy was making her wanton, she had discovered in surprise. She could have torn open her bodice to bare her body to him, could have taken him right here and now. That he had the same need was obvious, but here in his parents' house they could do nothing but kiss, and ache.

They moved apart. William said, "What was Mother whispering to you about?"

"How glad she is that you will have to give up your London ambitions."

"At first she tried to make my father refuse his consent to our marrying. Then she thought of that."

"She's in for a surprise, then, isn't she?"

"What do you mean?"

"That we'll see. Nothing says you have to stay here in Stratford, that *we* have to." She strolled about inspecting the room. It was not large, and it was at the front of the house, where it would catch all the noise and dirt from the street. Also it was over the workshop and wool store and smelt strongly of fleeces and curing hides. The little particles of dust in the air made Anne sneeze. The room was presently half-full of hampers and trunks, broken furniture, worn carpets; all the things no one could be bothered mending, burning, or hauling tidily to the attics. The floor needed scrubbing, the windows needed washing. There were cobwebs on the rafters. Anne ran her finger along the mantelpiece and looked with satisfaction at the dust.

"I'm sorry," William said awkwardly. "I suppose Mother should have…"

"Your mother probably knows full well that she is not losing a son so much as gaining an unpaid housemaid. But in return we get free lodging. It *is* free, isn't it?"

"Yes, but…"

"So, we live free. No expenses. I help in the house – well, I do that at home – and perhaps I could earn a little by brewing. I'm a good brewster. And I raise our child, you work at the school, and we save our money." She sat on the edge of the bed and gave an experimental bounce. The ropes needed tightening, and a cloud of dust drifted up from the sagging mattress.

"It's a rotten bed," William said, watching her. "Let's buy a new one."

"I can bring one from home."

"No, our marriage bed should be our own. Not," he said, turning aside to perch a buttock on the window sill, "that it will any fine sort of bed. One day I'll buy you the grandest bed in England. One day. I am going to be rich, Anne, I am going to make my way in the world. For now I can offer you nothing, but one day I will give you a fine house, fine furniture, the position my wife deserves. If our child's a boy he will have the best education, a future. I will get away from home, and Stratford and I'll be a rich man. One day. I've nothing to give you now except a second-best bed and a second-best life. But wait, Anne, and I'll take care of you."

"You're giving me your name so the child won't be born a bastard and I won't be branded a whore."

His face lightening into a smile, he said, "Well, it's my child too, after all."

"But to strip the matter to the bone, you do not love me." He flushed, and didn't answer. "But we must marry. People will laugh at you, married to a woman seven years your elder. Face that. So, Will, let me help you. Let me be your partner as well as your wife, and your friend, I hope."

"Always my friend."

"Yes, well, let's see if we say that in a few years time or a few months, with a squalling baby… No, Will, let me help. We've no choice for the present, but who knows. We can do what we like. It would be pleasant to be rich, but I would rather you were happy. Shall we say, five years?"

"Why five?"

"It's a good, round number, but very well, call it two or four or until you are of age; let's see what happens. You could write a lot of plays and poems in three years, five years."

Looking oddly at her he said, "Yes… yes, I shall, Anne. And, yes, we'll be partners and friends. A true marriage. Come, clap hands and a bargain."

She took his outstretched hand, looking steadily into his eyes. "A bargain."

Part Two

1587-1588

8.

The bed they had bought was second-hand – William persisted in calling it, snidely, second-best – but it had two great advantages. One: it was sturdy and didn't creak under lovemaking or childbirth; and two: its carved head concealed a hidey-hole with a lock.

Very quietly, afraid of waking William or the children, Anne knelt up in bed, opened the little cupboard and took out the bag of money.

Quite a lot of money now, after nearly five years – sixteen pounds. Ten marks of it was Anne's dowry, untouched all this time and a little left to Anne by her cousin. The rest they had saved from Anne's small earnings from selling ale, William's wages as a grammar school usher, the extra he sometimes earned writing letters or legal documents for people in the town, and the four pounds his friend, Richard Field, had got for selling three plays to theatre owners in London.

They had few expenses, but still it was money saved by going without new clothes, books, any amusement that cost money. Last Christmas their gifts to each other had been four pens, courtesy of the Christmas goose at Hewlands Farm, and a hair ribbon. Ink and paper could be afforded, just, as long as they were used only for money-making writing. At least there would be no more children; the twins' horrendous birth, in the third year of their marriage, had seen to that. Neither Anne nor William cared; three were enough. Anne had weaned Susanna at twelve months, and they had meant to take care, but there had been a languorous warm May night; one of the few nights they didn't both fall asleep the moment they went to bed. They had thought they could afford two children, but they hadn't counted on twins. Three children before William was twenty-one.

No prospect of a house of their own for at least two years more. William's father owned other houses in Stratford and he could have let them have one at a low rent, or no rent, but he had refused – afraid, Anne suspected, that William would do less to help him in his business. Twelve hours a day at school, and every night at least two hours on his father's letters or accounts; more time spent helping the lawyer.

Or perhaps Mr Shakspere feared to lose Anne because without her he would have to hire another maid. Anne was fond of her father-in-law, but there was no denying that these days he was close-fisted. Two more years, Anne thought grimly, three at most, and I'll be out of here to my own house.

Carefully she counted out the money, muffling it in the folds of her shift. Not carefully enough, for beside her William turned over, groaned and blinked at her.

"What are you doing?"

"Counting the money."

"So early?"

"Why not?"

He shrugged and turned over again. Anne stared at his bare, well-muscled back and thought how much she would like to plunge a knife into it.

"Will. The players are in town today. The Queen's Men."

"So?"

"So we can afford to go to the play. I have asked Joan to mind the children. Three hours to ourselves, seeing a play."

"I don't want to go. Save the money."

"Keep your voice down or you'll wake the children."

Too late. A thud, the patter of tiny feet, and the curtains at the foot of the bed parted on a shining morning face surrounded by russet curls.

"Good morning, Susanna."

"Good morning, Mama. Is Daddy awake?"

"Yes," Anne said meanly, and four-year-old Susanna scrambled up the bed beside her father.

"Dad-dee."

"I'm asleep."

"No you're not 'cause you're talking. Tell me a story."

"It's too early. God, it's barely dawn. No story."

"I'll wait till you're awake." Susanna snuggled into the middle of the bed between them. She had her father twisted around her little finger, and knew it. They tried to be strict with her and not let her grow spoiled, but she was so clever and pretty, and they loved her so desperately. She looked like William, she had his shape of face, his hazel eyes, his red-brown hair. Nothing about her was Anne's.

"Susanna," said Anne, "would you like to go and see a play today?" William's eyes snapped open.

"What's a play?"

"It's when a lot of people act out a story on a stage, in pretty costumes."

"I want to go."

"Good. You and I shall go; Daddy doesn't want to."

"Why not?"

"Ask him."

"Daddy?"

"Oh, very well, we'll go and see the play. But you'll have to sit very still and quietly, Susanna."

"I will. The twins can't come too, can they? They're too little."

"Much too little."

"You've woken them," William said resignedly, as again came the thud and patter and the flinging aside of the bed curtains. The two small faces that peered in were identical and blended their parents' features, but Hamnet had Anne's dark hair and brows and her dove-grey eyes, while Judith took after William's mother with blue eyes and fair hair. The twins were, this July, two years and five months old, and had an infinite capacity for noise.

Well-trained, they said a polite good morning, then bounced onto the bed. "Daddy tell us a story," Hamnet said confidently.

"Too early."

"He's been awake for a long time," said Susanna.

"And I must get up," Anne said, and swept all the money but two shillings back into the bag and locked it away. "Daddy will tell you a very quick story then you must go and wash and dress for breakfast."

It was going to be a hot day. The dawn mist had already burned off and the sky had the hard, clear look of intense sunshine ahead. Anne disliked summer in a town, the heat held in by the crowding houses, the air muggy and over-used; perhaps it was time to spend a few days at Hewlands Farm. Five years of respectable marriage, and the children, had improved matters between Anne and her stepmother. The children loved going to the farm. They had cousins there now, for Anne's brother Bartholomew had also made up his differences with their stepmother and brought his wife Isabel back. They had two babies now. Anne's sister Catherine had been less lucky; none of her children had lived. Idly planning as she dressed, Anne listened to the rise and fall of her husband's voice as he told a story – from the odd word she could catch she thought it was a version of *The Odyssey*.

Five years ago this month she had first met William Shakspere, just home from the north, and he had come to call on her and had told her old cousin that same story. Poor cousin Agnes had survived to see Susanna christened, and then had faded away as gently and undemandingly as she had lived. That same week, come to think of it, Davy Jones's mummers had put on another play, this time paid for by Stratford's council. The king and queen had been much admired, William had reported.

On that thought Anne turned back to the bed and chased the children away. "Go ask the maid for water to wash, and Aunt Joan will dress you. I will see you at the breakfast table." Susanna thought about arguing, caught her eye, and raced after the twins.

William lay back and folded his hands under his head. "Why this early-morning counting of money and this zeal to see the play?"

"Because if we don't do something now we never will. If *you* don't do something."

"Such as what?"

"Talk to the players. Ask them if they can take you on."

"Don't be ridiculous, playing companies don't recruit in country towns. They'd laugh in my face."

"And God forbid you take a risk, eh? Would you really rather live with a grudge than put your dream to the test? Much easier, isn't it, to rot here in Stratford blaming me for trapping you into marriage, than actually seeing if you have anything more than a boy's dream?"

Struggling upright he snapped, "That's unfair! I have never blamed you or thought of it as being trapped." Anne raised a sceptical eyebrow. He flushed. "Very well: sometimes I've thought that. As I'd bet you have too."

"Of course I have. Do you think this is a dream come true, living here, five of us in one room in your parents' house? Having three children so quickly? Working sixteen hours a day to save your parents paying for another maid? Training your baby brother to the pot? Letting your sister cry on my shoulder because she's eighteen and no man's offered for her? Wiping up your brother's puke when he comes home drunk? Feeding your mother herbals to get her through her change of life? Never having a new dress? Watching you write plays at ten o'clock at night to earn a few more shillings when you can't even afford a drink with friends? Listening to you, the few times you feel like talking to me, droning out how much you long to try your luck in London and how good you could be? Watching you posture and make mouths in the glass like a love-struck girl while I try to stay awake to read your plays for you, and knowing that's as close as you'll ever come to a real theatre or making an effort to be an actor because it's easier to stay here and be a schoolmaster, because you're afraid to try and because it is so, so much easier to blame me?"

She ran out of breath, and with it all her anger trickled away. Wearily she finished, "Whatever I say, you'll find some excuse, some very good *reason*, to do otherwise."

"I didn't know you were so unhappy."

"Did you not? Well, things could be worse. I've a decent home, even if it's not my own, and three healthy children I love. Remember how before we married we used to talk of how unhappy we were? We're five years older and no better off, except for the children. And sixteen pounds."

"Sixteen pounds would hire and furnish a house."

"Here in Stratford?"

"Wherever you wanted."

"London?"

"Do you want to go to London?"

"I'm not sure, Will." She sat on the side of the bed and ran her fingers through his hair. "I always wanted to see London, but live there? I don't know. But the players are in town, and if you don't at least talk to them and ask them their advice, I will take the children and go home to Hewlands Farm – not forever, not to leave you, but because I need a change. Because you are twenty-three and look forty, and you're unhappy and hard to live with."

"Am I really that bad? I work long hours, true, but that's for money for you and the children. We could have our own house."

"Before you woke up I was thinking how much I'd enjoy stabbing you to death. You're not so bad. I love you. But I won't live with an unhappy coward who lost his dream for lack of effort or courage, and punishes his wife for it."

Rather pale, watching her intently, he said, "What if I try, and fail?"

"At least you'd *know*. At least you will have tried. Better to be a glover or an usher in a school because that is what you do best. But Will, look – Dick Field said he had no trouble selling those plays you sent him, and I've always thought you could have got more for them if you had been in London yourself. Give it a try. Speak to the players today. Ask them for advice, ask what your chances are of a playing company taking you on. Show them your plays, tell them you sold two to Whatsisname."

"Henslowe."

"Whatever. Or, William, and you laughed at me last time I suggested this, you could write to Lord Strange, for whom you used to work in Lancashire, and ask him if his company of players would take you on."

"I could not write to a nobleman I've not seen in five, six years."

"Why not? I've never been more than five miles from Stratford but I know how things are done; country town or capital city, it's who you know, it's using people you've met, it's reminding useful people of old acquaintance or obligation. So, William, you can rot here blaming me or your stars for the rest of your life, or you can test out your dream. Start by coming to the play today."

It sounded like the sort of line on which players made their exit from a scene on stage, and so she exited, downstairs to feed her family their breakfast.

9.

The play ended. There was a moment's hush, then the audience burst into applause. As they stamped and whistled the players lined up to take their bows, again and again, then filed away through the curtains at the stage's sides. Spain became once more just some rickety boards on trestles, a painted backcloth and Stratford Guildhall.

"Did you like it, sweetheart?" Anne asked Susanna. The little girl had watched with her father's intensity, hardly breathing.

"Yes. Mama, that lady was a man. Why was she?"

"Women aren't allowed to act on the stage. Boys play all the ladies."

"Oh. Why?"

"It's simply not allowed," William said, standing up and easing his back; the wooden benches were no couches of luxury. "Shall I, after all…"

"Yes." Anne took her daughter's hand and marched around to the back of the Guildhall. William flapped along behind.

The players were bundling their materials into hampers, loading them onto a cart. Two of them were squabbling bitterly. Watching them was a rosy-faced man Anne recognised as Richard Tarleton, clown to the Queen's Men. On stage he made you want to laugh as soon as he put his head round the curtains; now he looked tired and as if laughter were the last thing on his mind. Smaller, too, than on stage.

"Excuse me, sirs," William began.

"If you're selling something," Mr Tarleton gave him a dismissive glance, "you've come to the wrong place. We're players. No money."

"Oh no, it's nothing like that. Sir, please could we – I mean, could I – speak privately? It's about a matter of business. I would be glad to take you to the inn and buy a drink."

Astonished, Tarleton's brows shot up and he glanced at Anne in a way she didn't quite like. She had worn her only 'best' dress, her wedding dress, and had thought its flowered linen and her little lace-edged cap modest enough. Surely she didn't deserve that appraising, almost salacious look. Was it common for men in country towns to pimp their women to travelling actors?

His voice steely, William introduced her and Susanna.

"Mr Tarleton," said Anne smoothly, "may I say how much I admired your performance? I'd heard yours is the best acting troupe in the land, and now I see it's true. And your performance, sir, was... was... incomparable." It was the right tack to take. He expanded like a watered flower. Well, she thought, I did like his performance.

"I thank you, madam. Now, your business?"

"Sir, we heard that in Thame one of your company was killed."

"Yes, William Knell, God rest him. Though Towne, who killed him, was acquitted. Self-defence. A quarrel. Yes, he's a loss to us." Real feeling lurked behind the mannered phrases.

"And you have our sorrow for it. And it may give offence to ask you this so soon after his death, but I want to be a player." William lifted his hand at the other man's instinctive protest. "Please, sir, hear me out. I daresay you get all sorts of people wanting to join your troupe."

"Aye, we do. Runaway apprentices, boys who've gone too far with a girl and have an irate father after them; sometimes even the girls. We are not recruiting, young man. And certainly not in a country town." He smiled, pleasantly but firmly, and began to turn away.

"Mr Tarleton, I ask you only for a few moments of your time to advise me over a drink. I was one of a private troupe of players in the north, I have performed for Lord Strange and Lord Derby among others, and I have sold two plays to Mr Henslowe at the...the..."

"The Curtain," said Tarleton, looking at him oddly. "What's your name?"

For a moment William couldn't remember. He looked blankly at Anne for help. She gave him a pitying smile.

"Shakspere. William Shakspere."

"You wrote that piece about King Henry the Sixth?"

"Yes, sir. You know of it?'

Tartleton made a mouth. "It was inexperienced, but not so bad. How much did they pay you for it?"

"A pound," he said proudly.

"Next time ask for more." There was a moment when he almost bade them good-day and left, then he said, "You offered

58

me a drink? I'll accept, gladly, and if I can advise you I will, but only for half an hour."

"That is more than I dared to hope. Thank you."

He wasn't home to supper, or by the time Anne went to bed. She tried to stay up but was too tired, and only woke at the sound of William's boots hitting the floor. She pulled back the bed-curtain and saw him in his shirt, stretching until his arms cracked.

"Will?"

"Did I wake you? Sorry." *Shorry*; he wasn't drunk, but nor was he quite sober.

Anne sat up, clasping her knees. "Where have you been all this time? What did Mr Tarleton say? Will?" Maddeningly he stopped to kiss the twins and tuck their covers in. "William!"

He collapsed into bed beside her, folding his arms behind his head. "I've been out walking. Nowhere much, just walking. Thinking. I stayed an hour or more with Tarleton and some other players. Drank too much, I suppose. Then I walked. Out in the forest. By the river. Thinking."

"Did Mr Tarleton not encourage you?"

"He was quite encouraging. He'd read the Henry play that Dick Field sold to Mr Henslowe, and he'd seen the comedy performed. I didn't know they had actually played it. He said it went well, the audience liked it. He said I have great promise as a writer for the theatre."

"Oh, Will!" In the moonlight she could see the silly great grin on his face. "What else did he say?"

"He asked if I could act. I told him of the little experience I've had and he made me read a piece through." The grin widened. "He said I show some promise." Suddenly he unclasped his hands and threw himself over to look at Anne. "He said I should try my luck in London. He can't take me on with the Queen's Men, it's not for him to do and they're the pick of England's players; 'sides, they've others waiting for their turn, men who've done their 'prenticeship. *Ap*-prenticeship. Three years, is usual."

Rather flattened, Anne said, "And was that all?"

"No, no. No. He says, said, I should go to London. Try my luck in London. He said, do I know anyone in London 'n I said, Dick Field, 'prentish to the printer. 'N he said, good, best to have some friends in the city. He said, when the Queen's Men are back from their tour, to come and see him at Henslowe's playhouse. But the best, the best..."

"Tell me or I'll smother you with the pillows."

"Smother me in my bed. Put out the light, and then put out the light... I'll use that one day. Anne, he gave me an introduction to James Burbage. He said you were quite right and I should approach Lord Strange because knowing someone like that helps, but still he gave me an introduction to Mr Burbage! Head player of the Earl of Leicester's Men! He wrote it down, it's in my purse. A letter, Anne! Said I'm a promising writer and a passable actor, and willing to do anything, and he'd take me on if he could but he can't so Burbage should. Wrote it down. Said I should try."

It was true you could feel more than one emotion at once. Joy, relief, sorrow, envy, cold and lonely misery. "I'm glad, Will."

His eyes held hers, some of his elation ebbing. Gently, commandingly, he said, "Are you? It would mean leaving you here. It would mean at least a year before I could send for you to come to London. I'd be paid for my work, but not enough, not yet, for you and the children. Or you'd have a miserable little lodging not fit for you. And the acting companies go on tour. In summer, they're on the road, travelling all over England, for months on end. I'd send you all the money I could, but we couldn't be together. You'd have to live here or with your step-mother."

"I know."

He turned over again and lay staring up at the tester. "You'd do that? Put up with that?"

"Yes. And when you were touring, you could come home now and again. Other times, perhaps. I could come to London."

"Four days on the road, at least. And what of the children?" Blindly he reached for her hand. "Anne, I want this so much, but I know how selfish it is. Five years, and I've given you no happiness."

"You have, Will. You have." All this time she'd been sitting up, her chin on her knees. She slid down beside him, resting her head on his shoulder. "I love you and I'd rather have you in London and happy, than here and miserable. Keeping her voice steady with an effort she said, "I want the lovely boy I married back again. I want that happy man."

"Even if my happiness takes me a hundred miles away and leaves you here?"

"Rather that than a bitter man who hates me after thirty years at each other's side."

"I could never hate you, Anne."

"But always in the back of your mind would be the knowledge that but for me… When would you go?"

"Mr Tarleton said the autumn would be best. London's unhealthy in summer. Plague always about. He suggested I go when the touring companies are coming back and the winter season's being planned."

"That's sense. It gives us time to plan. To get your clothes together, all that kind of thing. Time to write to Dick Field to find you a London lodging. Or do they put you up at the playhouse?"

"No, I'd need a lodging. Anne?'

"What?"

"Now it has almost happened, it frightens me. A dream come true, or a nightmare? What if I fail?"

"Then at least you'll know. You won't live all your life with what might have been."

"There is that. Yes. G'night." He was asleep almost before he'd finished the word. Anne lay awake all night.

10.

Two doublets, one of good green cloth with spare sleeves, the other of brown leather. Breeches and stockings, a new woollen cloak, a hat. Three pairs of gloves, two belts, a new purse, six handkerchiefs. Two pairs of boots. A knitted scarf. A brush, a comb, a razor. Cloths for cleaning teeth, two balls of soap. Paper, pens, a stoppered ink-pot. A knife, a spoon. A jar of herbal nostrum, sovereign against colds and coughs; a pot of goose-grease and wintergreen, cure for almost anything. Three books, the rest to be sent by carrier.

Anne had spread all these things, William's entire possessions, across the bed; the bed in which from now on she must sleep alone. The thought made her want to cry. Everything made her want to cry, these days. Two more days and William would be gone.

Mrs Shakspere came in, holding a pile of shirts and under-linen from the laundry. Susanna was with her, clinging to her, and their two faces wore, for their different reasons, identical expressions of mulish dislike. Mrs Shakspere disapproved of this whole venture of going to London. Disapproval was one thing, but Susanna's stark, painful disbelief that not even for her would her father stay, was almost beyond bearing. They both blamed Anne, and the two pairs of cold eyes fixed on her, day in, day out, rasped her nerves raw.

Mrs Shakspere put the linen on the bed. Only one of the shirts was new, Anne had only just finished making it, but everything was of good quality, beautifully mended, laundered snow-white, immaculately ironed. In that at least William's womenfolk saw eye-to-eye: he would go with the best clothes they could contrive.

Mrs Shakspere said nothing as she smoothed the shirts. Nor did Susanna. They hadn't spoken to Anne for a week. Suddenly it was more than she could take.

"I don't want it either. But I have to let him go, or make him miserable."

"You told me that if you married him he would never go away."

"I lied."

"So I see. It's not decent," said Mrs Shakspere. "If you were any sort of wife you'd stop him going."

Anne saw Susanna nodding smugly, so like her grandmother that Anne longed to slap her. "Would I? How? You say you love him, yet you'd see him unhappy because you're too selfish to part with him. I love him. I love him enough to let him go. And I think it will break my heart. And what do you think it is like for me, to mend his clothes and help him pack and see him longing to go away? And I have to bear it alone, for I've no one to comfort me, no one at all."

William came home that night cheerful, whistling as he bounded up the stairs. Free. His last day as a schoolteacher was over. In two days he'd be on the road to London.

The landing was poorly lit and he almost fell over Susanna, sitting on the top stair. "Darling, what are you doing there?" She bounced to her feet, looking reproachfully back at him.

"Mama's crying and Grandam's cross and I hate you and if you loved us you wouldn't go away!" Then, frightened by her defiance, she ran away down the stairs. William caught her halfway down, shook her, spun her around to face him.

"Don't ever say that! I love you. I love you all more dearly than anything in the world. Even if you hate me I'll still love you forever. Don't say that to me, Susanna." She stood rigid in his grasp, refusing to meet his eyes. "We explained it all to you, Susanna. I have to go to London to make more money for your mother and you children. I can only do that in London. It's not forever, I'll come home when I can, and when I'm settled in London your mother will bring you to me. It's what must be, Susanna."

He wanted to add, "And I can take no more tears and tantrums and ungiving silences," but his child's eyes were full of unshed tears. He loved her with that fearful, hopeless love that only parents know. He wanted to snatch her up in his arms, to take her with him, to change his mind and stay. He touched her face, angry when she shied back.

"I love you, Susanna, and I will miss you, but go I must." She tossed her head and marched off down the stairs; at the bottom she sped around the corner out of sight, to cry unobserved, he guessed. For a moment he was tempted to go after her. She was only four-and-a-half. But there was nothing more he could say to her.

In his bedroom he found Anne packing his bag. As he watched, she tucked a sachet of lavender and herbs, guaranteed to keep fleas and lice at bay, between two of his shirts. Her face was calm but her eyes had the sodden look that comes from secret crying.

"I have to go, Anne. It's what must be."

"Yes," she said tartly. "I heard your silver-tongued eloquence with Susanna. Much a four-year-old knows of 'what must be'. Oh, I know, I know, she's growing spoilt, and yes, it must be. But it is hard for me, Will; all adventure for you, all dreariness and loneliness for me. I've never said that to you before, but that too is what must be. And yes, I know it will be worth it in the end, and I believe in you and I'll make no attempt to stop you. But you're no child to think that what you do gives no hurt to others."

"I don't think that. God's nails, Anne! Adventure for me, yes, and fear and hardship and not knowing my way, and perhaps failing and having to slink home with my tail between my legs, the Warwickshire boy who thought he could succeed in London without money, influence, friends, education. Leaving my wife and children, living anyhow. Anne, don't send me away with tears and anger, I've had enough of that."

"Would you have me send you away indifferently?" But her anger had gone, and with it some of her misery. Uncertainly she held out her arms. He came to her, resting his head on her shoulder, holding her.

"If I could take you with me I would, but not this first time, my dear. Let me find a good lodging, let me begin to make my way a little. Then you shall come to me and bring the children."

"And you will write? Write to me, I mean?"

"Be sure of it."

He left next morning in the misty dawn. He kissed his father, who wept and tried to hide it. Kissed his mother, who turned her angry face away. Kissed his sister, who wept and blessed him through the tears. Kissed his brothers, who enviously hugged him.

"Mother..."

"Let her be," his father said, watching his wife flounce away inside. "Now, William, it's as well she's not looking, for I have this for you." It was a purse of money, pressed furtively into his hand. "I've saved a little for all you children and you might as well have this now. But spend it wisely, my boy."

"I will, Father. Thank you."

"And, William, remember London folk are not like us. Be careful. Give your trust sparingly and your friendship wisely, but work to keep the friends you have. Don't let yourself be drawn into quarrels; but if you must be, let people know where you stand and what your principles are. And never borrow money; nor lend it, for that makes as many troubles as debt. Let's see, what else? Curb your tongue; sometimes you talk too freely in exercising your wit. Listen more than you speak. And mind you keep up a good appearance; people judge by appearances. Dress well, but according to your station, avoid vulgarity and seeming to ape your betters. And, William, be true to yourself and then you'll be false to no one. And God save you, my son. God speed."

"God save you, Father." William hugged the old man. "Thank you." He kissed Anne and rubbed her cheek with the back of his fingers. They said nothing; their farewells were already done. The sleepy twins clung to him, kissing him sweetly. Susanna hung back, but at the last moment, as he shouldered his pack, she ran and flung her arms around him. She was crying, but she managed to say God speed.

Then he was gone, and the morning mist hid him from sight before he had reached the end of the street.

My dear wife:
This tells you I am safe in London. Dick Field gives me a bed in his lodging and I am comfortable. I have seen the Tower of London and the beasts in the menagerie in Lion Tower, and London Bridge. Also I have been to St Paul's, where all of London does its business, and where in Paul's Yard I fear I will spend too much on books.
I have seen my Lord Southampton's house, and Lord Essex's and Lord Leicester's, and Whitehall Palace and Westminster. I called on Master Alleyn the player. I have seen six plays. I went to Master Burbage, who had spoken to Mr Alleyn and Mr Henslowe of me, and he read my plays and liked them, and he has taken me on as dogsbody and sometime writer. I prompt the players, sort the properties and count the costumes. I am happy. Kiss my children for me.

My dearest wife:
Today I acted in a play, taking the part of a soldier who speaks no lines. I
have met Christopher Marlowe, the playwright, and we talked together. He is
of my age and from Kent. Tomorrow we play his Tamburlaine, *and Kit has*
given me an idea for a new play about a Roman, Titus Andronicus. The
Londoners like gore and tragedy, it seems, or a good comedy with clowns.
Have you heard that the Queen had her cousin Mary of Scotland put to death
at Fotheringhay Castle? London buzzes with talk of a Catholic uprising, but
I think it will come to nothing. I enclose three pounds.
Kiss my children.

My dear Anne:
All London is a-buzz with the fright of the Armada. It truly seemed these
Spanish swine would take our fleet and invade England, but Drake and
Howard and their fellows were too cunning for them and the danger is past.
My Roman play is finished, and Mr Burbage is pleased with it, but when it
will go into our repertoire *I have no idea. I send twenty marks with this.*

Dear Anne:
Today we leave London to tour the country. We go North first…

Part Three

1589-1593

11.

Susanna ran shrieking through the front door, sending her little brother flying. Ignoring his wail, she grabbed her mother's arm. "Mama, there's a troupe of players come. It's Daddy! The players have come!" On her last words she turned and ran out as tempestuously as she had entered, knocking Hamnet down again.

"Susanna, wait," Anne called, then *faute de mieux* ran after her. "Wait for me! Susanna, it might not be your father." Too late. She seized the twins' hands and pelted after the child.

The rattle of drums. The blare of trumpets. The clatter of the wagons. The voices, singing and crying their arrival. *Come see the play. In the Guildhall. Three o'clock in the afternoon this day. The players are here!* Her heart thudding, Anne shaded her eyes to look. The players were bright in some great lord's livery, but the jackets weren't scarlet and the badges weren't the Bear and Ragged Staff of Lord Leicester.

"Susanna, love, I'm sorry, but it's not Daddy, it's not Lord Leicester's Men. *Susanna!*"

The little girl was running desperately, straight for one of the players. A man with a tanned face, curled hair, an earring in one ear. And he was leaping down from the cart, running to catch Susanna in his arms.

"Daddy! Oh, Daddy, Daddy, Daddy."

"Sweetheart, yes it's me, Susanna my love." He swept her up and covered her face with kisses. "Susanna, yes it's truly me, but where are my twins? Where's your mother?"

Slowly, Anne stepped forward from the gathering crowd. Her eyes met her husband's, and a smile of extraordinary intimacy broke across his face. He said, "Anne, my dear," and, interested, the players and half of Stratford watched a long and passionate kiss. The players gave them a round of applause.

"Oh, Will," Anne whispered, "why didn't you tell us you were coming? I've missed you, my dear."

"And I've missed you. Anne, I've so much to tell you. Are these the twins? Judith, Hamnet, do you remember me? Come and kiss me." Susanna was still clinging like grim death, her legs around his waist and her arms tight around his neck. Awkwardly he hunkered down and held out his free arm to the twins. Not remembering him well, or not as this gay and buccaneering figure, they were more interested in the white-faced clown in motley, capering around them and playing a flute.

"I take it this is your family, Will?" said a new voice.

William stood up. "James, yes. My wife, my daughter Susanna, my twins, Judith and Hamnet. Anne, this is Master Burbage, the leader of our troupe."

With a flourish James Burbage bowed to Anne. "Madam, your most humble servant. Will is a lucky man." He lifted her hand and kissed it. The twins giggled. Anne curtsied back, smiling up at this glamorous man.

"I am honoured, Master Burbage. May I bid you welcome to Stratford?"

"Indeed you may, Mistress Shakspere. A fine town it is. Now, I must wait upon your Mayor – Bailiff, is it here? Will, you are exempted from helping with the setting-up, go greet your family. Be back by two at latest or pay your two shillings fine." He clapped William's shoulder and turned back to his troupe, urging them on like sheep, bawling did they think they were here to make holiday, get *on*, they had to be on the boards by three of the clock. Smugly William watched them scamper. One, a pretty boy in his teens, made a vulgar gesture. William bowed delightfully.

"But he makes a lovely girl," said William. "Put him in a dress and he'll break your heart. Well, wife... home?"

But his mother barred his way. "Well, son? Am I not worth a greeting?"

"Mother, forgive me, my mind was on the children. Good-day; God save you." He kissed her, and her face softened.

"It's good to have you back. You look well. Is this the fashion in London, for men to wear an earring?"

"It has been for some time. Yes, Hamnet, what is it?"

"I *said*, who's the man with the white face?"

"William Kemp, our clown; a fellow of infinite jest. Wait till you see him juggle."

"What's juggle?"

"He throws things up and catches them. Lots of things, knives and oranges, anything to hand, and keeps them spinning. I can do it too, a little. I'll show you at home. Oh, look, there are the Sadlers. Judith, Hamnet, bid them good day."

Many other neighbours had been lured out by the news of the players and were staying to greet this unfamiliar native son. By the door of the Henley Street house stood a knot of people, staring in disbelief, and William's sister Joan broke free and ran to hug him.

"Will, you're home! We didn't dare hope, they said Lord Strange's Men, not Lord Leicester's, but it's you, it's really you."

"Yes, it's me. It's good to see you, Joan. Father..." Hesitantly they embraced. "Father, you're well?"

"All the better for seeing you. Gilbert, run and fetch up the best wine. Let's celebrate."

"When I've greeted my brother." Gilbert grinned and threw a quick arm round William's neck. "So, William Shakspere the player. Can London spare you?"

"With embarrassing ease. Wine, yes please, Gil, and Anne, Mother, is there any food? We've been on the road since five."

Gilbert fetched the wine, Mrs Shakspere went to hurry dinner forward. They finally prised Susanna off her father, though she sat pressed close against him. Cramming down bread and cheese, William tried to answer all their questions.

"Lord Leicester died last year. You heard, of course?" His father nodded, crossing himself. At the gesture, William's eyes flicked up to Anne's, then blandly away. "They say the Queen was sorely grieved. They'd been friends since their youth, some say she wanted to marry him. And, through friends, our troupe passed to Lord Strange. D'you know who I mean? Ferdinando Stanley, the Earl of Derby's son, and so we wear his livery." He touched the eagle's foot badge on his jacket. "And we play under his name. This is excellent cheese, we get none so good in London. Yes please, that was a way of asking for more. That's the thing about touring, it gets us out of the city into the clean air and the sun, and we get good food."

"You look thin," his mother said.

"Oh, d'you think so? No, I'm well."

"But London is unhealthy. And where do you lodge, son? I don't like the sound of it at all."

"The playhouse is outside the city, Mother, in one of the Liberties. Out past Bishopsgate, in Shoreditch. My lodgings are none so bad, Burbage lives nearby in Holywell Street. Half the company do. The landlady is clean; and yes, she feeds me well." His mother's mouth turned down dubiously. Hastily Anne asked what the troupe had played.

"At the Theatre, oh, everything. I could recite you the bloody *Spanish Tragedy* in my sleep. I probably will." Under the table he took her hand, lacing his fingers tightly into hers. She returned the squeeze, trying not to blush. They'd sleep together tonight. Sleep, and more besides, with luck. "And, oh, works by Greene and Nashe, and by Kit Marlowe, of course. No-one can get enough of him. Old stuff and new, whatever pays best."

"Do you *get* any pay?" his mother asked, and once again Anne rushed into the breach.

"Madam, you know he does, I told you how much he sent me with his letters. It seems," she couldn't resist adding, "that the theatre is a paying concern."

William put his hand on her arm, hushing her. His eyes never leaving his mother's face, he took his purse from his belt and spilt its contents across the table. In reverent, astonished silence his family looked at the pile of coins. Gold coins. More money, in cash, than most of them had ever seen.

"There's eleven pounds and a bit more there," William said evenly. "Made from playing and writing and patching up other men's plays. I can, at last, provide properly for my wife and children." He lifted Anne's hand and piled the coins one by one into her palm. "It's yours, love. I've enough for the rest of the tour, and there's a bit more in London." Neatly he folded her fingers down over the money. "You see, we common players share the groundlings' gate. That's the money paid by the people who stand in the space before the stage. Penny a head, and we cram 'em in. Burbage and his partner in the Theatre share the takings from the galleries. It's tuppence up there and an extra penny for a cushion if your bum can't stand bare wood. Yes, it pays. Enough for now."

"So it seems. And what parts have you played?"

"A bit of everything. Well, not the leads, I'm too junior yet. Got to work my way up. Spear carrier. Deathless lines like 'Here comes the King of France.' Funny how there's always a king of somewhere. I've fought for every nation on the earth, often, *mutatis mutantur*, for two different sides in the same piece. I've murdered and lied, poured wine, carried letters, been a Jew, a Spaniard, once a king myself – oh, and the loveliest girl."

"I noticed the beard had gone," Anne said drily.

"It'll be back again. I'm too old to play girls now. That's what the boys are for. With a wimple I can play a nurse. Or a mother. Or a queen."

"Surely it would be simpler just to allow women to play?"

"Anne!" said her father-in-law, truly shocked. "It's against the law, and for another thing, not even the lewdest woman would think of treading the stage."

"No, sir. I'm sorry."

"Quite right," William said straight-faced. "Think of the havoc women would cause in a company. And we're such a sober, God-fearing lot, we actors. We have women seamstresses to make our costumes, but that's a different kettle of fish. Speaking of fish…"

"Yes, dinner is ready. Come to table. William, you'll say the blessing?"

Listening to him, Anne thought how he'd changed in voice as well as in appearance. Some of the Warwickshire burr had gone, he turned some words in what she guessed was the London way, but most of all he spoke more clearly, deliberately and with a deeper tone. If this was what he could do with a simple meal-blessing, he was probably a good actor. Which was a relief. He had a mannered, fluid way of moving, and his gestures were controlled. It was all art, now, whatever the matter. He was brisk and confident and polished, much different from the provincial boy she'd sent away two years ago. You'd take him for a courtier today.

Out of that thought she said, "Will, have you seen the Queen?"

"Once, in the distance. It's the Queen's Men who get the commands to play the Palace. I saw her once, on the river, in her barge."

"Tell us."

"Well, gorgeously dressed, of course, ablaze with diamonds and rubies. A silver gown with lace and gauze, a high-standing ruff behind her head like a frame. It was after Armada time and she had Drake and Howard, Essex and Raleigh, all of them, with her in her boat. Laughing, and music was playing. She's an old woman now, close to sixty. She wears a lot of face-paint, very white with rouge on her cheeks and lips, and her gowns are low-cut and show her bosom." His mother tsked with shock. "She is a law unto herself, Mother. Gorgeous, and every inch a prince."

"Yet she put her cousin Mary of Scotland to death two years ago." Again John Shakspere made the sign of the Cross. William studied him for a moment, then turned away and cut another slice of pie.

"Yes, she did. It was put about that her secretary tricked her into signing the execution warrant. I don't know the truth, of course. But they say Mary was involved in plots, neck-deep in treason against our Queen and the peace of our realm."

"Faked evidence, an excuse to do her to death."

"Perhaps, Father. Or perhaps it's the truth. But her death has made her a martyr and the centre for Catholic sedition." For a long moment his eyes held his father's, whether in query or warning Anne wasn't sure. Then he said, lightly, "But I didn't finish telling you of my glories in the theatre. All London rings with my fame as a prompter, giving the actors their cues. Not to mention my way with managing the props and counting the cash. And, Father, when the costume gloves need mending or Master Burbage is going out in style, no one else will do."

"And do you write, Will? Do they act your work?"

"Sometimes. Audiences like works by names they know, and bums on seats is what matters in the theatre. In the Theatre. Perceive the difference the capital makes, Anne, for Burbage calls his theatre the Theatre."

"I perceive that the capital has made a vast difference, Will. But I hope your work is acted soon. Do you still write?" Thinking of all those nights when, however tired he was, he would find an hour or two to write; how often had she fallen asleep to the scratch of his pen, and woken to hear it still and see the candles guttered.

"Oh yes. And in the intervals I press my work on Burbage and Henslowe. If Marlowe can do it, so can I. But he, of course, is a Master of Arts from Cambridge and, therefore, taken seriously."

"A man of birth?" Anne had thought it was the ordinary sort who wrote for the stage.

"No, his father's a shoemaker, I think; he had a scholarship to university. Between us, if we can't furnish out the stage with plays, we could furnish out the players with shoes and gloves." Broodingly he said, "He's good, is Kit. His *Tamburlaine* is the most popular play in London. But yes, Anne, I go on writing when I can. And I know what *plays*, you see, I know what people like and what works on stage. Not everyone has that in their quiver. My stuff would do for the ordinary people, but the intellectuals want their plays written by one of the university wits to flatter themselves."

"You'll succeed yet, my dear."

"I daresay." Again that almost shifty look passed across his face. "Are you all coming to the play this afternoon? Oh, God's wounds, what's the time?"

"Not two yet."

"Oh, good." He settled back into his chair but shook his head when Gilbert made to fill his cup again. "So, are you coming to the play?"

"Can the children come?"

"If they're quiet. Which you will be, won't you, my loves? Good and quiet in the Guildhall to see your father act? Though you can cry bravo all you like, and clap, and boo the villain."

"See Daddy juggle?" Hamnet asked.

"Not in the play, darling. Will Kemp attends to the funny business."

"Juggle now, then. You *said*."

"You did, Will," Anne reminded him.

"I'm not very good at it. I can only manage three." Instantly the children pressed apples upon him. And he juggled. More than adequately, it seemed to Anne as she choked with laughter and applauded. He ended by bouncing an apple into each child's lap. "There, that's all for now. I must go soon to help set up for the play. Who's coming?"

"Me for one," said Gilbert.

"And I," said Joan. "A shame Richard and Edmund are in school; perhaps they can play truant and come to the play tomorrow."

"We-ell…" His parents consulted with a glance, then to Anne's surprise said yes, they would come. They'd always gone to the travelling companies' performances in the past, especially when John Shakspere was Bailiff, but the theatre had taken on the evil glimmer of Sodom and Gomorrah, luring their eldest son away. It was hard for them to hold up their heads when everyone knew their boy was a common hired player. They blamed themselves. But now, Anne noted, they were oddly, shyly proud of William. London fame meant little in Stratford, but hard cash was different. So yes, they said, they would go to the play.

"Then I'll see you all there." William kissed the children. "Ugh, wash your hands and faces first." Kissing Anne, he whispered in her ear, "I have a thing for you."

She glanced up through her lashes. "I certainly hope so."

"No, you shameless woman, not that. Well, that too. A thing at the theatre. You'll see."

They were in good time, it lacked half an hour to three when the Shaksperes filed into the Guildhall. Clutching the twins' hands Anne asked her mother-in-law to take a playbill; whether or not it listed William's name among the players, it would be something to put away and keep, a memory.

"Anne?" An uncertain reader, Mrs Shakspere turned a bewildered face on her. "Anne, can this be right?"

"Can what be right?"

"Well, look. Judith, give me your hand, let your mother see." She thrust the paper at Anne. Anne read it, and her jaw dropped.

"Lord Strange's Men present… under James Burbage… *The Two Gentlemen of Verona*. Look, O, look – *A play by William Shakspere*. Why didn't he say? A surprise, he said."

Gently her mother-in-law said, "My dear, he meant it as a compliment to you. After all, you believed in him all those years."

"You didn't want me to encourage him."

"No I did not, for it's not what we ever wanted for one of our children, but here he is with money in his purse and the good will of his fellows; and he is happy. It's given to few enough of us to be happy." She took the play-bill back from Anne and read it through again. "And after all, they could hardly come to Stratford with a play by John Shakspere's son and not perform it. And," she said confidently, "I am sure it is very good. Come along, children."

There was a painted backcloth and they had rigged some curtains at the sides to hide the actors' comings and goings. Wings, William had told her they were called. It was a shabby little makeshift arrangement, yet it held a magic. The audience hummed with anticipation. Sharp as the market clock struck three, a fanfare sounded and James Burbage strode onto the stage. Everyone clapped. He bowed his thanks then spread his hands.

"Gentles all," he flattered, "today we are honoured to play this gracious town of Stratford." (More applause.) "And it is meet that here we present a play by one of your own. My lords, ladies and gentlemen, Lord Strange's Men present a new work: *The Two Gentlemen of Verona*, by your own William Shakspere."

"My daddy!" Hamnet yelled then ducked into Anne's lap when everyone turned to look.

"Indeed." Burbage bowed to William's family, and again especially to Anne. "And now let us take you to Verona."

As writers say, as the most forward bud is eaten by the canker ere it blow, Even so by love the young and tender wit is turn'd to folly, blasting in the bud. Anne glanced at her mother-in-law's rapt face, saw the same enchantment on all the other faces. They weren't in Stratford any more, they were in Verona, and glovers had become lovers, hatters had become wits, solid matrons pretty girls.

Then Anne forgot who and where she was and let the play transport her.

"Was it good?"

"Wonderful."

"I meant the play."

"So did I."

"Ha!" William turned over, pulling Anne into his arms. He kissed her breast. "So you no longer call my loving wonderful? Yet I made you moan. Was *I* good?"

"In bed and on the stage, you were wonderful. But different, Will. It seems you've learned more in London than how to shape a play."

"Ah." She felt his lashes flutter in a guilty blink. "It's been two years, Anne, and I am a man."

"That excuses anything?"

"No. But explains it. I haven't taken a mistress, Anne, there's no-one who holds my heart. You're my wife. When I can bear it no longer alone, yes, I lie with others."

"And bring what they teach you home to me."

Angrily he said, "I wanted to give you pleasure. There's more to this business than four bare legs in a bed, much more than I ever knew here in Stratford. You always pleased me, Anne, but I've learnt more. I wanted to give you pleasure," he repeated.

"Well, you did. Yes. And you're a man. Yes. Just don't tell me anything of who else you take to bed."

"I wouldn't."

But after a moment's stolid silence she said, "Are there many other women?"

"No. Leave it at that, Anne. You're my wife and dear to me."

Wisely she did leave it at that. They lay, still embraced, saying nothing. She thought he was nearly asleep when he said, "Anne, is my father still deep in the old religion?"

"He doesn't speak of it to me for he knows I don't approve. But yes. Is it dangerous, Will? He's been fined for not attending church, but is it worse than that?"

"Yes," he said soberly. "It's very dangerous. God knows there are plenty of recusants all over the country, but most of them have the sense to show outward conformity. The Queen prefers tolerance, but her patience has its limits and there are men in her government who aren't minded to be tolerant or patient. I hear a lot in London, Anne. Some of it is gossip and silly rumour, some's spite; but the Catholics are active and running into danger. It's worse since Mary of Scotland died. God's nails, between the Puritans and the Catholics a man doesn't know what innocent remark might run him into trouble. The Puritans spend their entire time trying to close the playhouses, afraid people might enjoy themselves. But dabbling in the old religion is as dangerous as witchcraft, Anne. Many people see no difference between the two."

Curiously, because they'd never much discussed these matters, Anne asked, "And what are your beliefs, Will, deep in your secret heart?"

"I wish people could be left alone to worship as they like. What does it *matter*, when you come down to it?"

"The Queen is head of the English church, so it matters. It's close to treason not to follow the Anglican way."

"But in the end, if one's a Christian, what does the form matter? It's all a way for the government to hold people in control."

"I hope you don't go around London saying that."

"Oh no. I go to church on Sunday, I take my communion three times a year; we theatre people come under enough suspicion as it is. Conformity is all. Queen Elizabeth is God's Anointed and Head of the Church. Once we die, the rest is silence. But I must warn my father not to meddle openly with Catholicism. Thanks be, we'll never have the Inquisition in England and Bloody Mary's days won't come back, but between the government men looking for sedition and the Puritans and the other fanatics, even a Stratford glover must be careful."

"Tell him so."

"Aye, I will. And Anne, make sure no-one can reproach you with lack of conformity. Obey the law. Go to church, praise God and the Queen, see the children learn their Catechism, speak openly against the old religion. *Do* the children know their Catechism?"

"Of course, do you take me for a fool? Church twice on Sunday, all the proper teachings. Hamnet starts next year at the petty school, remember."

"Oh God do I remember. ABCs and horn books, letters in the cross-row, why don't you know your lesson, William, over the bench with you, here's a way to make you learn. And then on to the upper school and rhetoric and bloody logic and bloody Latin and here's a thrashing for you, boy, and conjugate the verb, and why are we muffing our construe, Master William, over the bench for a reminder of the ablative bloody absolute, and spare the rod and spoil the child, let's hear the Catechism... You're lucky you didn't go to school."

"So it seems. Bartholomew was very gentle in teaching me to read. Did you thrash the boys you taught?"

"Only if they gave me cheek. And then I chastised their cheeks. I'd better write some more plays, for if I ever have to go back to being an usher in a school I'll hang myself. I still need a patron, Anne, some nobleman who'll let me use his name and who'll accept my poems. And, it's to be hoped, pay me well."

"Would Lord Strange do it? Have you met him again?"

Yawning, William said, "Yes, briefly. Yes, he might. But he's in bad odour with the government at present." He yawned again, and slid his arms out from around Anne to turn over.

Snuggling against his back, wrapping her feet around his, she said, "Why is he?"

"Suspected of Catholic sympathies. And he's got a claim to the throne, which under a Tudor monarch means you're for the block."

Nearly asleep Anne said, "What claim? How?"

"His mother was a Clifford. Descended from Henry the Seventh, I think. Perhaps even worse, from the Plantagenets. Can't remember. A distant claim, but enough in the Queen's eyes. He's suspect. The Tudors like to get rid of anyone with the shadow of a claim; wonder he's left alive. And the Stanleys are famous for turning their coats. The Queen won't believe he's loyal just because he says so. Though I think he is. He's not stupid. A pleasant man. Might ask him, be my patron, poems. G'night, my love."

"Goodnight, my dear." As she slid over the edge into sleep she thought, that's only about the second time he's ever called me 'my love'.

12.

The children had misunderstood, they had thought their father back for good. Susanna's eyes, William's eyes, were huge in her stricken face as she cried, "But I don't want you to go away! I love you, Daddy."

William squatted down and put his hands on her shoulders. "Sweetheart, I love you too, of course I do. But I must go. I never meant to stay; I cannot. Child, I explained this when first I went to London. This is how I earn my living. I have to go on touring, then back to London. And now, I can come home more often, and perhaps your mother will bring you to London."

"I want you to stay. Now. Don't go."

Straightening up he said, "I must, Susanna. Be brave, be good. Needs must. And I must go today, with the players."

"I hate them. Stay. Please!"

"I cannot."

"But I want you to."

"Then want must be your master, Susanna."

He had never spoken to her so harshly. Mama and Grandam were the ones for firmness and discipline, her father the one for indulgence. She had always been his pet, and thought she could do as she liked with him.

"I hate you," she said, and stamped her foot. William looked coolly down at her.

"Never say that, Susanna. I love you very much. But I must go. And I don't want to take away the memory of a spoiled and insolent child. Come now, love, you're seven, you can read, you're a clever girl. Be a good one too, and sensible. I have to go and there's an end to it."

No colour in her face she stared for a moment then spun around and raced off up the stairs. William sighed and looked at Anne. "I thought she understood."

"She didn't want to. She loves you so dearly, Will. They all do."

"And I love them, but love won't pay the bills."

"I know."

He put his hand on her shoulder. She turned away.

"What, Anne?"

"What do you *think!*" she cried, shaking off his hand. "Susanna said it for all of us. You have to go, yes, but *let us come too!*"

"But..."

"Oh, but me no buts, William. Don't you know, can't you imagine, how boring my life is here? How much I miss you? How sick I am of lodging in your parents' house? How much I want a change and some fun? And do you know, do you care, that your only son never quite believes you exist because he couldn't remember you? And now you are a god to him, he adores you, and you are going to go away and leave me to explain to him why you're no longer here. Hamnet is four and a half years old, William, and you are about to break his heart."

Again his hand fell on her shoulder, hard this time, gripping, turning her about to face him. "Lovely speech. Thank you. I love my children."

"I know, but –"

"You said it: but me no buts. Have you thought, Anne, of what it would be like to live in London?"

"Of nothing else. You fool."

"How dirty it is, how unwholesome the air, how bad for children, how expensive, how you'd know no one there?"

"Yet it's full of families. Other players' wives and children live there."

"I'm on the road half the year."

"Half a loaf's better than no bread."

"God save me from platitudes!"

"We could come home when you went on tour. We could manage. Will, please. Or by God *you* will go and tell your son goodbye for another two years, *you* will explain it to him as you did, so charmingly, to poor Susanna. *You* will be the one who hurts them and I, for once, will be the one who blames you."

His mouth twisted as he thought it over. "You strike a hard bargain."

"Perhaps it is about time I did."

"You really want this?"

"Yes."

"Very well. When the summer's over. I'll see about a lodging."

"You mean it?"

"Yes, my dear, I do. And to prove it I'll go tell the children."

13.

Six weeks later William wrote that he had found a house. It was in Shoreditch, near the playhouses, with open fields at its back. A kitchen and two rooms downstairs, three rooms upstairs, a privy in the garden and a wash-house at the back. It had some furniture, he wrote, beds and tables, but Anne must bring all her household stuff.

Household stuff, she thought; did she have enough? She routed out her trousseau goods, most of which had lain untouched in boxes in the attic all these years. Cooking pans, pewter and earthenware plates and cups, towels, two precious crystal glasses, some cushions and, most special of all, a tapestry. Little enough. The blankets and bed curtains, the painted wall-hanging and the rug which she had brought to her marriage had seen hard wear. Ruthlessly she threw out anything too shabby and bought new, spending some of the extra money William had sent with his letter. It meant paying for carriage to London, but that was better than arriving in the city, with winter coming on, without enough warm blankets and curtains. Her stepmother combed Hewlands Farm for goods and sent in a wagon loaded with three chairs, a table, a court cupboard, a hamper of hangings and a carpet, a lot of bottled fruit, some excellent copper pans, a ham and two hard cheeses. Mrs Shakspere and Joan worked day and night with Anne, washing and polishing, and sewing new clothes for the children and the only new dress Anne had had since her wedding.

At the middle of October they set out. Held down to the slow pace of the wagon, they were lucky to make ten or twelve miles a day; a good thing, Anne believed, that they were travelling before the worst of winter made the roads into quagmires. She spared a thought for William and the other players who did this sort of journey year in, year out, in the heat of summer or through the worst weather, trudging beside their carts from one country town to another, lucky to find a decent inn at the end of the day.

The children soon grew bored with travelling and squabbled endlessly over who was to ride on the cart and who up behind Anne or their uncle Gilbert (Mr Shakspere would not hear of a woman and children travelling alone, not these days, you never knew). Anne made them walk most of the time it wasn't raining, because it left them too tired at nightfall to quarrel.

Ten days on the road, then they saw London ahead.

The children had envisaged an instant visit to the menagerie in the Tower, and they were disappointed to enter from the north by the road which, through the wall of the City proper, became Bishopsgate Street. William's letter had given careful directions but still Anne couldn't believe this was the right house. It was almost new, not more than fifty years old. And fine. Too fine. Newly whitewashed, the windows gleaming; more broad windows upstairs. But there was William lounging through the front door, a smug smile on his face.

"Welcome home, Mrs Shakspere. Will it do?"

"Do? Oh, Will. Can we afford it?"

"Yes," he said negligently. "It's been empty some time and the landlord was glad to let it. Hello, my darlings, like your new home?" They did. Pausing only to hug William, they raced inside to explore, their shoes echoing on the floors and stairs. "You look tired," William told Anne, giving her a kiss. "A hard journey?"

"Tiresome more than hard. It's good to see you. Well, let's see this house."

It was splendid. Two spacious rooms downstairs and a kitchen with a clear-burning hearth; upstairs, a big room overlooking the street and two smaller rooms for the children. Up in the roof were another two tiny rooms for servants. William had had a woman come in to scrub, he proudly told Anne, and the maid was at the market even as they spoke.

"So all you need do is make the beds. Gil and I will bring all these goods in. Look, Mistress Burbage sent a basket of wafers, and these flowers, to welcome you, and she'll call tomorrow when you've had a chance to settle in. Dick Field's wife, too, and Ned Alleyn's. You won't be without friends here, Anne."

"How kind," Anne said dazedly. The scrub-woman had missed a few cobwebs high up, she noted, but it would be churlish to mention it. The children thundered back down the stairs and out through the kitchen, Judith screeching about the garden.

"They're happy. Come, let's have a glass of wine to christen the house."

"No cups till we unpack."

"Damn. Then come on, brother, let's to it."

That night Anne lay wakeful beside her snoring husband, listening to London. At Stratford a fox barking in the distance was a din; here, despite the curfew, people never seemed to go to bed. A horse clopped past, a cat yowled the agonies of love, two people across the way started a violent argument. Hamnet stirred in his sleep, whimpering with a dream. Anne tried to ease her body, aching from the journey and the rush of unpacking. She felt deadly tired yet wide awake.

She tried planning the things needed in the house: the kitchen walls washing, shelves to be put up for William's books and her pieces of pewter and glass. Another clothes chest for the twins' room. And really they were too old now to share a bed. Judith must be made to move to Susanna's room. Where are the best shops and who are the reliable tradesmen? Put up that extra hanging in here, although it was a good room, high and wide, with a really handsome bed. Some new curtains wouldn't hurt. Speak to William about money and get a household allowance. Get Gilbert to nail down some squeaky floorboards; he was good with his hands. Plant out winter vegetables.

In everything, it was a new life. And William would not have wanted her to come to London if there was anything... anyone...

14.

Another new play, and Anne was going to the theatre. Hamnet was at school, Susanna and Judith spending the day with the family of one of the other players. For any housewife with children, a day to herself was a holiday, and Anne sang under her breath as she dressed. In Stratford a woman who used face-paint was rated as a whore, but in London a touch of rouge and black on the eyelashes was permissible. At thirty-six she had some fine lines around her eyes, but her skin was clear and soft, she had no need of the white-lead pastes and vivid stains of city women. On the whole, she thought as she peered at her reflection in William's small mirror, not too bad for a middle-aged woman. A dab of scent behind the ears, and she was ready.

Hearing the knock on the door she pulled on her new green coat and hat and hurried down the stairs. One thing London was not, was a place where a woman could safely go about alone, and William paid one of the theatre boys, a Cockney hanger-on who did rather well out of holding horses and running messages, to escort her to the playhouse. She liked this boy, whose only name seemed to be Nol, and he was a good escort, although she would not have cared to translate some of his advice to people who jostled her.

When first she came to the capital she had expected shining white towers and a silken ribbon of blue for a river, people in bright clothes, scented air. What she had found was a tangle of little streets under a haze of smoke; mud and middens; coarse-voiced people drably dressed; and the chance of losing your purse or your life if you didn't look lively. It was filthy and stinking, a hotbed of vice and crime, and at first she had hated it. But soon the city had won her round. It had life. Only in London could you find such shops and grand palaces among the warrens, or see ships in from Venice, Spain, Turkey. Only here could you take a boat idly on the river to see the sights, and find yourself waving to the Queen as her barge passed on a wave of music and scent. Only here could you rub elbows with the men whose names rang around England: Raleigh, Drake, Howard, Essex, Cecil, Walsingham. And only here were the playhouses.

At The Theatre, Nol saw her to her seat, paid the extra penny for a cushion, bought her a poke of hazelnuts and a mug of ale and gave a little more advice to a man who thought a woman coming alone to the playhouse must be plying for trade.

"Better sit wiv you, Mrs S, keep fellows like that away." His eyes shone with longing as he looked at the stage, and solemnly Anne agreed that would be best.

"Have you seen this play, Nol?"

"*Richard Free*? Only in rehearsal, like. It's Master Will's best, they say. 'E packs 'em in, does Master Will. they take more money off of 'is plays than all the rest. Nor it ain't just the take. 'E's good."

In his way this boy was a connoisseur. He'd been hanging around playhouses since he was old enough to pick a pocket. He must have seen every play put on in London in his lifetime.

"He is good," Anne agreed, and companionably they shared the hazelnuts. "Not a bad house. Nearly full."

"They'll pack a few more in. Oi, Kit Marlowe's in."

"Wants to find out how it's done, no doubt. Where? I don't see him."

"Down the front. See?"

Anne peered, and located Christopher Marlowe by his bobbing black head. He was talking (but when was he not?) to someone, his hands flying as he rattled earnestly on. Anne caught his eye and waved. He blew her a kiss, and indicated by a complex gesture that the playhouse was too full for him to join her. "See you afterwards?" she made out, and nodded.

She liked Kit Marlowe; impossible not to, for all he was the most notorious bugger in London and almost certainly one of Walsingham's spies. He had been kind to Will when he first came to London, reading his work and approving it, and he showed commendably little resentment that his one-time protégé was rapidly overtaking him in fame. He had charm, that was the thing. He flirted outrageously with Anne, which she enjoyed because it was safe, but under the flirting and the loudly paraded atheism and love of boys he had a keen mind and a surprising gentleness. William trusted him and was his friend, which was good enough for Anne, even if she hadn't liked him for his own sake.

Nol tugged at her sleeve. "There's a feller over there wavin' at you, Mrs S. Shall I go an' give 'im what for?"

"No," Anne said hastily. "I know him." She waved back to Sir George Carewe; he was one of the richest men from Stratford way, he had married a Clopton heiress. Bowing, he beckoned to her: come join me. There was just time before the play started. With Nol clearing a way for her, Anne threaded through the crowded galleries, clutching her penny cushion, and sat down beside Sir George.

"My dear Mistress Anne, how pleasant to see you." He leaned forward a little to speak to the lady on his other side. "Your ladyship, your lordship, may I present to you Mrs Shakspere?" The blue hat with the fantastically long, curving feathers turned, revealing a tired, pretty, face. Without much interest, but willing to be pleasant, the lady nodded to Anne. Beside her a very young man whose auburn hair fell to his shoulders, turned also. Anne bowed. "Her ladyship the Dowager Countess of Southampton," said Sir George, "and her son the Lord Southampton." Astounded, Anne bowed again, more deeply, murmuring a greeting.

"Shakspere?" said the young man, and his cornflower eyes sparked. "Are you related to the playwright?"

"I am his wife, my lord."

"Then it is an honour to meet you. I greatly admire your husband's work. I've seen all his plays. I think him a good actor, too."

"Thank you, my lord."

"Yes," said the Countess, "his plays always entertain. We have thought of asking this company to enact a play for us, privately. I believe they do that. In private houses."

"Indeed they do, my lady."

"Then we shall see to it. But hush, it's starting."

Expectation fell over the audience. Anne knew William came on early in the play, and she knew he would be waiting behind the curtains, trying to calm the stage-fright that still came over him. Other actors, Anne knew, needed a drink or a pipe of tobacco – or other things – before they went on; William's stage-fright took the form of intense sleepiness. It vanished the moment he went on stage, but between his scenes he had to fight to stay awake.

Outside a clock chimed the hour. The trumpets blew. The audience rustled into silence, then gasped as an evil, black, hunchbacked creature lurched onto the stage:

"Now is the winter of our discontent made glorious summer by this Sun of York, and all the clouds that lour'd upon our house are in the deep bosom of the ocean buried."

Anne almost forgot to look for William, realised he was playing Clarence, shoved her knuckles in her mouth when the guards hauled him away to prison and death. Then the wooing scene took her breath away, even if she'd laughed when William read her the scene: what woman, she had mocked, could fall so instantly in love with the man who'd killed her family? William had sulked. And he'd been right, for the scene worked on stage. It worked superbly.

The play sped on, the bottled spider dominating every scene and making the audience like him for all his wickedness. Yes, Anne thought, this is good, it's his best, it will live and live. William was back as Tyrell, then as a soldier in the final battle, and then it was over. On her feet with the rest, applauding, shouting, Anne knew she had seen a great play, a superb play, a play for all time. And that word-struck boy I loved in Stratford wrote it. The man capable of writing this play married me, Anne Hathaway the farmer's daughter. I was right to send him away. For all it cost me, I was right. And had I not encouraged him, would he still be making gloves in Stratford, a bitter man with failed longing in his eyes?

"Mrs S?" Nol gingerly touched her elbow. "Mrs S? You want to go back stage? I'll take you."

"Yes. Yes, Nol, I do. It was good, wasn't it?

"It's 'is best. See Buckin'am forget 'is lines? I thought Master Will'd belt 'im one in the chops."

"No, I didn't notice. It was wonderful. Come, then, let's go behind. Lady Southampton, Lord Southampton, it was my great honour to meet you. Good day to you. And to you, Sir George. Perhaps we will meet again while I'm here." With a final bow she gathered up her skirts to leave.

"Mistress Anne," Sir George's voice halted her. "If you go behind scenes, would you be so kind as to allow his lordship to accompany you? I will see her ladyship home, but Lord Southampton has the fancy to pay his compliments to the players."

If the Earl of Southampton had not been so young, Anne would have felt overwhelmed; nervous, too, lest she commit some dreadful *faux pas* that would disgrace her husband. But he *was* young, just a boy, and so clearly eager to be pleased. Hamnet looked so like that when offered a treat that it was impossible for Anne be shy. Curtsying again she said, "Of course, sir. My lord, they will be delighted and honoured. But if you've not been back-stage before, be prepared, it can be noisy. You will think them all mad."

People knew Southampton and there was no need to clear the way for him. But at the bottom of the steps Christopher Marlowe waited, so that Anne walked almost into his arms.

"Your lordship," she turned to Southampton, "are you acquainted with Master Marlowe?"

With a shy smile the young earl said, "We have met, yes. Do you also go behind scenes, Master Marlowe?"

"Indeed I do, my lord. Anne, my lovely girl, light of my life, come kiss your humble servant."

"The day Kit Marlow's humble we can look for a hot January." She kissed him.

"Yet Chaucer tells us January ran hot for a lovesome maid."

"But I'm no maid."

"But as lovely as May. Excellent play, isn't it. That husband of yours is good. *Some* people even speak of him as a second Marlowe. Did you see that clodhopper playing Lady Anne get his dress stuck in his bum-crack? Come along, we'll go behind and I'll compliment your husband; through clenched teeth." Serious for a moment he said, "He *is* good, Anne."

"Better than you?" she teased.

Still serious, he said, "One day he will be. I'd better kill him, I think."

"Would you widow me, Christopher?"

"Only if you would then marry me and bring me Will's luck. Oh dear, oh dear, such fun we have back-stage."

Southampton looked taken aback, as well he might. A stranger might have thought the company all at odds, might have expected drawn swords and sent for the Watch. Anne knew it was only the euphoria and irresponsible high spirits of the good performance of a successful play, and here and there the free and frank exchange of views, meaning nothing but given meaning by the actors being still in their stage voices.

The 'tire-master was shrieking to have a care of the costumes as people jostled, the stage manager was counting the props back into the hamper, the actors congratulating themselves and each other, visitors trying to throng into the cramped confines backstage. Cries rang in Anne's ears: *Well done, a perfect play. I look hideous in this dress. He missed my cue again, Will. Did you see that girl in the front, the one with the tits? Will, we must talk. Nearly ten pounds we took today. Early call tomorrow, gentlemen, to rehearse the new piece. I say well done, absolutely superb. It's too long, Will, we have to cut it.*

That last caught William's attention. "Cut it? Never."

"But Will..."

"Cut a play by William Shakspere? Think what you say!"

"But Will..."

"Go." William had seen his wife. "Anne, my dear. What did you think?"

"It was good, Will."

"Well of course it was. I wrote it."

"Yes, and it is truly good. I'm proud of you. And you were right about the wooing scene."

"I'm always right, I'm Shakspere. Yes, Kit, what *is* it? Don't pluck my sleeve like that."

"No, don't, Master Marlowe," said the passing 'tire-master. "It's costume. Give it back, Will, before it's damaged."

Ignoring him, Kit said, "We bring you an admirer, Will. My lord, William Shakspere, author of this piece. William, His Worship the Lord Southampton."

That brought a silence as perhaps nothing else could have done just then. Into the silence the Earl's soft voice spoke. "I do not mean to intrude upon you, gentlemen. I wish to present my compliments. A wonderful play, wonderfully acted, and written by a master."

William smiled. Christopher Marlowe did not.

"I have to thank you," Southampton continued, "for three hours' delight. And more than three hours, in the past, and I hope more than three hours again. A brilliant play."

William bowed his thanks, staring at the Earl. As well he might, thought Anne, for Southampton was very, very beautiful. Close-to like this, one saw the face of a very young man – eighteen? less? – still with the epicene beauty of adolescence; but for all that it was a man's face. He was tall and slim in the way that said he hadn't finished growing. The long hair falling over his shoulders was a gleaming auburn gold, his eyes the colour of cornflowers, thickly, silkily lashed. His clothes were dove-grey and tawny velvet, studded with jewels and laced with gold no brighter than his hair. A pearl and gold brooch starred his hat and a pearl drop hung in his ear. He smelt of sandalwood and chypre, and when he smiled, as he did now at William, his teeth showed white and even as more pearls.

"Will, get that costume *off*," said Dick Burbage Then, "Oh, my Lord Southampton. My pardon, I did not see you at first. Good day to Your Worship." True actor, he added, "You saw our play today? Did you enjoy it?"

"Greatly, Master Burbage. Your performance was beyond praise. They say King Richard was a wicked man but tell me, do you believe a hunchback could ride into battle and fight as manfully as the records tell us he did?"

"My lord, speaking after three hours laced into that hunchback costume, I doubt it. But then, I doubt he really was a hunchback. People still remember him, you know. Perhaps Will should give him some different deformity to prove his mind's wickedness?"

"What do you want of me, Dick? A good play or a history lesson?

"A good play every time, Will; drama. And that costume, thank you." Grumpily William peeled it off and stuffed it into Burbage's arms. Anne handed him his own shirt. Someone shouted to Burbage to hurry up, the alehouse would be drunk dry by the time they got there.

"Are you," Southampton wistfully asked, "going to the tavern?"

"Yes?"

"Then may I come too?"

Flabbergasted, William said, "But my lord, we go to a common place. It's all players and common folk. It's not fit for you."

"I've been in taverns before. I'm not a schoolboy. I would like it."

And now, thought Anne, who had smacked just such lordly sulks out of Hamnet, you'll stamp your foot and shout that you *will* have your way.

Caught between caution and the need to please a nobleman William said, "My lord, you are Lord Burghley's ward, and I have my way to make. I don't want to explain to the most powerful man in England that I let his ward be robbed or murdered in a London alehouse."

"When I went before I did have my tutor – my secretary – with me," Southampton admitted, the sulks clearing, "and he soon took me away. I should not have asked you, should I? You'll want to be alone with your fellows."

He looked so downcast that William said, "You are most welcome to bear us company. But not to the tavern, I think. My lodgings are humble, but I would be honoured to receive you there."

Southampton blushed. "If you mean it, the honour is mine."

"Then come along." But William dropped back to murmur to Anne, "Is the place tidy enough?"
Somehow regaining her breath she said, "It is, but Will, how can you invite *the Earl of Southampton* there? Think who he is!"

"He's a boy, and stage-struck, and he admires my work. A possible patron, Anne. God knows I could do with one."

"Ah," said Anne, and snapped her fingers to the boy Nol, silently trailing them. "Here's some money; go buy good ale and the best wine you can, Malmsey or Canary wine, French claret; no rot-gut, mind, his lordship is used to the best. And some Ginevers and brandy."

"Tell Sarfampton to keep 'is 'and on 'is purse." The boy scampered away. Reminded, Will and Anne closed in on the Earl. Kit Marlowe, shuffling moodily along behind, filled and lit his tobacco pipe and, in a cloud of smoke, they finished the short journey to William's lodgings.

Anne had seen Southampton House up on High Holborn; no doubt its smallest chamber was bigger than her entire home. She wondered what the Earl had expected. But the rooms were, if plain, clean and tidy and they had the grace notes of a Turkey carpet, some silver plate, brocade and velvet cushions. And books. Last winter William had paid the theatre carpenter to nail up shelves for him wherever there was room, and the books had been busily breeding ever since. After one interested glance about, Southampton doffed his hat and cloak and began to inspect the books. Once or twice his brows rose in surprise; occasionally he took down a favourite.

"You have wide interests, Master Shakspere."

"Here in my home, my lord, call me Will, everyone does. I've a magpie's tastes, I read anything and everything. London's booksellers all know me and they keep books for me. Wine, your lordship?"

"Harry. If you are Will, then I am Harry." As he took the glass from William he gave him such a sweet and piercing smile that Anne felt as if the world had for a moment spun in reverse.

She was glad when Southampton moved on to look down at the papers to William's writing table. "Have you a new work in preparation? Could I hear some of it?"

"That's an appeal that never fails," Anne said drily. She could have added, "Nor does flattery, to a writer". Aloud, she said, "Read him your *Lover's Complaint*, Will."

"It's not finished."

"But it's good," Kit said. "You're fast overtaking me, Will my friend. Read it."

Three hours later the boy Nol was asleep on cushions in the corner, the room was hot from the fire and clouded with Kit's tobacco smoke. Most of the wine had been drunk, and all of the ale; crusts and bones on platters showed that they must have eaten, though none of them could remember doing so. The men were all in their shirtsleeves. Anne sat with her head on William's shoulder and his arm around her; Harry sat literally at William's feet, curled up on a cushion before the fire. They had heard *The Lover's Complaint*, Kit's half-written *Hero and Leander*, sonnets, parts of William's and Kit's new plays. None of them was drunk, except on words, but an intimacy had sprung up among them that had something of drink's enchantment to it.

"They want me to marry," Southampton said reflectively into the silence. "They nag, they cozen, they beguile, they order me. *You must marry and beget an heir*, is all I hear. My mother, Lord Burghley, my friends. Burghley wants me to wed his granddaughter."

"Then why not do it?"

"I'm only nineteen."

"I was married at eighteen," William said, "and a father at nineteen."

"But you married for love. Didn't you? People like you can, you see. And you're happy in your marriage, I can see that."

"Yes," said William, and stroked Anne's cheek. "Yes I married for love, and we are happy."

Now why, wondered Anne, does he say that as if it's a prayer, an invocation, rather than a statement of fact? Yet it's the first time he has said it.

"Then there's your answer!" cried the Earl. "I will not marry where I do not love. I will not be sold into marriage to make Burghley's granddaughter a countess. And I've no reason to think well of marriage."

"Yet rank has its obligations," William said gently. "And when you hold your newborn child in your arms, everything, anything, is worthwhile, for then you know the meaning of love."

"Even a child begotten in dislike? For cold duty?"

"Now there I can't answer you from personal experience. But yes, I suspect so."

Southampton swivelled around to look at Marlowe. "And you? What do you say in this debate?"

"I? I'm not qualified to speak. Marriage is not for me." At Southampton's uncertain glance towards Anne he said, "Oh, our lovely Anne knows what I am. A ganymede; a sodomite; a practitioner of the Greek vice."

"Sweet Hellene, make me immortal with a kiss," murmured William, and Southampton laughed until he cried.

"So marriage is not for me," Kit went on, "but I agree that a man of your standing and rank will have to wed, and soon; also, Burghley will have his way. He is the most powerful man in England. Have a care for those around you who may be... vulnerable."

"Yes, yes. But I will not be sold." As if in comment, outside a clock struck nine. Reluctantly Harry Southampton rose to his feet. "I must go. I am expected at home, where I have never enjoyed myself so much as here. This has been the best of times. Thank you. Mrs Shakspere – Anne – I trust we will meet again." To her pleasure he kissed her hand. "It has been a delight to meet you. Will, Kit, I bid you goodnight."

"But you can't go alone through London," William exclaimed. "Not after dark. I'll come with you. Kit, you will bear Anne company for half an hour?"

"With pleasure."

"Then it's settled. Where's my cloak?" William gave Anne a hasty kiss and ushered Southampton out.

Anne opened a window, not that London's night air was the perfumed exhalation of the gods, and stirred up the fire. When she went to check on the sleeping children their tabby cat rushed in to the warmth, paraded around the hearthrug then tucked itself up, purring.

"Kit," said Anne, "you know all the London gossip. What do you know of Lord Southampton?"

"I've met him a time or two. I like him. A sweet-tempered boy, although spoilt. Clever, learned, educated."

"I could surmise so much for myself. What else do you know? Why did he say he's no reason to think well of marriage?"

"Ah. His parents married young. Not a successful marriage. By the time Harry was, oh, four, his parents were at odds. His father accused his mother of adultery, she accused him of being under the thumb of one of his servants; perhaps under a little more than that. They parted, Harry was sent to live with his father, and both he and his sister, Lady Mary, were forbidden to see their mother. I heard that in his will Harry's father left ludicrous signs of favour to his servant and stated that his daughter was not so much as to be in the same house as her mother."

"A hard man, then. Unforgiving. Spiteful, even."

"Perhaps. He died when Harry was eight. Left enormous debts, I believe. Lands, of course, because the Wriothesleys own half England, and castles, houses. But the old earl had lived past his income. Harry's wardship was sold to one of the Howards, I believe, then Burghley snapped it up. Let's be fair; Burghley's keen for money and to marry his jumped-up family into the nobility, but he's a good man, and he takes good care of his wards. Harry had the best education, first at Burghley's own school then St John's at Cambridge and Gray's Inn. Probably he had a happy home life with the Burghleys. But when you've spent the first eight years of your life as a pawn in your parents' quarrels, never seeing your mother and being taught to think her an adulterous shrew, no, you would not think well of marriage."

"I daresay not," Anne agreed. "Poor boy."

"Yes. My family's nothing. My father's a shoemaker, there's no money, there were all the usual troubles and quarrels, but I had a happy enough childhood. My parents are proud of me, so far as they can understand." He stroked the cat with his foot, and it looked up at him, its eyes half-closed. There was something cat-like about Kit himself, Anne mused. His face was triangular or heart-shaped, wide across the eyes and slanting down to a small chin. His hair was black and very silky, like a cat's fur, and his eyes a feline green. He could claw on occasions, too, and purr.

"For all that," Kit went on, "Harry Wriothesley is a beautiful boy who one day should be rich, he's been an earl since he was eight and he's been petted and flattered all his life."

"Spoilt."

"It's to his credit that he's not, or not more than tolerably so. I daresay he's vain, but who wouldn't be if they've been compared all their life to Adonis, Apollo, Narcissus, called beautiful, been courted for their influence and favour? The nobility of England, Anne, are a law unto themselves. They are, or would like to be, soldiers and statesmen, advisers to the Queen. They are, or would like to be, poets and word-spinners. They go to plays, they discuss books, they are familiar with the classics and the new sciences, they toss recondite allusions about and cap one another's quotations. They like to have a pet poet or playwright."

"Like you. Or Will."

"Yes, indeed. We too are courted and petted and flattered. We reflect glory on our friends and patrons."

"So Will may find in Southampton the patron he wants?"

"Yes he may. Anne, does Will's father still practice the old religion?"

He had slid that question very deftly into the sleepy, slow companionship. Startled, as he no doubt intended, Anne kept her wits about her.

"Still? I didn't know he ever had. I live in his house, Kit, and I have never seen anything but the observances of the established Church. Why do you do it, Kit?"

"Do what?"

"Don't fence with me. Why do you spy for Walsingham? Why do you persecute Catholics? The man who said 'I count religion but a childish toy and hold there is no sin but ignorance', the man who proudly proclaims his atheism and love of tobacco and boys and upholds freedom of thought is surely not the man to believe in religious persecution."

"But Catholics are traitors. They plot against our lawful monarch Queen Elizabeth."

"I daresay some do, but a government man whose life and reputation depends on discovering Catholic plots is bound to discover them, isn't he? Or to manufacture them."

"Dangerous talk, Anne. What if I went straight to Walsingham with that remark?"

"I'd be in the Tower, being tortured. But you won't carry tales to Walsingham, will you? Not of me, or Will?"

"*Are* there tales to carry?"

"No, as you know well. We're no Papists. Nor are we traitors, although a jesting remark such as I made just now can be twisted into a case against an innocent person. Why do you do it, Kit? Do you like the danger? Are you playing both sides against each other? An atheistical sodomite is flirting with danger by his mere existence. Why add to it? Or do you protect yourself by working for Walsingham?"

"Perhaps. And you, Anne Shakspere, are not supposed to know I work for Walsingham. Did Will tell you?"

"The entire country knows it," she said scornfully. "Well, all of London, at least. And I wonder why you, a brilliant man, our friend, a good man in so many ways, spy and help harass people who are innocent of treason and want nothing but to worship as they believe. Didn't the Queen herself once say that she has no window to see into people's hearts and if they are loyal to her, she cares not how they worship?"

"Will talks too much."

"After ten years of marriage I often agree, but not in the way you mean." With growing anger she went on, "You, Christopher Marlowe, you who never venture outside London or Cambridge unless it's to go overseas on these spying missions, you don't know what ordinary people think and feel and believe. Ordinary people – the Marlowes in Canterbury, the Shaksperes in Stratford, the cordwainers and glovers, the labourers, the burghers, the merchants and shopkeepers, the women, the shepherds – these people love the Queen, they admire her, they think of her with almost religious awe; at worst they believe she's a good monarch and they are loyal to her, even if they follow the old religion."

"Yet Catholics," Kit flashed back at her, "take their orders from the Pope and from the Catholic monarchs of Catholic countries. If the Pope says, as he does, that our Queen is a bastard and a usurper and that to disobey her laws or work to overthrow her is no crime, then that is what they believe. What they do."

"Not all of them."

"So you say. But enough of them. We spoke of Harry Southampton – his father was rabidly Catholic, his mother's the same. His father was involved in plots against the Queen. He was arrested for taking counsel from a Catholic priest who told him he need not obey the Queen. That's why his family's so eager to keep in favour with Burghley by marrying the boy off to his granddaughter. And that is just the sort of person Spain, to take but one example, uses. Wouldn't Spain love to overthrow – by which of course I mean assassinate – our Queen and install a Catholic monarch on her throne? A puppet monarch, of course. Lord Strange, say, or another of the Plantagenet pretenders if one can be found; or Mary of Scotland."

"Who's been dead five years. And her son is Protestant."

"There are always candidates. Would you see England Catholic again?"

"Bloody Mary's long dead too, Kit, and England will have no more of her kind, no more martyrdoms or burnings. Queen Elizabeth has been our Queen for thirty-four years because she is tolerant and wants her people's love. And I don't think you believe a word of what you're saying."

Kit threw back his head and laughed. "Whether I do or don't is not for you to know, Anne. Perhaps, though, I like the danger. The intellectual challenge."

"Playing with people's lives? When a man, or even a woman, goes to the torture chambers because of you? How can you do it?"

"Perhaps," Kit spoke very softly, "I have no choice."

"Ah. And your conscience is your own?"

"Precisely. But be warned, Anne, Will's father is listed as a recusant. He does not attend church, he is known to be in sympathy, at the least, with the Papist cause. Where does all his money go, Anne? For years he's been running into debt, selling off land, trying to raise mortgages. Yet he should be a rich man. Is he keeping a priest?"

"No. And I would know, Kit."

"Sending money to priests in hiding? Sending money overseas to Catholic supporters?"

"No. I think he's simply not very good at handling money. Or… well, you probably know more of this than I do: he supported his wife's family, the great and glorious Arden – not that his wife is very closely connected to them – in their quarrels with some important people, the late Lord Leicester for one. And those important people ruined him financially. The little illegalities that are winked at in others with more influence, like wool and malt dealing and usury, were used to ruin him." She leaned forward, holding Kit's green eyes with her own. "Go tell your spy-master and his nephew who gossip says is your lover, that John Shakspere is no Papist. Nor is William Shakspere, nor his wife or children. Remind the Walsinghams and whoever else must be told that John Shakspere's ancestor fought for Henry Tudor at Bosworth Field under Lord Derby."

"I shall. And in return, you tell your father-in-law that he is under suspicion and to mind what he does."

"I'll pass the message on, though he does nothing to earn suspicion. Have you ever tried to recruit Will into your unpleasant little gang?"

"Dropped a hint, once," Kit admitted. "He laughed in my face. And I've never quite managed to find out what he believes."

"He believes in England, in our queen, in love, in loyalty, in charity."

"Yes," agreed Kit. "Depressing, isn't it, in such a clever man."

Anne laughed, and through her laughter heard the sound of feet on the stairs. "Here comes the clever man. Will, my dear, come to the fire, you look cold."

"I am. A horrible night." He threw down his cloak and came to hold his hands out to the fire.

"And, judging from the shiny, dreamy smile," said Kit, "you've found your patron?"

"Yes. I have. I've promised him a poem, dedicated to him as my patron."

"You'll be trampled to death in the crowd," warned Kit. "That boy's already had more works dedicated to him than you can shake a stick at. All by people wanting him for their patron. He is, after all, the Earl of Southampton."

"But the difference is, "said Will, "that I am William Shakspere."

"All the same," he said to Anne later that night, in bed, "I'm going to be busy, aren't I. Harry has invited me to Titchfield in the summer when they have a party of guests. His mother would like the company to do a new play, a comedy. A comedy for Lady Southampton, a poem for Harry, and Burbage is nagging me for a new play to go into *repertoire* as soon as can be done, acting six days a week…"

"Will he pay you?" *Harry*, she thought, as if that boy were just anyone.

"Reluctantly."

"Not Burbage; Lord Southampton, I mean. For this poem singing his praises."

William rolled over and gave her a reproachful look. "The poem doesn't have to sing his praises. No. The dedication, the fact that I write it for him, in his honour, does that. I like him, Anne."

"So do I. But will he do what he promises? Might he not lose interest? People like that are fickle."

"Oh, not Harry, I think. He admires me. And yes, he'll pay me. Perhaps even enough to buy a share in the playing company. A hired player no longer, Anne, nor a jobbing playwright – a stakeholder in a playing company, part-owner of a theatre, that company's permanent writer. It's the start I've wanted, love. It's what we waited and planned and worked for all those dreary Stratford years. I'm becoming famous for my plays, but this new chance means *money*. And reputation. It means being established, no longer living hand-to-mouth. We can buy our own house in a year or two."

"In London?" It crossed her mind that they would have had much more money had she not insisted on living here. London was expensive and, at home, they lived free. But at home the children would have seen their father for perhaps four weeks a year. Also, somehow, she had never quite thought of London as home.

"No, lodgings are enough. Unless you want a London house. No, a place in Stratford."

"But you love London!"

"I enjoy it. I don't love it. Stratford's home. I'll buy you a house, Anne, one suitable for you and the children. Something grand."

"Then you'd better get busy writing."

"Mmm, yes."

Anne would have liked to make love again, but when she moved against him and touched him, all she got was her hand held, and a rough draft of his dedication to Southampton.

15.

Two days later Anne heard a peremptory knocking on the front door of the house. Intent on mending the lace collar on her husband's best shirt, she paid no particular attention; William paid it none at all, he probably didn't hear it. He was writing and lost in the world he was creating. Then feet clomped up the stairs and the parlour door shook under the hammering.

William's friends usually breezed straight in. Half-afraid, Anne put down her sewing. She looked at William as the hammering came again, and this time a cry of "Open in the Queen's name!" Even William heard that. He threw down his pen and signed to Anne to open the door.

Three men stood there. A messenger and two men who were unmistakably guards. Armed.

"William Shakspere?"

"I am he." William put Anne behind him. "What do you want of me?"

"You are bidden to Lord Burghley."

"*Burghley*? Why?"

"At once. Is this woman your wife?"

Even in that moment of fear Anne noted that you could actually *see* someone's hackles rise. Silently she begged her husband to be careful. He said, quietly enough, "This lady is my wife, yes."

"She too is bidden to Lord Burghley."

"But..."

"At once."

"Are we under arrest?" William asked.

"Not yet," the messenger said. "You may fetch your cloaks."

"Our children?"

"Tell your maid to watch them."

There was no time, or safety, for them to talk. Anne's conversation with Kit Marlowe was burning in her. But if it was some such matter, it would have been Walsingham's men who came for them, wouldn't it? And their destination would be the Tower. Or perhaps it still was. Her hands shook so much she couldn't fasten her cloak. William did it for her, and kissed her as he draped the cloak around her. She mouthed, "Kit?" and he shook his head. "It's all a mistake, darling. Any imagined fault must be mine alone. Tell the truth." Swinging his own cloak around him, he led her back to the outer room. "Are you sure," he asked the messenger, "that my wife is sent for?"

"His lordship's instructions were quite clear. Both of you. Come."

They were marched, ignominiously under guard, through London. Word of this would get around within the hour, Anne knew. By dinner time Burbage would have William's understudy ready for the afternoon's performance. By supper time the landlady, weeping behind closed doors when they left, would have re-let William's rooms and put the children onto the street. Anne glimpsed the lad Nol lurking in the crowd and mouthed "Burghley" at him. Let him make of that what he would.

They were going westward. Not to the Tower, then. Away from London Bridge, where the severed head of William's maternal ancestor Edward Arden had rotted for years, the treatment meted out to traitors. Perhaps William's head would soon be there. A shame, people would say for a day or two, he showed promise. Then they'd tear up his plays and forget him. What a world we live in, Anne thought, where innocent people can be arrested without explanation and a case trumped up against them. Or perhaps it's merely that something in one of William's plays displeased the Queen and he is to receive an official reproof. But in that case, why send for me? O God, my children.

But at Whitehall they were shown into a small anteroom and left alone. No thumbscrews, no rack. Yet. No torture but the silent waiting to play on their nerves.

After almost half an hour, a quietly dressed man came in, said, "Master and Mistress Shakspere?" and directed them into another room. It was a pin-neat mirror of William's room with books crowding the walls, orderly piles of papers on the writing table, a rich carpet, good chairs. It smelt of old leather, beeswax polish and lavender.

Rising from the table, coming to greet them, was the Father of England. The Queen's Right Hand. The Lord Treasurer of England. William Cecil, Lord Burghley, was white-bearded, not tall, well but plainly dressed in a long robe. He looked tired and rather ill, but his eyes were bright with intelligence and a sharp and not unkindly interest.

Anne curtsied as she would to the Queen. William bowed.

"Master Shakspere. Mrs Shakspere. I am sorry to have to meet you here in my business apartments and not at Cecil House, but needs must when business presses. Pray take a seat. May I present my son Robert Cecil?"

The dark, small young man bowed as well as he could with his twisted body and hunched back. His eyes too shone with interest, and gave them a small, charming smile. "I saw one of your plays once, Master Shakspere." He sounded surprised at himself. "I enjoyed it."

William bowed, for once bereft of words.

"May I offer you wine?" Lord Burghley said, and when they nodded dumbly a pageboy handed them fine crystal glasses of ruby wine.

"Are we then not under arrest?" William asked.

"Arrest? Of course not. What made you think so?" Lord Burghley sat down wrapping the skirts of his robe cosily over his knees.

"With respect, your lordship, when a messenger comes with two armed guards and conducts one without explanation, in haste, to you, even the easiest conscience must feel unease."

"Yes, I see. But my intention was not to frighten you. On the contrary. Master Shakspere, my ward the Earl of Southampton tells me he has met you and your wife."

Burghley paused to sip his wine. Anne suspected it was a deliberate pause, as practised as any actor's, for effect. Most people would rush into speech in the face of that pause, in the face of what had just been said. But William said nothing, studying this famous statesman; perhaps one day a version of him would appear in one of his plays.

"Yes," Burghley continued, "Lord Southampton told me of his visit to you. He has rarely mixed with ordinary people, and it was a pleasant time for him. He enjoys plays. He has a great love of literature as well."

"So I understand, my lord. He spoke of his time at your Cecil House school, of the fine education he received there, and of his time at Cambridge."

"Ah, yes. Yes, I have been at pains to give all my wards the best education. Lord Southampton is young, of course, and not yet wise in the ways of the world, but he feels some friendship for you."

"You object to that, your lordship?"

"Not in the slightest now that I have met you and your wife."

Well, of course Burghley didn't have to strike bargains with common people, but there was more to this than inspecting his ward's friends. For a moment a glint of humour, or appreciation, showed in his faded eyes, and at his nod his son refilled their glasses.

"You have been married some ten years, I believe?" he asked, glancing at Anne, who had the passing thought that he knew to the hour when they'd married.

"Ten years in November, My Lord. We have three children," she added when his look of gentle enquiry became a surprisingly warm smile. "A girl of nine, twins of seven."

"And you are often in London, Mistress Shakspere?"

"For much of the year, yes. In summer I take the children home to Stratford-upon-Avon."

"Because in summer the players go on tour, I believe?"

"Yes, my lord."

"But you have a son at school, I believe? Does your arrangement not interfere with his education?"

Oh yes, this is normal, thought Anne, discussing education with the Queen's chief minister. "He is a clever boy, Lord Burghley, and does well at his books, and we believe that a boy should not grow up with only one parent. That outweighs the week or two of school he misses when we move."

With another smile Burghley turned back to William. "I have heard your mother is an Arden, is that correct? An old family."

"Quite correct, and yes, an old family. The Arden were lords of Warwickshire before the Conquest."

"Indeed. Now, pleasant though it is to sit and talk, I'm sure you are a busy man, as am I, so I will be frank with you. You have the reputation, Mister Shakspere, of a clever man. Are you a discreet one?"

"I can keep a secret apart from the rest of the world."

The dark Cecil son laughed. His father was a moment behind him in seeing the joke.

"Ah, yes, a pun. Discreet, discrete. Words are your business, of course. So let us come to business. I feel great affection for my

Lord Southampton and it grieves me that he has stubbornly turned his face against marriage. I gather he touched on the matter when he visited you. It seems you spoke so warmly of marriage and fatherhood that he came home with his mind somewhat changed; something neither his mother nor I have achieved." Pulling his robe closer over his knees the old man said, almost petulantly, "It's the boy's *duty* to marry. And so, Mister Shakspere, I have a commission for you."

"Poems." William said. He flung himself down into the chair before the fire and started to laugh. "Poems! To convince that boy to marry." He reached for Anne's hand, and together they gave themselves up to laughter. There was a wild edge to it that had nothing to do with amusement; they had been too much frightened. "After all that, being hauled to Lord Burghley, fearing for our lives, he wants nothing but poems."

"And offers the favour of the most powerful man in England, remember."

"Oh yes, yes. Yes, the *entrée* to the world of Court favour, of the aristocracy. And money. I was going to write Harry Southampton a poem that would live forever and make us both immortal, and now I'm a paid hack again, writing poems to make Burghley's granddaughter a countess." He broke into an excellent mimicry of Lord Burghley's precise, pedantic tones. "'The boy is susceptible to flattery, Master Shakspere and, straight talk of duty and honour having failed, we are disposed to try a more – ah – *honeyed* route. Lord Southampton likes and admires you, Master S, so let us see if your honeyed words cannot convince him to do his duty.' Ha!"

"You'll have to do it, though."

"Yes, of course I will. I can't afford to be in disfavour with Burghley. I'd bet that in that tidy desk of his he had a *dossier* about us. He probably he knows what we had for breakfast this morning. He might have turned to threats – cunningly veiled ones, of course – had he not summed us up and decided frankness was the better way. Yes, he decided not to mention that my father's under some suspicion of recusancy or that he could ruin me with a word. Close down the theatres, disband the playing companies, forbid me London; whatever he chose. So yes, I'll write his poems."

"And the one you planned for Lord Southampton."

"That will come all the sweeter for being entirely my own. Oh, I want his patronage, and some money would be welcome, but it's not the same as this… *commission*."

"Your poems will be just as good."

"Probably. But it's like being back at school, doing set work. Yes, they'll be good. Won't change Harry Southampton's mind, of course."

"Lord Burghley doesn't expect a miracle, Will."

"Just as well." He rose and pottered over to his writing table. Staring down at the papers there he said, "After Kit read us his *Hero and Leander* the other night, I had an idea. A theme of Venus and Adonis." Absently he reached for a pen and paper.

"Not now, Will. Not if you're to play this afternoon."

"What? God's teeth, what's the time? I'll be late, Burbage will fine me. Anne, you'll come? We're playing Marlowe today." In a whirl he seized cloak and hat, bustled Anne about, clapped her hat on her head and led her out the door. When she protested she'd eaten nothing since breakfast he said, nor had he, and welcome to the life of a jobbing actor. "I'll buy you a pie at the cook shop."

"Better have one yourself or Kit's finest lines will be drowned by your stomach rumbling."

"It'd be an improvement. Hurry, Anne. O for *time*; time to write, to think, to read."

At the playhouse Burbage, in a fine old frenzy, grabbed William and thrust his costume into his arms. "You're late."

"Not my fault."

"Never mind that. Hurry. And make it good, Will. This could be our last performance for a time. I've heard there's plague in the eastern parts of the city."

"*Plague*," Anne whispered in fear. The great killer, the terror. It travelled on the breath, doctors said. You could even carry it on your clothes. If she took it home to her children… This was why she refused to live year-round in the capital, why she timed her visits here with care. Plague was usually at a different time of year, though it knew no rules.

"Don't worry, it's not yet widespread. You're in no danger. It may come to nothing. It may be some other disease."

"You'll leave tomorrow," William told Anne. "But Dick is right, there's no immediate fear. Go watch the play, Anne, and don't fear."

But it wasn't plague that closed the playhouses. Anne never got the bottom of the matter, but there was some riot among apprentices and the City authorities leapt at the excuse to close places of entertainment.

"Until Michaelmas," William fumed. "What are we to do? Bloody Puritans, any excuse. An apprentices' riot, nothing new there, but they'd like to get rid of the playhouses altogether. That's why the theatres were built outside the City. In the Liberties where the City's authority doesn't run, we should be safe. But no. Christ's nails, what are we to do? Go on the road again? Damned if I will."

"Well, my love," said Anne, "you've been given your time to write your poems. Come home."

16.

"William," said his mother, "there is a gentleman downstairs asking for you. He says his name is Marlowe."

William swung around in astonishment, spilling ink over Hamnet's Latin exercises. "Marlowe? *Christopher* Marlowe? Here? Small, black hair?"

"Yes. Will he want to stop here? Shall I make up a bed?"

"I don't know. I'll go down, Mother. Leave it to me."

Almost as surprised as William by Christopher Marlowe's arrival in Stratford, Anne tidied away her mending. She was reassuring Hamnet about the spoilt exercises when the memory of her last long talk with Kit Marlowe froze the words in her mouth. John Shakspere was listed as a recusant. Marlowe worked for Walsingham. He wouldn't have come here with a warrant of arrest – not Kit, not to William's father – so perhaps he had come to warn them. All is discovered. Flee.

"Nonsense," she said aloud, and Hamnet stared up, hurt, his lip quivering.

"The master will say I spoilt the book. He will! I'll be beaten!"

"What? Oh, no, darling, I was thinking aloud about something else. Daddy will make it right with the master, don't worry." All *what* is discovered? Nonsense.

And William came back in with Kit, both smiling all over their faces, laughing at something. "Anne!" said Kit, bowing elaborately then kissing her. "I hope I see you well?"

"Entirely well. And you? What brings you to Stratford?"

"Oh, business." His feline eyes read her face. "Between me and Will. Holloa there, young Hamnet, stewing inside on a lovely day like this? Ah, Latin; I remember. Susanna, Judith, you've both grown prettier. Here's sixpence, go and treat yourselves to something your mother says you mustn't have." You always forgot that Kit was the eldest of several brothers and sisters, he was at ease with children. Anne's three thought he was wonderful, not only because he always gave them sixpence. Anne had worried a little: Hamnet was seven: but Kit was no pederast. He liked men, not boys. And certainly not his friend's child. The thought would appal him.

"And do I too get sixpence to take myself off?" she asked, watching the two men settle down in their chairs.

"No, Anne, stay. It's not private from you. But it's a serious matter. Will, we have been defamed. Libelled. Belittled."

"What? *We* have? Kit?"

"Yes. You remember Robert Greene?"

"If you mean that snide, stinking, sneaking little ginger-headed whoremonger who imagines he can write plays, yes I do. Isn't he dead?"

"Yes, of the pox. God must be a critic. But before he went to his reward he found time to sit up in his beggar's bed and pen a little tract, a pamphlet, a book. Here." He whipped it out from inside his doublet and passed it across to William. "I have marked the relevant passage."

"*A Groat's-worth of Witte,*" William read the crudely printed cover. "Yes, that's about all Robert Greene ever had of wit." He flicked to Kit's marker. At the expressions playing over his face – amazement; shock, anger; disgust; petulance – Anne longed to go and read over his shoulder. Kit winked at her. "*Listen to this*! 'Trust them not.' He's talking of people like *me*, Anne, men without university degrees who dare to come to London and write plays. 'Trust them not: for there is an upstart crow, beautified with our feathers' – *beautified;* beautified is a vile phrase – 'our feathers, that with his tiger's heart wrapped in a player's hide, supposes he is as well able to bombast out' – *bombast* – 'a blank verse as the best of you, and being an absolute Johannes Fac Totum, is in his own conceit the only Shake-scene in the country.' The bastard, how dare he? It's tantamount to accusing me of plagiarism. And it's me he means: not only 'Shake-scene' but 'tiger's heart'. My *Henry the Sixth*, that phrase is from. *Tiger's heart wrap't in a woman's hide.*"

Anne hadn't missed that. She thought it rather funny, but kept a straight face of shocked disapproval.

"I own," William went on, angrily pacing the floor, "that the story of that play was not original. Of course I used an old source as we all do. But I did not *steal* it."

"Bar a line or two from my *Edward II*," murmured Kit.

"Homage to the master," snapped William. "As you've used a line or two of mine. It's inevitable; things stick in one's mind. But I will not have anyone, let alone a talentless, filthy, pox-ridden, whoreson prick like Robert Greene, say I steal other men's work."

"No, it's bad, Will. Greene doesn't hesitate to take a hit at me, later in his little work." William glanced at another marked passage, nodded soberly, and ruffled Kit's hair. "What are we to do? Who printed this rubbish, by the way? Henry Chettle. Hmm. Another playwright. Do you suppose he wrote this himself? Though Greene could never forgive me that my plays take more money than his, and him a *university* man and, therefore, a *gentleman*. He tried to borrow money from me once. I refused and he never forgave me." He flung himself into a chair. "What are we to do, Christopher? *Can* we do anything? I can't afford to go to law, even if an action would lie."

"Nor can I. But I had a good idea, Will, I think I've been rather clever. Harry Southampton."

"Lord Southampton?" asked Anne. "What of him?"

"Well, I had made up my mind to write to Will about this, then I thought, why not ride to Stratford and talk it over; it's fine weather for riding." William made an impatient gesture. "Oxford is on the way to Stratford; on one way, at least. And the Queen is at Oxford. And Harry Southampton has been bidden there to dance attendance on Her Majesty. He liked you, Will, when he met you in London. So, what simpler than to stop in Oxford, find Southampton and put the matter to him?"

"But Kit..."

"Oh, he was glad to help. He will help. He was at Gray's Inn; not that that qualifies him for more than play-going and tobacco-smoking. But he was shocked at the affront to England's two premier poets. His words, dear Will, not mine."

"But what can he do?"

"Make representations to Chettle, make him regret he ever published this trash. After all, Will, an *earl*, and Lord Burghley's ward. The mere hint of his displeasure would make any printer blench."

"And will he do it? Why should he bother?"

"I told you, he idolises us. He likes you, admires your plays rather more than he does mine, I think. More to the point, he once sat through half of one of Greene's efforts." William laughed aloud. "So, of course, he will help us. He will send representations to Chettle and obtain an apology, a retraction."

"How very kind of Lord Southampton."

"Oh, I nearly forgot," Kit said. "Lord Southampton sent you a letter." Forgot, my bum, thought Anne, and wondered what Kit thought he was up to.

"How very kind," William said in a stunned voice when he'd read the letter.

"What is it?"

"Lord Southampton invites me to his home, to Titchfield, in Hampshire, to discuss the poem I'm to write and dedicate to him. Also he speaks of a party of guests later and they, or his mother the Countess, would like a play, a new play. At a fee, of course. It's a commission." He looked at Anne as if asking her blessing.

"Of course you must go. You can hardly refuse."

"No," said Kit, very blandly. "He cannot."

17.

It happened that William's visit had to be postponed. He was about to set out when a letter came: Harry Southampton's maternal grandfather, Viscount Montague, had died in the first week of October. *But please come,* wrote Harry, *for to have a friend by my side would be a comfort.* Details about the funeral followed, then, *I will look for you in a week or two from the date of this letter. Please do not fail me.*

William wondered if it were unseemly to go to a house in mourning, but another letter begged him yet again to come, and he set out in the middle of October.

Titchfield was not the largest or grandest house William had visited, but it was the first of its kind he had come to as a guest rather than a hired entertainer. He thought it handsome, a pleasant seat in fine countryside, its mellow stone glowing honey-gold in the afternoon sun. For a moment he thought he should go to the back entrance, then thought, No, I am a guest, and rode boldly up to the front door.

A footman greeted him, called for a groom to take his horse, said that His Lordship was out riding but expected back shortly, and handed him on to the butler. The butler said that His Lordship was out riding but expected back shortly, and handed him on to John Florio, Southampton's Italian secretary. He said that Ees Lordship was out ridingue, but was expected back shortly, and handed William on to a footman, who conducted him at last to his room, saying, "His Lordship is –"

"I know. Out riding, but expected home –"

"Momently."

"You amaze me."

"Will you require water for washing?" The man's tone meant, if you players know what washing is, and he left a space where 'sir' or a title might have fitted.

"Of course," said William with a haughty surprise that wiped the half-smirk off the servant's face. After all, as his mother had said before he left Stratford, who, a hundred years ago, had heard of the Wriothesleys? Rich they might be, powerful they might be, but they were upstarts whose money came from old King Harry's destroying the monasteries, and William must never forget he was an Arden by descent.

His room was in the same wing as Harry's, a mark of signal favour. Hired players usually bedded down wherever they could find a horizontal space. But he was here as a friend, not player or servant. The room was small but gracefully furnished with everything a sensible man could want. Best of all, it had a large writing table in the window with a cushioned chair.

There was water for washing, valets to unpack. He needed do nothing himself. William was not unused to the gentilities of life, but this was another realm. Dreamily he washed, put on the clothes the valet laid out for him, then went to the writing table. One of the serving men was looking doubtfully at the small leathern trunk in which William kept his books and papers. "Leave that to me." He disliked other people touching these things, except Anne. He arranged his books, the ones he had to have to hand while he worked, his precious copy of Ovid's *Metamorphoses*, Boccaccio, Ronsard and Montaigne, a few others, and laid out his paper and pens just so, inkstand to the right. A smaller box with a clicket lock held his current work, and the key to that stayed in his belt-purse. It would be a strange thing to work in someone else's house, but this room had windows to the south and east, and the garden below. He could work here. What he did here would be good.

He was looking idly through Ovid when Harry came quickly into the room. "Will, my dear friend. I'm so glad you've come." He put a quick kiss on William's cheek. He was in riding clothes, and the exercise in the brisk air had brought unusual colour to his face. Here on his own territory he was more self-assured, quicker moving, and seemed less boyish.

William had forgotten how beautiful he was.

"Come to my room, I long to talk with you."

"My lord."

"Harry, remember? Or are we no longer friends?"

"We are friends. Harry. I want to thank you for your help with that pamphlet of Greene's."

"But I was glad to help," Harry said earnestly. "Such an insult to you couldn't be left alone. And all it took was a visit from my man of law. A humble retraction will be published."

"It was kind of you to help. And to invite me here."

"No, quite selfish of me. The pleasure is mine. Come, now. I'm three doors along. We'll take glass of wine together. Our time's our own. My mother is away, so's my sister."

Harry's room was a nest of silk and velvet, gold brocade and crystal. Of course there was water ready, valets to attend his every need. Having his hair combed, Harry looked at William in the glass, and smiled. "Let's have that wine." On his words he hurried William into the adjoining room, where he flung himself down on a divan. This room was a salon, long and high, lined with books, furnished with chairs, several tables and lecterns, two more of the velvet divans. Windows looked to the formal gardens at the front of the house. Portraits and looking-glasses framed in gold decked the walls. Already, though it was not yet twilight, servants were lighting the candles that stood everywhere, while others brought manchet bread, cheese and fruit, and poured wine.

"Your health," said Harry, dismissing the servants.

"And yours." The wine was unremarkable; someone fiddling the household books, William surmised.

"Now, the poem?" Harry prompted.

"Yes." William sat down opposite him. "*Venus and Adonis*."

"A good title. A good theme." Harry's long, beautiful mouth twisted. "One of Burghley's secretaries wrote a work and dedicated it to me, not long ago. The theme was Narcissus."

"Not flattering."

"No. It was not meant to be. Oh, fine words, pretty phrases; shame there was no talent. And – *Narcissus*. Vain I may be; girlish I know I look. Proved myself as a man, I have not; not for want of trying. Eager to marry I am not. Deal in country matters with women, I do not. But *Narcissus*?"

"Yet Narcissus was beautiful," William said and couldn't keep from smiling.

"And am I beautiful?"

"You have a glass: you know you are. Do you have nymphs in love with you?"

Harry shrugged. "For all I know. There was no Echo in the work I speak of. Insultingly no Echo. But I love no nymph. Am I Adonis in your poem, Will?"

"Do you wish to be?"

"I think," said Harry gravely, "that I wish to be your Adonis."

"And yield to Venus?"

"That is up to you, my Will."

"No, my lord. *Your* will."

"Venus or Cupid. And no more 'my lord'."

"I'll remember. Harry, Lord Burghley is to pay me to write poems urging you to marry."

Southampton lay back on his cushions, gazing narrow-eyed at William. "Harry, marry. A vile rhyme. You can do better. I know about your bargain with Burghley. The man never gives up, does he?"

"He would have you give yourself up to marriage. How did you know?"

"His son told me. Robert Cecil likes me. I wondered if you would tell me, or gravely write your poems and wonder why I was not pleased."

"I was unsure about telling you. But I prefer honesty."

"Between friends?"

"Between friends. But many people would think ours an odd friendship, Harry."

Lifting his wine cup to his lips Harry paused and said, "How old are you?"

"Twenty-eight. Nine years your senior. Ten years married. Three times a father."

"Then that should remove one barb from the quiver of popular disapproval. Patron and poet. A simple relation. You shall pierce me with your... poetry and all the world may see. What the world does not see, is no concern of the world's. Write your poems for Burghley, Will, and take his payment. I'll like them nonetheless. I shall even pretend they move me to do my duty. Perhaps they shall. To love, at least. And now, to *Venus and Adonis.* Is it written yet?"

"Only a stanza. But it's planned in my mind."

Sounding suddenly very boyish in his earnestness Harry said, "Here you will have all the time and peace and inspiration, I trust, to write what you will. And pens, ink and paper. Books. And pleasure. You are my honoured guest here, Will."

"And *I* am honoured."

"If so, repay me with a poem the world will remember. Make me immortal." He turned over, laughing again as he reached for William's hand. "And read me it, every day."

18.

But at first the poem made slow progress. What Harry was giving William, and a greater gift than he knew, was leisure. The first carefree time of his life. The first holiday. From habit he woke early, before six, but now he could go back to sleep or lie in the drowsy pleasure of having no duties, no calls on his time. No school to teach, no plays to write against the clock, no rehearsals or performances. No travelling. Quiet and peace. And Harry.

Harry Wriothesley could be childish, selfish, capricious and stubborn. He was in many ways unworldly; sheltered. He could be as easily amused as William's son Hamnet by a play on words, a bawdy song, a story. He could also be sophisticated and subtle, a clever disputant, an erudite listener. He was also kind, generous and sweet-natured, with the makings of a good man. In those first few days, and before they knew it, those first few weeks, they rode out every day, they went to the sea-shore, played tennis and bowls, walked for hours. Autumn it might be, yet it seemed the sun always shone, the sky was always an azure bowl flecked with scribbles of fluffy cloud, the sea always calm. Both fair-skinned men with auburn hair, they grew red from sun, then gently brown.

Despite possessing countless houses all over England Harry was a London boy, a city child whose nose had been kept to the grindstone of learning. He had never, until now, gone out on foot in the woods, had never run through the early dew on the grass, had never set a snare for a rabbit. He knew the sea as something to comment upon in *terza rima* or to sail across, not as something to plunge into, naked, in the warmth of noon. What hunting he'd done had been the formal affair, with other courtiers all with an eye to ritual and who had the best horse, not the exhilarating scramble on foot or, as the whim took him, on horseback. He had never watched harvesters at work or plucked fruit straight from the tree or bush and eaten it in the open air, washed down with ale bought in a village.

"How do you know all these things?" he asked one day, lying back in the grass in his shirtsleeves, the juice from an apple running down his face.

"I was a boy in the country. An ordinary boy."

"And free."

"Free to play truant from school sometimes or to go out poaching with my friends if I could get away with it."

"And chasing girls?"

"Sometimes." William rolled over onto his front, propping his chin on his hands. "But I never knew the freedom of money or of university life. I had to leave school at sixteen and work for my father."

"In the glover's shop."

"And as a tutor and schoolmaster. I could still make you a fine pair of gloves, Harry." Harry looked struck by this; as well he might, a man who'd never so much as dressed himself. "We're very different, my dear. You grew up to inherit this..."He waved a hand, taking in the great house in the distance, all the lands it surmounted "... and I in a glover's and wool-dealer's house in a provincial town. A tradesman's son. Nearly a tradesman myself."

"But you are not."

"Play-writing is a trade. So is playing. Six performances a week, week in, week out. Writing when I can snatch a moment, usually at the cost of sleep. Touring in the summers. And what I could tell you of the roads in England, and the lodgings! Why can't we have better roads, Harry? When you take your seat in Parliament, bring a Bill to improve the roads."

"I shall. Though you'll have to wait two years till I'm of age." Harry moved to rest his head in the small of William's back. "I grew up knowing I would inherit all this, yes, but I never knew a happy family life. My parents quarrelled, they parted, they used me as go-between. My father kept me and my sister from our mother. And living with my father was no holiday. Fanatical Catholic, did you know? Narrow and righteous, involved in plots and treason. A foolish man. And spiteful. Also under the thumb of his servant – for which you may read his lover – Dymock, who had to be obeyed in everything. *He* was king in the Southampton houses. I never heard my mother spoken of but as an adulterous whore. And my father left me little but debts."

"But you love your mother?" William rather liked the Countess. She was, although a silly, tactless woman, kind-hearted.

"I suppose I do. One does, after all. She irritates me, often. She's discontented, not that I can blame her after the life my father gave her. My grandfather was the point of security to me when I was a child; he was a good man. My mother fancies herself in love with Sir Thomas Heneage. Perhaps they'll marry. Although she's old to marry, in her thirties."

Amused, William said, "So is my wife."

"So much? She doesn't look it. Then she's older than you?"

"Nearly seven years older."

"Why'd you marry her? Sorry, was that tactless?"

"A little. She was with child. That's why we married."

"Ah."

"Not that we married without love, Harry. I loved her more than I knew at the time. She encouraged me, let me read her my work, advised me, comforted me when everyone else was telling me to forget my wild dreams of London and theatres and poetry. I called her my Muse." He turned over again, taking his friend's head upon his belly. Absently stroking the long gold-auburn hair he said, "I've written little since I've been here. I've enjoyed myself too much."

"Enjoyed yourself with me?"

"Yes," William said, laughing. "You're eager for flattery, aren't you?"

"Flattery? Or liking. Knowing I am liked. Or loved?"

"Liked. Loved. You are my dear golden lad, my friend."

Now it was Harry's turn to spin over, so that he looked into William's eyes. "In this light," he said, "your eyes are grey, and gold, and green and azure. *Am* I your dear lad?"

"You know you are."

"Say it. Say you love me."

"But of course I love you. My dear lad, my dear lord." The moment held, and stretched, as they stared into one another's eyes. William could feel his flesh coming alive, as if he had been physically caressed. The beauty of the day, of this boy who looked at him so meltingly, coalesced. This was happiness, this was freedom, this was love. Shyly, as if he weren't the elder, he said, "And you, Harry? Do you love me? Older though I am, autumn to your spring, world-worn, do you love me?"

"Dearly. Dearly. You make me happy, Will." Harry had to move only a hand's span closer to kiss him. Their lips met, lightly, sweetly, with a power that shook them both. No more than that, just a kiss. Just love.

"You make me happy too." He kissed Harry's eyes, the corner of his mouth. Harry laid his head back down, over William's heart.

He sighed. William stroked his hair and the soft white skin under it.

"What think'st thou?" Harry's tone made it a caress, or a promise.

"That I am happy. That thou art my heart's desire. And that for the first time since I came here I have my poem clear in my mind."

"Tell me."

"Not yet." William was silent so long that Harry leaned up on his elbow to look at him.

"I thought you'd gone to sleep. Tell me the poem, Will. Talk to me. Or kiss me again."

"No. And don't be peevish. There, a kiss." His lips lingered for a moment, then he put his hand on Harry's cheek and drew away to sit up. "It's time for me to work, Harry. Time to begin."

Harry lay there, leaning on his elbow, frowning up at him. "You would end this day?"

"God, or Apollo Phoebus, will. It is near day's end, Harry, and I must write. Come, love, nothing will end our love, but I must write." And Harry saw it, saw the withdrawal into a world he knew nothing of, the passion and need that were not for him. Accepting it, and maturing with the acceptance, he laughed and stood up, brushing the grass from his clothes.

"Then come home, Will, and write."

But he had pictured a cosy scene, William pausing every second moment to read his work, to ask Harry's opinion, to intersperse his work with kisses. Alas. He was in the same room as William, but another world. He doubted William even knew he was there. The servants came, enquiring about supper. Would his lordship come to the dining salon? Should they serve the meal here? William paid them no attention. "Here," Harry said, and saw that William didn't even smell the food. Dismissing the servants, Harry himself put food on a plate, put it beside his friend. He got a grunt of vague acknowledgement and had eaten his entire meal before he saw William's left hand move our, absently, to take the first morsel.

"Eat, Will. Take a moment. Eat your supper."

"What?"

"The food is growing cold. *Is* cold. Take a moment, leave your work and eat."

"Ah." And, moments later, "What? Food? You should have told me. What's so funny?"

"Nothing, Will. Nothing, my dear. Shall I send for more food? That's quite cold now."

"No, it will serve." William stood up, stretching to ease his back, shaking out his cramped hand. He came to the table and began to eat rapidly. He looked up once, smiling at Harry. "Have you been here all the time?"

"Yes. I gave you," he said pointedly, "three cups of wine, which you drank without knowing where they came from. Would you rather I went away? Do you rather work alone?"

"Oh no, you don't bother me. This pie's excellent."

"I'll tell the cook."

"Now what's the matter?" William asked, cramming in more food. "I said you don't bother me. That's a compliment, Harry. There are few people I can bear in the room while I work."

"Is your wife one of them?"

"Oh yes, Anne understands. At least you can be quiet, my dear, unlike most people. You share that with Anne. You understand."

About to say he'd spoken many times, that he could have danced naked around the room while the Queen's minstrels played and William would not have noticed, Harry took the compliment and nodded gravely.

"I like to have you here," William said, sounding surprised. "But don't look for company from me. Not when I am writing. I can't explain it."

"You needn't. I've seen. It's quite late, Will. You've worked three hours."

"But I'll work on a little." He stretched again, groaning as stiffened muscles pulled. Again he shook his right hand. "Cramped."

"Let me ease it." Instantly William held out his hand, leaning back with a sigh of pleasure as Harry began to rub it. "Oh, that's good. Harder."

"You've knotted muscles, calluses too. I can feel where you hold your pen, the raised skin. Is it better?"

"Better." William's eyes strayed back to his writing table and the pile of finished pages there. Resigned to the inevitable, Harry kissed the palm of his hand and gave it back to him. With a vague murmur of thanks William wandered back to his work. Harry knew better than to ask to see what he'd done.

Doggedly Harry sat on, determined to do what he could to be a Muse. At ten the servants brought more wine and food, at eleven fresh candles. At midnight William asked for more paper. At one he went to the privy. At two he needed ink and drank a cup of wine, not knowing it was his fifth. At three he scratched his head, damned his pen, looked for another and found none.

"You've used them all," said Harry.

"Then sharpen me some more."

And Harry, an earl, who had never sharpened his own pens or done a service for another person, meekly cut new quills. At four he gave in, put down his book and said he was going to bed. "Will? Won't you finish for now? You've worked all the night."

"Have I?"

"Ah, you heard me. Will, you're exhausted. How can you work like this?"

"I always do while it's hot in me. Only another writer can understand. But you're right. I'm too tired." He glanced over the last page and, with an exclamation, threw it on the fire. "Far too tired, that's plain. I'm writing rubbish and wasting paper."

"Never."

"Oh yes. Very well, then, bed."

He was reeling with exhaustion, nearly asleep on his feet. Harry gripped his arm and guided him through the connecting door and sat him on the bed.

"No, my room. Lock my papers away. Always do. Can't sleep 'less they're safe." But his eyes were closing as he spoke.

"I'll put them safely away, look, here in my cupboard with my private papers. No one will touch them. Will, lift your feet, let me take your boots off. There." Awkwardly Harry undid buttons and laces, William obeying like a child, then swung him around, still in shirt and under-linen, and tucked him under the covers. "Go to sleep, Will, my love."

"To sleep. To dream. Perchance to dream. My hand aches. My eyes ache."

"I'll rub your hand. Sleep, Will." Harry tossed off his own clothes, extinguished the candles and climbed into bed. He took William in his arms, drawing him close, laying his head on his shoulder. William gave a long sleepy sigh of pleasure. It made

Harry feel protective, responsible as he'd never been for another human creature. William was not the first man who had shared his bed, but he was the first to lie defenceless in Harry's arms, wanting nothing but comfort and sleep. Gently he took William's right hand and began to massage it. William purred. Harry stroked the hair back from his brow and kissed him. Love filled him. William said, "My love," then something that sounded like "Windsor". Then he snored.

19.

That first all-night white heat of creation was not repeated, but after that William worked every day on his poem. Much of what he'd written that first night went on the fire, but much was kept, revised, rewritten. Harry became used to it – the slow drifting into silent thought, then the hours of writing in which he ceased, with the rest of the world, to exist, except as provider of paper, pencils, sharpened pens and food. Anne Shakspere must know this exclusion, he reflected; she'd had ten years of it. Did William make love to her sometimes, when he fell into bed in the satisfied glow of creation? Did he give her more than kisses and words of love? Or less than that? Did William talk to her as he did to Harry? *Could* one talk to a woman of emotions and things of the mind, of books and poetry and ideas? If one could find a woman like that, instead of a man…

"What about the poems for Burghley?" he asked one day. "He'll want to know, Will; he expects value for his money." They were at the shore, looking across to the Isle of Wight. Their horses cropped peacefully above them. Sea birds mewed overhead. A brisk breeze ruffled the water, splashing their bare feet. William tipped his head back to follow a bird's flight before saying,

"I've not seen the colour of his money yet. But the poems are being written."

"Oh?"

"Yes. Harry:
From fairest creature we desire increase,
That thereby beauty's rose might never die,
But as the riper should by time decease,
His tender heir might bear his memory;
But thou, contracted to thine own bright eyes,
Feed'st thy light's flame with self-substantial fuel,
Making a famine where abundance lies,
Thyself thy foe, to thy sweet self too cruel.
That thou art now the world's fresh ornament
And only herald to the gaudy spring,
Within thine own bud buriest thy content,
And, tender churl, mak'st waste in niggarding.

Pity the world, or else this glutton be,
To eat the world's due, by the grave and thee."

After quite a time Harry said, "It's Narcissus again. 'Contracted to thine own bright eyes.' And 'self-substantial fuel.' Still, Burghley will like it."

"You don't?"

"It's a good sonnet."

"Don't sulk."

"I am not sulking."

"No? Oh well. What about: *Look in thy glass, and tell the face thou viewest/Now is the time that face should form another...* The next lines I'm not sure of, but... *For where is she so fair whose unear'd womb/Disdains the tillage of thy husbandry?"*

"An agricultural metaphor," said Harry coldly. "Vulgar. It needs work. Do you think I'm so vain? Conceited?"

"No more than you should be."

"Your meaning?"

"That you are beautiful, and know it."

"And vain. And spoilt."

"Your words, not mine."

"Well, no one can say you're not earning your pay from Burghley. *Show* me that woman so fair, and it would be a different matter."

"Have you," William enquired, "never lain with a woman?"

"No. And don't use that voice, like a kindly older brother or an uncle. Next you'll say I don't know what I'm missing."

"Perhaps you don't."

"I do." They were sitting so close together that Harry had only to turn to take William in his arms and kiss him. This was no light, gentle kiss of purest love, but a kiss of passion, deep, demanding, longing. "I do know," Harry said against William's mouth. "I do know what I am missing. You. All of you."

"Harry..."

"You liked my kisses. You responded."

"Who could not? But Harry, listen:
A woman's face, with Nature's own hand painted,
Hast thou, the Master-Mistress of my passion;
A woman's gentle heart, but not acquainted
With shifting change, as is false woman's fashion;
An eye more bright than theirs, less false in rolling,

Gilding the object whereupon it gazeth;
A man in hue all hues in his controlling,
Which steals men's eyes and women's souls amazeth."

Harry smiled, enchanted. William took the boy's face in his hands and continued, *"And for a woman wert thou first created;*
Till Nature, as she wrought thee, fell a-doting,
And by addition me of thee defeated
By adding one thing to my purpose nothing.
But since she prick'd thee out for women's pleasure,
Mine be thy love, and thy love's use their treasure."

There was a long silence. "I see," Harry said at last. "That one thing is no-thing to your purpose: a double meaning. But I love you and I'll have you."

"Oh, be content, boy!" William cried, and stood up. "Love lasts; passion doesn't. Lust doesn't."

"You know that, do you? From your wealth of age's experience?"

"Yes."

Harry scrambled to his feet. He stood facing William, still close enough to touch or kiss. "But cannot one have both? Love and passion? And if the passion dies, the love will last?"

"Perhaps."

"Then why should it not for us? And in that sonnet you're not too complimentary to women, William. What did you say? Woman's shifting heart? False woman's fashion? You cannot have it both ways, dear Will. You cannot urge me to a woman, yet point out that women are inconstant, fickle, false."

"It's only a poem," William said feebly.

"And perhaps you are not so eager as you make out to urge me into the nearest woman's bed?" William looked away. Angrily Harry seized his chin and forced him to look back. Blue eyes stared into hazel ones, and Harry's anger fled. "William, you love me."

"You know I do. But I am married."

"Yet you write of women's falsity. Is your Anne false?"

"No. And I will not hurt her by..."

"By giving me your love? But haven't you done that already? Haven't you hurt her by loving me? By bedding all those women – and, by repute, not only women – in London?"

"Yes."

"That's honesty at last. Let's have some more. Can you deny you want me in every way, as I want you?"

"Leave be, Harry."

"No. You've broken your marriage vows by taking other women. Surely it is less of an offence to take me, your own kind and one who loves you?"

"I don't know," William said helplessly. "I love you. I long for you. Yet you have been trusted to me. I can't. Harry, leave be. Let me be. Please, if you love me."

Again silence fell and held between them. Again Harry was the first to speak. "I do love you. Very well. See? You've taught me I can't have everything I want."

"Conscience doth make cowards of us all."

"A fine line. You'll use it one day. Come, Will, let's go home."

Neither spoke on the ride back. Things had changed, perhaps been spoiled. Neither of them knew. And, for the first time, they were fully conscious that winter was nearly upon them; the wind blew chill and breathed of rain, the sky was dark with thunderclouds.

"The good weather is over," William said dully.

"Of course it is. It's December, Will. It has rained every night the last fortnight."

"Has it? I didn't notice."

"No, you were writing. Soon it will snow."

"Yes. December. I must go home for Christmas."

"Yes of course," Harry agreed a little too readily. "But will you come back? The theatres are closed, you've no occupation in London. Come back after Christmas. The players, your company, are coming in February. We look for your new play then, Will. There will be others here then. Essex, I think, and Kit Marlowe speaks of coming; also Thomas Nashe."

The mention of rival poets stung William. "With Marlowe and Nashe, what need have you of Shakspere?"

"I have need of the best. Come back. Please. After all, you haven't finished my poem."

"Nor I have," said William. "Very well. After Christmas, I'll come back."

20.

William was not expected home so soon. He walked into the house in Henley Street to find the family at supper, and in the middle of some argument. The dining parlour was decked with holly and ivy for Christmas, there was mistletoe over the door. Susanna was the first to see him, shocking her grandmother by spilling her plate as she leapt up and ran for the door.

"But it's Daddy. He's home!" She flung herself on her father, squirreling her arms and legs around him. She was really too old to be so boisterous and let her skirts fly up like that, but no one had the heart to reprimand her. The twins came more slowly, looking shyly up at their father. One arm still around Susanna, he crouched and drew all three children into his embrace. My beautiful children, he thought, feeling tears prickling his eyes. My darlings, my life.

"You've grown, you've all grown. Hamnet, darling boy, give me a kiss. Judith, my precious, you too. My sweethearts, I've missed you so."

John Shakspere kissed his son as best he could and lifted Susanna away from William. "A delightful surprise, son. Welcome home. Come, sit down. Mother, wine, our best wine. Children, make a place for your father."

"Father, God's day to you. You're well? Mother, how good to see you. And Anne," said William. "My dear, I've missed you. Come kiss me." She did so, thinking how brown and young he looked. And happy.

"You look well. You've enjoyed yourself?"

"Very much. But I missed you and the children. I wrote a good deal."

The rest of the family had waited their turn, but now came the kisses and handclasps, the barrage of questions. Are you well, did you have much snow on the journey, what news, how long can you stay, did you bring us presents, have you heard, what have you written? Tell us about the Earl.

A twin on either side, Susanna staring enraptured, chin on hands, from the other side of the table, William did his best to talk, drink wine and eat his supper all at once. Anne ate her meal in silence and let him answer all the questions, retail the news.

"I'm home for Christmas, then I join my fellow-players at Titchfield." Usually they were in London for the Christmas season, the Queen held court in her capital and wanted entertainment. "No one knows when the theatres will open again. And what news here?"

They told him, all speaking at once, and Anne watched his eyes narrow with interest. He'd come from the company of earls and poets, but he was enchanted with all these small Stratford doings; a fire, a marriage, a quarrel, an adultery, the state of trade.

"But it's late," he said at last, "and I've been on the road a long time. Time for bed."

His mother exclaimed to find it was past eight o'clock and the children still up. The three of them sat tight, identical mulish expressions on their faces.

"If you're in bed by the time I've finished my wine," said William, "I'll come and tell you a story. Kiss your mother goodnight, she's for her bed."

Transformed into angels, the children filed away upstairs. Anne said her goodnights and went thoughtfully up to her room. There she washed, brushed out her hair, put rosewater on her wrists and throat. She heard William bidding his family goodnight, then his voice falling into story-telling rhythm in the twins' room. Susanna shared her aunt Joan's room, and Judith should by rights have joined her while Hamnet moved up to a bed in his uncles' room, but the twins had refused to be parted. Saying they were as stubborn as their father, Mrs Shakspere had given them a little room at the back of the house. Susanna would be there, perched on the end of their bed, watching her father like a starving man given food, listening to the story to keep herself awake.

Anne heard William go through to Joan's room, speak to his sister. "Fast asleep for all she could do..." Joan laughed and murmured goodnight. A candle briefly flared, then William lowered himself into bed with a sigh.

"Awake, love?"

"Yes."

He turned over, put his arm around her waist. "The children are asleep. It's good to be home. This bed's begun to creak. Let's have a new one."

"But I like this one. Remember how we could afford almost nothing but we wanted a new bed? We spent our wedding night in it, I birthed the children in it. I like it. But I admit it could do with new curtains. And if you tighten the ropes under the mattress it won't creak."

"All right. And buy new curtains, get the best. And here's an idea; while I'm here, let us look about for a house. We need not commit ourselves at once but we can make enquiries, look about."

"Do you mean, to live here and not in London any longer?"

"I mean nothing in particular, not yet. Just looking ahead. Making plans." His voice had begun to trail away. "Tired. Good to be home. Goodnight, Anne. Sleep well."

"And you." So there was to be no homecoming lovemaking. Disappointed, Anne snuggled back against him, and let sleep claim her.

William had meant it about house-hunting. His first day in Stratford they pottered about the town, greeting friends, listening to gossip, but always with an eye out for suitable houses. Joan shared the secret, though William had warned her to say nothing to the rest of the family yet. He enjoyed planning, but he wasn't a man to spend money until it was in his hand. Nor did he care to figure in Stratford gossip as the man who came home from London full of high talk and empty promises. Still, he was right: one could plan. Or dream. University for Hamnet, yes, for the boy was clever. Dowries for the girls, yes, that too, for they were pretty, and with a little money they would make good matches.

Watching them as they walked ahead, clutching William's hands, Anne noticed how unusually talkative Judith was in his company. She was an odd little girl, quite unlike her sister or brother. Not stupid, not at all, but entirely uninterested in learning to write more than her name, and she could read only by following the words with her finger and speaking them aloud; often she muddled the letters. She liked stories and plays but she had no faculty of imagination, none at all. Perhaps, Anne mused, if Judith saw more of her father she would learn, to please him.

She was good at figuring, which was rare in a girl, and she had learnt scraps of Latin by hearing Hamnet repeat his lessons, but being pushed to learn more turned her mulish and sulky. Housewifery was her pleasure. She delighted to help in the house, and at seven she was a more than passable cook and deft with a needle. Her greatest delight was to go to Anne's stepmother at Hewlands Farm and help with the harvest, joining the local children in following the reapers, stooking the corn and gleaning, or picking fruit and vegetables and helping to salt or bottle them. She was a dab hand with the animals, nursing orphaned lambs, following the stockmen until she knew how to doctor sick beasts.

In fact, Anne thought, watching the child's bobbing fair curls as she turned her face up to William to chatter, Judith was a sweet, good-natured little girl who took after her yeoman and artisan grandparents more than her parents. She would make a good wife. She would have a little money from her grandparents, in time, and if William prospered as he hoped, both Judith and Susanna could marry well. Very well indeed. And if John Shakspere renewed his request for a coat of arms… John Shakspere, gentleman. Mister Shakspere. Mister William Shakspere, gentleman. *Sir* William Shakspere, with the two handsome daughters and the son, M.A., from Cambridge (though Oxford was nearer to home), a writer like his father as well as a Privy Councillor – Lord Chancellor – Lord Treasurer – Lord Shakspere, the Queen's favourite. (Or the King's, a thought not to be spoken for fear of a treason indictment.) The Right Honourable Hamnet Shakspere, Earl of Stratford…

"Anne? What are you staring at?"

"You're standing there like a block, Mama, we had to come back for you."

"Oh, I was thinking."

"And how do you like it so far?" said the wittiest poet in England. Ignoring him, Anne with dignity gathered up her skirts and moved on. Not far, because they were stopped in front of a corner house.

"This is one I've always liked," said William, taking Anne's arm to make amends.

"New Place? It's the biggest house in Stratford."

"And I like it."

"It's changed hands often. They say it's an unlucky house."

"Fiddlesticks. A handsome place."

"And how many poems would it take to pay for it?"

"Many. Many. But a man can dream. If I can make enough money to buy a share in a theatre… Well, one day, perhaps. Let's look further before it rains, then it's dinner with Hamnet and Judith Sadler, remember."

"Will," Anne said that night when the bed curtains were drawn, "you talk of buying New Place. Just how much money do you expect to make? I think you're living in a fool's paradise. We can't afford a house like that."

"Why not? Lord Burghley has given me twenty pounds for the poems I've written."

"Twenty pounds won't buy a house. Or, at least, not New Place."

"I know, but that's only the start."

"Why? Have you persuaded Lord Southampton to wed Lady Elizabeth Vere?"

"Not yet."

"No, I daresay not." She had meant to speak calmly, but even to herself her voice was sharp with malice.

"What does that mean?" William asked dangerously.

"I mean that you love that boy yourself."

There was a brittle silence before William said, "Of course I love him. We are friends. I love my friends."

"Like Christopher Marlowe?"

"Of course I love Kit." He turned over, wrapping a skein of Anne's hair round his hand. Painfully. "But if you mean I'm a boy-lover like Kit, madam, let me tell you: no such thing."

"I'd almost rather you were."

"Anne!"

"If you were like Kit and went around sodomising every pretty face you saw..." She heard his gasping intake of breath, and said through her teeth, "*Don't laugh*. I warn you. Make a joke of me, William, and I will divorce you. I mean it."

Weakly he said, "A decent woman shouldn't even know of such things."

"Oh, moralising now, is it? Well, ten years ago I knew nothing of 'such things', but you took an ignorant farmer's daughter and made her into something of a woman of the world. A player's wife, a poet's wife. Aye, I know about such things and not only from Kit Marlowe. And I know you love Harry Southampton and want him for yourself. It shines out of you every time you say his name, every time you touch that pearl earring he gave you or that gold ring on your hand, when you tell your brothers about the horse he lent you, when you talk about Titchfield. You want him and you're taking money from him. You whore, William. You whore."

He tightened his hand in her hair, dragging her bodily across the bed against him. "Take that back. Bitch. Take that back."

"Why should I?" She kicked him, hard.

"Because he's not my lover."

"But you wish he were."

William didn't answer. Held against him, unable to move for his grip in her hair and on her arm, Anne listened to that silence and felt the tears start to her eyes. She also, for some reason, felt aroused. William also. She felt it. She heard his quickened breathing.

"You brown-haired witch," he said against her mouth. "Yes, I wish it."

"And I would rather you took him to bed than loved him." She bit his lower lip, viciously.

"Ouch. You bitch." Keeping his hand in her hair he let go of her arm to reach under her nightgown, at the same time pulling her on top of him. "Why?"

"Because I love you and if I lose you I'll die."

"You'll die and right now. Come, Anne." He touched her intimately, laughing at her squirming gasp. "Die, Anne. Come and die for me. I love you. I love Harry. You're my wife." He'd come naked to bed, there was no clothing in the way of her hands.

"Not that I can blame you."

"*Gently!* Not blame me for what?"

"Loving that beautiful boy. After all, *I* fell in love with him too." He gasped in pure shock. "What is it? Words failing William Shakspere for once? Shocked that I dare love your lovely boy? That your wife dares love another man?"

"Both. Neither. Did you..."

"Bed him? Chance would be a fine thing. A boy like that and a woman like me? But had he asked, for all I love you..." He bucked under her grasping, stroking hands; his turn to be held helpless. "You whore, William. You might not sell your body, but you sell what's dearer to you. Your words."

"Not selling. Giving. Out of love."

"Then do it thoroughly. Bring me the money and bring me home enough of your love."

"I do. Oh *Christ*. You love him?"

"Fell in love with him. There's a difference. A fine difference. Words matter."

"Aye, they do, and I will attend to the words, fine or otherwise. Use your mouth for other things, Anne."

"As you would Harry did?"

"As you would Harry did. Let me at you. Oh God you bitch, you whore, you witch..."

"...your wife. Touch me there. As you can't with Harry. And there."

"And there. *Anne*. Oh, Anne. Oh God. Jesus. Take another man and I'll kill you."

"Take another woman and I'll kill you."

"Not with you in my bed, like this. Do it. Do it, Anne. Do everything."

"Like this? And this?"

"And this, and this, and this. You bitch, I love you."

A long time later, she said, "You're right, this bed does creak."

"Under that treatment, you're surprised? Jesus, Anne. Ten years married."

"Jealousy makes a good spice." She turned on her back, stretching, trying to pull up the tangled sheets. William flapped a moment, dragging the blankets up, throwing her pillow up from the centre of the bed.

"Did you really fall in love with Harry?"

"Did you?"

"I asked first."

"Then I think I'll leave you wondering." Neatly she turned on her side, her back to him. "Goodnight, husband."

"Goodnight," said William.

21.

Only a fool would travel in winter unless by dire necessity. So William told himself through the miserable days of his journey from London. The roads were foul, the weather worse. Often he could see only a few paces ahead through the flurries of snow. Once he lost the road entirely and wasted half a day. The inns he stayed at were dirty, cold and crammed with travellers in as bad a case as he. Despite his leather jerkin and oiled-wool cloak he was wet and chilled to the bone by the time he reached Titchfield, and was wondering why he'd come.

But he was taken inside at once, an honoured guest, and in the hall a huge fire blazed, and there was Harry, kissing his cheek and thrusting a mug of hot spiced wine into his hand.

"A bad journey?" he said sympathetically.

"Beyond telling." William's teeth chattered so much that he could hardly say the words. He downed his wine in two gulps and held his tankard out for more. Only then did he notice the other people in the hall. Most of them were unknown to him, or no more than vaguely familiar. He bowed, generally, as Harry mentioned his name, and heard some offensively warm, clean gallant say, "Oh, yes, the play-writing fellow," and laugh and turn away to nudge the Earl of Essex.

"Would you like a hot bath?" Harry asked quietly. William nodded. Harry murmured to a servant. "Come," he said to William. "The least I can do is thaw you out."

The organisation of great households like this was an awesome thing. How much money did it cost, William wondered, and how many servants, to keep rooms ready for guests who might arrive this week, next week, never? For his room was all prepared for him, the bed made and turned down, the fire alight, a jug of wine to hand. Above all, it was warm. Before he'd properly toasted his hands at the fire, servants were bringing in a bathtub and copper jugs of hot water.

Soaking, feeling the chill leave his bones, William so nearly fell asleep that he had to ask Harry to repeat something he had said.

"Christopher Marlowe has been here, and is expected again soon." Harry turned away as he said this.

"Oh?"

"He said he would come. Nashe too, perhaps."

"A plethora of poets."

"None so good as you. And also we have that strange Spaniard Essex thinks so well of. Perez or some such name." Placatingly, Harry took the sponge and began to wash William's back. "Did you have a merry Christmas?"

"Merry enough, and a pleasant time at home. You?"

"Yes, but it was dull without you. Did your family like the gifts I sent?" He was after all, very young.

"Yes," William said gently. "They liked them very much. It was a kindly thought, Harry."

Harry had sent silver lockets for the little girls, with a flower and their initials in enamel; also a dress length of velvet each, blue for Judith, green for Susanna, and nothing would do but that Anne and William's mother immediately begin to make the material up. For Hamnet, who liked animals, a Bestiary and a sheathed dagger sworn to have been captured from a Spaniard. Hamnet had been enchanted. For Anne there had been a bolt of kingfisher-coloured changeable silk and a pair of Turkish slippers with curling toes. She had been moderately charmed, given the source of the gift.

Remembering that, and Anne stitching at her daughters' new dresses, William said, "I brought you a gift, Harry."

"You needn't have. What is it?"

"In my bag, on top of my clothes." Craning around he saw that the valet had finished unpacking, and the gift lay on the table. "In the muslin, there."

Eager as a child Harry unwrapped it. "Oh, Will. Gloves. How beautiful." He turned them over, admiring the fine cheveril leather and the quilted, scented satin lining, the cuffs embroidered in gold.

Watching him, William said, "Remember we spoke of my boyhood and I said I could still make you a pair of gloves? Well, so I did." With it in mind, he had carefully measured Harry's hand against his own before he left. Harry's hand was narrower than his own, with very long thin fingers. "Not that I would rush to tell your friends I made them myself. It's enough they're forced to mix with a hireling player, let alone an artisan smelling of his father's workshop."

"But the gloves are beautiful. Finer than any I've ever seen. And you truly made them yourself?"

"With my own fair hands. In between making you a fine new play and more sonnets."

"A play? And more poems? Will, how can I thank you? And for the gloves, which I will wear with pride and tell everyone to shop for their gloves in Stratford."

"Be specific. Tell them, John Shakspere's shop. You can thank me by handing me a towel, I must get out." But Harry held the towel out wide and as William left the tub he wrapped it around him, thus holding him imprisoned in his arms. Very lightly he kissed the corner of William's mouth. They stared for a long moment into each other's eyes. Then William bowed his head onto Harry's shoulder. "I had forgotten how much I love you."

"I had not. But I have been so very alone all these weeks."

"Alone? With your mother and sister, with Lord Essex, with all your friends?"

"It is different. I thought – I feared – you might not love me any more."

"You need not have. For I do love you, Harry."

"And I you."

A bell rang, severing the moment. "Supper," said Harry, annoyed.

William glanced, up, laughing. "I need it. I've been on the road since first light. I've a dim memory of an equally dim pork pie at noon."

"Then dress, quickly, and come have your supper. And during it you'll tell us of this new play. Please."

"It's of some gentlemen," William said along the table as the servants brought the second course. "Gentlemen who foreswear the company of women for a year while they study."

"No women in it?" someone asked. "Sounds dull."

"Ah, but they cannot keep their oath." Boiled mutton, William saw, with caper sauce, and boiled fowls, pies, baked fish, blancmanges and creams, fritters. Excellent. "I call it *Love's Labour's Lost.*"

"Good title," said the critic.

"There's a room," Harry excitedly interrupted, "by the front door, facing the front of the house. I've ordered it cleaned and readied, it will be excellent for playing."

"When do the players arrive?"

"Soon. February."

"And are we merely to watch or can we take part?"

Harry knew Will's views on amateurs and studiously refrained from catching his eye. "We shall see," he said. "To amuse ourselves we could perform one of Will's old pieces. The *Shrew,* perhaps."

"No. It's too countrified," said the same man, "but *Titus Andronicus;* now that has a pleasing touch of Marlowe to it."

"And Marlowe's touch must please anyone," William said evilly.

Trying not to laugh, Harry suggested that such ideas were for later. After supper they would have music.

"And perhaps," said John Florio, his accented Italian voice lilting, "Master William would be so kind as to read us some of his poems. He has a most poetic touch." And Will, his mouth unpoetically full of mutton, could only nod agreeably.

And that's what I am, he thought that night, in bed. A hireling. A player. Someone to amuse the guests. A winter house party while there's plague in London. Guests at a loose end? Send for Whatisname, Shakspere, that's right, he's your man. Make extempore words to a song. Read a poem. Tell amusing anecdotes about touring. Teach some mincing lordling how to play Katerina. Trot out your Latin, your French, your Greek and your little Italian. Make a classical allusion, cap a quotation. Earn your keep, Will Shakspere. Sing for your supper.

The thought drove him out of bed and over to his writing table. He lit two candles and stirred up the fire. He pulled on his dressing gown and, absently, his best cloak over the top. He thrust his feet into the fur-lined boots Harry had given him in autumn. Harry, who had paid him no more attention all evening than to pull his strings for his guests' amusement. No better than a dancing bear. Harry, who wanted to be made immortal by his words.

So, all through the icy night, William wrote. Words poured from his pen, coming ready-made, it seemed. Once he rose to use the close-stool and kick the sulking fire to life, and went back to work with the thick velvet coverlet wrapped around him. He hardly felt the cold, or not until he saw the uneven lines of writing and realised his hand was shaking. His whole body was. But the bed was also cold; empty, its sheets a clammy embrace, the warming pan without a hint of heat. Harry's bed would be warm from the boy's sweet sleeping body. Or warm perhaps from Essex's body.

William remembered talk about those two in the past. Or someone else. I could be home, he thought, snug in my marital bed with my wife. I am a married man. I love my wife, who loves me. Who loves Harry Southampton. Or did she merely say so to punish me? She had said, at parting, "Go to your lovely boy and do whatever you must for fame and money. I'd rather you took him than loved him. But do what you must and bring me the money. I have been a player's wife too long. It is time I was a theatre-owner's wife, a poet's wife. And rich." His wife, his Anne. The shy farmer's daughter. *You took an ignorant farmer's daughter…* And gave her nothing. No house, no fine clothes, no ease. Friendship, yes. Enough of love. Little enough of love. But more than he had known until she said she loved another man.

William took up his pen again but his hand refused to answer him. Ink blots slashed across the page, the pen fell. He wanted to write of honour and corruption and could not. Miserably he rolled into bed, wrapping his diverse coverings about him. It was nearly dawn, a winter dawn of grey and frost. It would be a brave bird that heralded this dawn from an ice-hung tree. *It is the nightingale and not the lark, that pierced the something hollow of thine ear.* No – *it is the owl…* No… *Like to the lark, at break of day arising, sings hymns at heaven's gate…* Better… Birds chirping. Cawing. *The rook makes wing…* William slept.

He woke to warmth and pleasant smells and quiet breathing beside him. Most of all, to warmth. Through his closed eyelids he could see the flicker of the fire, and when he moved his feet they met the cosiness of a hot brick wrapped in cloths. Lazily he opened his eyes. Yes, a blazing fire and the thin light of a winter morning well advanced. His cloak was still around him, but someone had straightened the bed and tucked him snugly in.

"Good morning." Harry was lying beside him on top of the covers. He put down the sheaf of loose papers he was reading and grinned. "You worked all night again, it seems."

"Till dawn. I was so cold. Harry?"

"When you didn't come down to breakfast I came to see. Found the candles burnt out, the table covered with papers, you all bundled up and shivering in your sleep. I hope you haven't taken a chill. There's breakfast there if you're hungry."

William sat up. A tray on the bedside chest held covered dishes of eggs, slices of beef, bread so new it was still steaming, ale. "What time is it? I must get up. Aren't your guests looking for you?"

"They've gone out hunting. It's past nine. Eat it here, on the tray." Companionably Harry plumped his pillows for him.

"I've never eaten a meal in bed." But he did so. It was much too pleasant to move. "By the way, what's that you're reading?"

"For once you didn't lock your work away. You've finished *Venus and Adonis*, Will. And it is superb. What genius you have." His mouth full, William made a modest noise. "It really is good beyond praise. I am honoured. Dedicate this to me and I'll be immortal. And these other poems, did you write them last night too? And this fragment of a play?"

"I hardly know. I must have if it was out on the table. You've seen what it's like with me, Harry; the urge to write comes, the Muse comes." He reached for the sheet of paper in Harry's hand. Harry held it away, saying no, his fingers were buttery. To read it, William leaned his head on Harry's shoulder.

"Ah yes, I remember that idea coming to me. It's not well written, though. Needs work. It was just a night-time fancy."

"No, it's good." Harry shuffled the papers together, made a long arm to put them on the table, weighted down with a candlestick. He lay back, his arms folded behind his head, watching William finish his food. "I didn't give you a Christmas gift."

"You did, this ring, the pearl earring."

"Trinkets. I can't give you poetry or work a pair of exquisite gloves. All I have is my patronage and to use my rank to help you if I can. And money for *Venus and Adonis*."

"Those are very large gifts, my dear. My future. Fame, perhaps."

"Will you," Harry slanted a glance at him, "let me give you something else? For Christmas, for our love? Out of love?"

"Harry..."

"Listen. Will you let me buy you a share in the playing company?"

There was a long silence. William said softly, "To be no longer a hired player and play-maker? To be a share-holder, a house-keeper in a theatre? To be an established man, secure, with a steady income? You *ask* if you can give me that?"

"I thought you might be offended. It smacks of trade between us. But money is all I have to give. That and love. *With* love."

"But my lord, my love, we are talking of perhaps a hundred pounds, and you're not yet of age. Have you that much?"

"Yes. Will you accept it?"

"Of course. It's my hope, my dream. My future. I can't thank you." On a wave of huge delight he flung his arm around Harry and kissed him. Broke away. Looked at him. Saw the need and longing and love, and the defence against rejection. Kissed him again, and this time William's tongue parted Harry's lips and probed his mouth. Harry made a little sound in his throat. William took him firmly in his arms, kissed him harder, held him close and felt all his responses. In the back of William's mind a voice said sourly, *You whore, William;* and *do what you must. Bring me the money.*

"But it's not," he said aloud. "It's not the money. It is love. Just love. And because I have finished that poem and somehow that makes us less unequal."

"I know it's not the money," Harry muttered. "It's love. I love you."

"And I love you. I love thee, thou art my love. Harry my dear, my sweet love, give me time to wash my face and clean my teeth then if you love me, if you want me, go bolt the door then take off your clothes and get into this bed with me and make love to me."

"Yes," Harry whispered, enchanted. "Yes, my love." Later he said, "At last, my heart. At last." Swiftly Harry moved on top of him, matching their bodies so their mouths met and their hearts beat together. Then he began to move, hands following mouth and the long silky hair trailing a third sensation. Soon there were no sounds but kisses, and hands moving on flesh, each other's name enough endearment now, in the panting breath of passion.

Afterwards, when they lay holding each other, Harry said, "Why now, Will? Why did you resist me so long and give in now? Didn't you love me enough before?"

"I loved you more than enough. Wanted you very much, too. Couldn't let myself. I don't know, Harry. Perhaps it's because I've finished that poem and have something to give you at last. Perhaps it's because you brought me breakfast and tucked me up snugly."

Harry lifted his head, laughing. "I didn't go to the kitchen and cook the food myself."

"No, but you were kind. You took thought for me. Cared for me in that little way."

Baffled, Harry lay down again and kissed William's collarbone. "And now I know you truly love me. Now we're truly one."

"I always loved you," William said sharply. "And now you will break my heart."

"Oh no, love. No." Then, petulantly, he added, "Why don't you think you'll break mine? I do love you, Will."

"Yes, but I'm middle-aged, and married and not of your world or rank or kind, and you're young and very beautiful. Whether it's a man or a woman you find, yes, you'll break my heart, Harry."

"I won't. And you're not middle-aged."

"Half your age again. Twenty-nine, come April. Losing my hair."

"If you were *seventy*-nine and bald I'd still love you. I would love my clever poet."

"And if your clever poet stops praising you in his clever poems?"

"Still I will love you."

"I hope so."

"I know so." Harry started to kiss him again, but there came the sound of horses' hooves, of hounds baying, and a lot of hallooing. "Hey-up, our merry hunting party's returned. And I'm afraid I must go down and play the gallant host."

"Yes you must. Harry. You won't speak of this to anyone?"

"No, my dear. But tonight? Again?"

"Yes," William said with a faint sigh. "Tonight. Again. For I cannot resist you, my dearest love."

22.

It had set in to snow. The guests were confined to the house and desperate for amusement. Nothing would do but that they should put on a play. It would have to be one of William's. He had brought his own fair copies of *The Taming of the Shrew* and *Two Gentlemen of Verona*. The man who had complained the *Shrew* was too countrified must have done a little reading and discovered the play's sources, for now he was all for it. The *Shrew* let it be. So down they all went to what Harry called the playhouse room. He declared it perfect and ran about looking for properties and costumes and clamouring for their parts to be written out for them to learn.

"O God, your only jig-maker," William muttered when at eleven o'clock at night he was not in bed with Harry but sitting up copying out his play.

"What?" Harry said absently beside him, doing his best to help.

"Nothing." But William noted down what he'd said. It sounded rather well. "How far have we got?" He looked at the sheets written out in Harry's sloping, large, Italianate hand, comparing them with his own smaller, more accustomed writing.

"Last three scenes, now you've cut it so much."

"Had to, if they want to do it in two days' time. These aren't professional players who can con a long part inside a week and have it ready."

"How *do* you players remember all the words? You always have, what, twenty or thirty plays in your repertoire?"

"Practice. Keep writing."

Harry gave him a kiss and kept writing. He was as engaged as a child with the idea of doing the play, willing to put in all this dull work to make it a success. He was playing Katerina. He was by far too tall to play a girl, but it added to the part. His Katerina would be a gangling, awkward girl, all the more vulnerable by contrast to her pretty little feminine sister. John Florio was playing their father and Essex was parted as Petruchio.

"You don't really object to this, do you?" Harry asked when they'd copied the last scenes.

"No."

"Good. Then come to bed."

"Oh no, Harry," William smiled. "We haven't finished yet. We have to paste up all the separate bits to make a complete part for each person. So fetch out the glue-pot and paper, my sweet, and get to work."

"Oh well, waiting will make it all the sweeter," said Harry, and fetched out the glue pot.

As performances went, it was a dog's dinner, but they enjoyed themselves. Even William did, reluctantly.

"And the thing that stands out," Harry said, "is what a good actor you are. Of course I have seen you on stage times enough, but I'd never before watched you stop being yourself and become another person. How do you do it?"

"That I can't tell you. But you were a touching Katerina. And you kissed Petruchio far too heartily."

"Acting."

"Well, come kiss *me*, Kate." William pulled the other man down on top of him and all the new pleasures began again.

But, heady with success, the house party wanted to do the *Two Gentlemen* the following week and began to talk of William writing out his other plays for them to do. The players arrived just in time.

Watching them unload their wagon, William knew that they were his people. The hampers held not just clothes and props but his world. This Titchfield interlude had been a delight, but he did not belong in that world. Startled at the relief he felt, he ran down the steps to greet his friends.

"James. Dick. Welcome. What news of London? Will the playhouses be open soon?"

"Not for a while, it seems. Pembroke's Men are having a hard time of it on the road. Developments. I'll talk to you later, in private, about that." Burbage gave him a wink. "I'd better greet our gracious host."

"Yes, come inside where it's warm. My lords, my ladies, may I present Lord Strange's Men: James Burbage, Richard Burbage, Augustine Phillips, Will Kemp our clown, John Heminges,

Richard Condell, John Sinclo, Ned and Will our boy-players. And Dominus Marlowe you know." While everyone bowed William hooked his arm in Marlowe's and took him aside. "Christopher, what are you doing here? With *my* company?"

"Don't worry, William, they feel for some strange reason that they will persist with you as their play-maker. Lord Harry invited me and I also find it convenient to be out of London at present and to make holiday, *gratis*. You look well, my friend. Hampshire must agree with you. Or Southampton, at least."

"Hampshire is a most pleasant county. Kit, I want to know what you're doing here."

"I'm not here on… business, so calm down." Of course that had been in William's mind. Lady Southampton was as fervent a Catholic as her late husband had been. Harry's views on the burning question were unknown.

"No, John Florio takes care of spying on the Southamptons."

"How did you know?" Kit asked, startled out of his irritating sang-froid.

"He told me. Back when I wrote that sonnet introducing his *Second Fruits*. He invited me to join his little game, just as you did. I declined."

"Ah, yes. So honourable, our William. Yes, that sonnet, *Phaeton*, so quaint. No doubt the last piece William Shakspere doesn't sign. Your sugared sonnets for our lovely friend are becoming famous. I long to read them. Finished *Psyche and Cupid* yet?"

"If you mean *Venus and Adonis*, yes I have. It's good, Kit."

Proving again why he kept William's friendship, Kit said gently, "If you wrote it, it is more than good. You'll outstrip me altogether soon."

"Never. Though I would like to be known for my poetry more than for running off plays for the public theatre, mending other men's work."

"And so you shall be. We will both be great names. Ah, my lord, I trust I see you well?"

"Thank you, yes," said Harry. "What is this, a play-writers' conferring? Come, I have sent for hot wine before these players go to their quarters."

As he led them back to the party Kit flicked an eyebrow at William. Yes, William longed to say, I didn't miss that: *These players. To their quarters.* So my two worlds meet and recoil. Harry had meant nothing by it, except inadvertently to compliment William by distinguishing him from his fellows. But they *were* his fellows, his peers. Harry was not and never could be.

"With your permission, my lord, I will go with them." Hurt flashed in Harry's eyes. "We must discuss the new play," William softened it, and Harry's face cleared.

"Of course. But I will see you later." He meant to be discreet, but Kit's face was full of knowledge.

Besides the playhouse room and several small bedrooms up in the attics, the players were given a large, disused room on the ground floor, tellingly near the domestic quarters. But it had a good fire and a table and enough stools and chairs, and the servants brought food and more wine.

"Comfortable," James Burbage said, stretching out his feet to the fire. "Well, it's a good play, Will, *Love's Labour's Lost.* Very good. It plays well. We ran it through once before we left London, once we had our parts down. You're playing the schoolmaster, the pedant?"

"Takes me back."

"Yes, you had some fun writing that. Dick, pull my boots off, please; they're wet. Rotten journey down, Will. Now, some news. Word is that the Lord Chamberlain is looking to form a new playing company."

"A new one? I thought the authorities were keen to keep a check on us?"

"Yes and that's part of it, no doubt. But old Hunsdon wants to form a particular company, to be called the Lord Chamberlain's Men. It's to be the best, the *crème de la crème*. Most of us. Some of the Admiral's Men, if they're lucky. You, for our playwright."

"Ah. Would that be why Kit Marlowe is hanging around you?"

"Could be, could be. But he and Henslowe are like that." Burbage held up two twined fingers. "And it seems to suit them. Kit writes for Ned Alleyn's style. Will, it did cross my mind that Lord Southampton is Governor of the Isle of Wight, yes? And George Carey's his deputy, yes? And Carey is Lord Hunsdon's kinsman and also Her Majesty's. Southampton is Lord Burghley's ward. It makes a neat connection; Southampton, Burghley, Carey, the Lord Chamberlain, the Queen. Kit Marlowe could be looking after himself, trying to wriggle his way into that connection. He's been playing too many dangerous games lately, has Kit – or perhaps he's merely trying to be the play-maker for this new playing company. Keep your eye on him. But we don't want him, good though he is. You suit us, Will. So stay on your toes and you'll be in this new company. And it will have Her Majesty's favour."

"I see," William said thoughtfully. "James, I might soon have enough money put by to purchase a share in a company. In this new one, with luck, if not, in our present one. What say you to that?"

Burbage studied him for a moment. "We can always do with new stakeholders, Will. You know what the money side of it's like. But it would cost you a hundred pounds for a share."

"I can manage that, I think."

"If you can, you're in. You'd go on writing for us?"

"Oh yes, of course."

"Good, for I want to retain our own writer. Three for the price of one, eh? Actor, play-maker and shareholder."

"If all goes well. When would the new company start?"

"That's anyone's guess. The plague's still about in London, of course, but they're using that as an excuse to keep the theatres shut. The Puritans are up to their usual tricks and the government's playing coy. I wouldn't count on seeing the theatres open this year."

"So long?"

"Aye. We'll be on the road again come Spring." Suddenly not quite meeting William's eyes he said, "You'll be with us still?"

"Of course." William knew that quite definitely. He loved Harry, but he couldn't continue to live here, known at Southampton's catamite, living off the crumbs from his table. "Of course I'll be touring. Come Spring."

Over the next few days William had little time for anything but his play. The Southamptons had invited people from London and from the neighbouring great houses to make it a splendid occasion as well as a diversion from the dumps of winter.

William was busy. But not too busy to note that Harry was spending a great deal of time with Christopher Marlowe. While William directed rehearsals, practised his own part, re-wrote the play, smoothed ruffled feathers and answered questions, Harry and Kit were snug in Harry's reading room, talking over the dear old days at Cambridge, reading Greek, discussing literature or, with Essex, slandering Sir Walter Raleigh and Francis Bacon. When the weather cleared they walked out together, or rode. There was talk of a new play from Kit. He begged his lordship's permission to dedicate *Hero and Leander* to him when it was finished. At night, William several times found Harry's door locked. People began to whisper behind their hands and shot curious or relieved looks at William. The few times he was alone with Harry, they were busy with love, not questions. William began to contemplate writing a poem, or perhaps a play, about jealousy.

The new play was a success. Cheered to the echo. For a week the players stayed, putting on a play each night, ending again with *Love's Labour's Lost.* Then it was March and time for them to go.

"And for me to go too," William told Harry.

"Stay."

"I must go to London to see *Venus and Adonis* into print. And then I go on the road with the players."

"Why? You needn't. I'll give you all the money you need. You can live here. Plenty of people keep a writer to –"

"My love, no." Lovingly William stroked the golden head nestled on his shoulder.

"Why not?"

"I doubt you'll understand, Harry. I need my own world and my own people."

"You mean to go back to your wife?"

"Of course, when I can. I want to see her and the children. This was only a holiday here."

"I thought it more. If you're afraid of talk, I'll make you my secretary, put you on my staff with a salary, set up a players' company of my own. You mustn't leave me. You can't leave me!"

"Yes, I must. I can. Must, while I *still* can. I daresay there's talk enough already, but what's done is done."

Harry stopped his nuzzling caresses. He sat up, thrusting the hair back from his face. In these last few months his looks had matured, William noted. He looked much less girlish, fully a man now. And still beautiful. All the more beautiful. Even when he was petulant with anger. "If you leave me," he said, "you can't love me. What if I refuse to pay you for that poem? Refuse you my patronage? Refuse the money to buy a share in the theatre? If you don't stay, you can kiss those things goodbye. Because I gave them out of love, and if you leave me you don't love me."

"That is how a child reasons."

"I am not a child!" Harry shouted, childishly. "I'm a man."

"Then act like one." Harry gasped as if William had slapped him. "Refuse me the money and I'll still love you. But you will despise yourself and, therefore, me. Yes, you're a man and you know that what we have is between men. It's love, Harry. Don't spoil it. I have duties and responsibilities. So have you. And what sort of love cannot bear a parting? Parting's a sweet sorrow, Harry, when it's not forever."

"But you will come back to me?"

"If you want me. When you want me. But remember I have a life outside these walls and this bed and your arms."

"If I come to London will you...?"

"Harry, I will be in London until the Spring. Come to London if you wish. But then I go on tour. That's flat. It's what I must do."

"And I must bear it."

"As must I."

"Well, then." Harry lay down again, taking William sweetly in his arms. "I must accept it. I do. And what I said about the money was anger. Spite. Misery. You'll dedicate your wonderful poem to me and I'll buy you your share in the playing company. Because I love you. But when you go home to your wife..."

But William cut him off by laying his finger across his lips. "When I go home to her I won't forget you. And that is all you can know of what's between Anne and me. We're doing a lot of talking, Harry, when I must leave in a day or two. Come here and love me."

23.

"So," said Kit, "you're famous. All London rings with your name." He sauntered across to William's writing table and picked up one of the copies of *Venus and Adonis*. "Dick Field did you proud. It's a handsome publication."

"We old Stratford men must stick together. But yes, it looks well. What do you think of the dedication?"

"Properly obsequious and respectful. Obsequious to the point of arse-licking. Which reminds me; word is that Harry Southampton's given you a thousand pounds."

"A *thousand!*" William swivelled further around to look at his friend, but Kit was standing before the window, his face in shadow. "No, Kit. I doubt he's *got* a thousand pounds till he comes of age." William thought of the money he had recently sent home to Anne. Not a thousand, of course, but nearly three hundred, for the play, for the sonnets, from Lord Burghley, and a clear hundred to buy his share in the playing company.

"Ah, yes, I did wonder. A thousand pounds would make you the most expensive whore in Christendom."

"Will you get out," William courteously enquired, "or be thrown out?"

"Touched you on the raw? I see. It's as he says. You're in love with him."

William began an angry retort and saw the malice in Kit's eyes fade. "I love him," he said. "Yes, I'm in love with him. Did you two talk of me, then?"

"He didn't tell me anything intimate. He talked of you with love. And what of your wife in all this, Will?"

"That is my concern."

"And I hope you have it well in hand. A fine woman, Anne. I envy you her. You know you won't keep Harry, don't you?"

"Yes," said William, knowing an infinity of pain. "Yes, I know it. Kit, why did you go to Titchfield?"

"To see if I too can win Harry's, er, patronage. See how frank I am with you?"

"Be more frank. Are you his lover?"

Kit let a moment go by before he said, "I have been. Welcome, Will, to the company of those who are hurt. Like Anne."

William saw the book quivering in his hands. "You're an odd person to give a moral lesson. Suppose we leave Anne out of this?"

To his surprise Kit said, "Very well." He came to sit beside William, clasping his hands behind his head. "*Venus and Adonis* is a great work, Will. It will live. A fine and witty work."

"Thank you."

"I mean it. Will, I'm afraid."

"Of what?"

"I have," Kit said slowly, "got myself into a dangerous spot. I can't tell you. Best you know nothing. At Titchfield I watched Will Kempe preparing his act. He juggled seven balls and never let one fall. I'm not the juggler I thought I was. Stay out of the spying game, Will. And watch that your father goes no further into recusancy. Stay away from Raleigh's circle." Unshed tears made emeralds of his dark-lashed eyes. His hand crept out and closed over William's.

"Kit, my dear friend."

"Oh, it may come to nothing. But if you hear I am dead, don't believe it until you view the body. If anyone comes to you asking of me, you know nothing. There is nothing to know. No secrets. No papers. Mourn me if you will. Then forget me."

"I could never forget you. Nor could the world forget you. Kit, if it's a matter of leaving the country, that kind of thing, I can give you money."

"You need not. It may come to nothing. But remember I loved you. For all that I sought to win Harry Southampton, as patron and lover, from you, I have loved you." In one lithe movement he stood up, gave William a kiss and went.

After a moment William leapt out of his chair and ran down the stairs after him, but by the time he reached the street Kit was nowhere in sight.

Anne looked at the letter the messenger had brought. She ran her finger over the seal, tracing the unfamiliar coat of arms imprinted there. "From Lord Southampton? And for me, not my husband?"

"Yes, ma'am. I'm to say, if there is a reply, you may send it with me."

"Will you wait a few moments?"

The man nodded. Anne directed the maid to take him to the back parlour and give him some ale. Then, slowly, she climbed the stairs to her bedroom. The children were clamouring around her. A letter must be from their father. What did he say, was he coming home? She shooed them away and locked her door.

Why did a man write to his lover's wife? With news of his death? That he was never coming home again? Abruptly she broke the seal and unfolded the paper.

The letter was formal, pleasant. And, as gently as possible, it told her that Christopher Marlowe was dead.

"Christopher," she whispered. "Oh, Kit."

...in a tavern brawl at Deptford, or so the common fame runs. If there is more behind it, no one is admitting it. It might be wise not to enquire too closely. Thinking you might not have had the news, I thought it best to write to you. I do not know where Lord Strange's Men will be at present. It is possible your husband will not hear until he returns to London or comes to Stratford. It is a great loss to all who knew Christopher Marlowe, and to England.

He had signed it, formally, *Southampton.*

Well. Kind of him to write. A great loss indeed. Dear, witty, malicious, kindly Kit with his green cat's eyes. He had liked her. She had liked him. He had been a friend. This would hit William hard. Did he know, or was he touring contentedly, looking forward to seeing Kit when he returned to London? At least he evidently was touring, not summering again with Southampton.

Anne had never written to a nobleman. In fact, her only letters had been to her husband, who would never criticise her mistakes. At William's writing desk she took out paper and hesitantly inked a pen. In a careful, childish hand, she wrote a few words of thanks for the news, of her loss, of her gratitude for his kindness in telling her. She did not, she finished, know where her husband would be at present or whether he had heard about Marlowe.

That would have to do. She folded the letter and gave it to the messenger. And wondered who William would turn to for comfort; her or Harry Southampton.

William came home a bare week later. Anne was dusting the parlour when two arms closed around her and a kiss was planted on the back of her neck.

"Will, it's you!"

"Who else, sneaking up to kiss you?" He spun her around, kissed her lips. "I've today and tonight. We're at Oxford and I begged some leave. You're well?"

"Oh yes, Will. And you?" Though she had little need to ask. More richly dressed than she was used to, brown from sun, dusty from the road, content and full of health. Glad to be home. Her heart soared. "My dear."

But their daughters had seen him come. They were all over him, and from then on there was no time for private talk. Hamnet was in school. "So we'll fetch him home," said William. "I've only today and I've missed him. Send Richard with a message, urgent trouble at home." And by the time he'd greeted his parents and brothers and sisters and had a mug of ale, Hamnet was home, flinging himself on his father, half-crying with joy. Then it was dinner time, and still no chance to be alone.

In the afternoon they went to the back garden, under the shade of the fruit trees, and there were strawberries with cream and wine kept cold in the well. Anne took her shoes and stockings off. William lay in his shirtsleeves on the daisy-starred grass, Judith weaving a daisy crown for his hair. Hamnet cuddled against his shoulder. Susanna hugged her knees, listening to him talk.

"The new play?" William answered Hamnet. "A success. Picture, Hamnet love, a room in a great house, a room big as this house, the curtains drawn and more candles than you've ever seen, all blazing. And two-score men all in silken clothes and jewels, and pretty ladies."

"As pretty as Mama?"

William gave it due thought. "Not *quite* as pretty," he decided, and added aside to Anne, his eyes full of promise, "You're looking very handsome, Mrs Shakspere. A new way of doing your hair. I like it. And a new dress."

"I spent some of the money."

"Excellent. There'll be more. *Venus and Adonis* is selling like hot cakes. It's a success, a *success d'éstime*, I'm becoming famous for it. People talk of 'sweet Mr Shakspere'. All those same people who despised me as a would-be playwright, a would-be poet, trying to make my way with no university education, no connections. What did you think of it, Anne?"

"I liked it. Admired it. Pagan. Passionate. Sweet. Country love. And I wonder if people think I am Venus, the rampaging country hussy."

"No hussy. Country matters… What, Hamnet? Oh yes, the play. Did you read the fair copy I sent home?"

"Yes but I didn't understand some of it. Mama said they were probably jokes."

"Mama was right. I had some fun with that play. Holofernes is… well, I won't say his name, but someone I know."

"I liked him, the schoolmaster," said Hamnet. "He was funny. He was a bit like the one at school, the new one."

"And a bit like one I had when I was your age. Prosing old pedant. So the play went very well. Master Burbage was excellent as always. We all were. And the audience liked it. We did it a second time that week, and it will go into our *repertoire*. Kit Marlowe was there and he liked it."

Judith put the daisy crown on her father's hair. "Master Marlowe's dead," she said.

"Why didn't you tell me?" William repeated. He had stopped pacing the bedroom and was slumped on the edge of the bed, his face still marked with tears. He had looked not to Anne for solace, but to his mother. Anne had been left to comfort the children. Poor Judith had been weeping desperately because she thought William was angry with her and her twin had scolded her. Susanna was crying because she heard her father crying. Hamnet was grave-faced, looking in his sensitivity more than ever like William. All of them desolate that their lovely day was spoiled. Anne tried not to cry because William had looked at her with hatred.

His mother had taken Anne's part. How could Anne tell him? She hadn't had a moment. He'd sent for Hamnet, then it had been dinner, then there were the other children. Anne had been biding her time, waiting to tell him in private. She had liked Master Marlowe, and a friend's death was always a grief, but there was no call to take it out on Anne.

William made his peace with the children. He ate dinner quietly and then told them a bedtime story. Not a word to Anne, until now, when the household was to bed and he came at last to her room.

"Why didn't you tell me? Do you hold that much spite against me, that you couldn't tell me of my best friend's death?"

"He was my friend too."

"A passing friend. He was my mentor, my friend, my colleague, the one I tried to emulate, the one I admired above all others. When first I went to London, when first I met him, he talked to me – *talked!* – we talked the stars to bed, all one night, the first night we met, because each of us had discovered perhaps the only one who could understand. He helped me, he read my work, he wasn't envious or spiteful, he..."

"He loved you. And you loved him. I know that. I liked him better than almost anyone I know. And I didn't tell you because, as your mother said, what chance did I have? I was going to tell you as soon as we were alone. Spite? Never spite between us, whatever you do when you're away from me."

To her annoyance Anne was also weeping now. She bent and retrieved Southampton's letter, lying crumpled where William had tossed it once he had finished reading it. "And if we're to strip the matter to the bone, if even Harry didn't know where you were, how much less could I know? I couldn't send a letter. I could only wait to hear from you. It was kind of Harry to write. I think he knew I loved Kit Marlowe too."

"Harry can be kind," William said cruelly, then threw her his sodden handkerchief. "Oh, blow your nose, woman. Don't snivel at me. I was unfair. But oh Jesus, *Kit*. Christopher Marlowe. Dead. That golden voice silenced forever. My friend gone."

"Mine too." Anne blew her nose, then with distaste put the handkerchief aside and fetched out two clean ones. "Here."

"Thank you."

Wearily Anne turned aside and began to undress for the night. "Will you come to bed? If you have to start back early tomorrow you should get some sleep."

"I won't sleep." But he took off his clothes and climbed into the bed. It was a hot night and they lay naked, only a sheet over them. Almost crying again Anne thought how, so few hours before, she had looked forward to this moment when they would go to bed and make sweet, languorous summer love. Or William would explain that because of Harry there would be no more lovemaking with her. He would have told her kindly, with all the love he could find. Not with anger and contempt.

She put out the candle. They lay in silence. Each knew the other was still awake, but neither wanted to be the first to speak. After half an hour by the chime of the town clock, William's hand slid across the bed and took hers.

"I'm sorry," he said. "I know it wasn't spite. That was grief talking. And shock. I think Kit half expected something to happen, Anne. He said in London, the last time I saw him, that he was perhaps in danger. Said if I heard of his death I wasn't to believe it unless I'd viewed his body for myself! So perhaps..."

"But Lord Southampton said in his letter there had been an inquest. A crowner's court."

"Proves nothing. If Kit was as deep in secret matters as he sometimes said, what easier for the people concerned to fake a death, give false evidence? Harry's letter said Frizer was there at that tavern, and Poley; two nasty little pieces of work, deep in spying. Or," the febrile hope left his voice, "perhaps that's it. They did it. Kit was assassinated. To stop his mouth. To fake up a case against someone else." William turned on his side, towards Anne. "I told him that if he needed money to leave England I would provide it. He refused. Perhaps I could have helped him more. Done something."

"He knew you would have, had he needed it."

William's hand reached out blindly and touched Anne's stomach. He rested it there. "Kit asked me if I loved Harry. When I said yes, he said, 'And what of Anne in all this?' He said he envied me for having you. He liked you."

"Was he ever your lover?"

"No," William said on the ghost of a laugh. "No. Although he asked. He was Harry's lover."

"Ah." The grunt of surprise was forced out of Anne. In this night time, emotion-stripped honesty she could ask, "Did that make you jealous?"

"Yes, Anne, it did. I've learnt what jealousy is."

"I could have told you."

"Yes."

"And did you take that lovely boy to your bed? Was he your lover?"

"Yes. I've hurt you, haven't I?"

155

"Yes. But I was complicit. I spent the money he gave you."

"The money he gave me for plays and poems. Not quite immoral earnings."

A little time went past before Anne asked, oddly urgent, "What do you do with Harry? What do men do together? Do you take him like a woman? Does he take you like that? Do you hold each other and kiss? *Is it better*? Better than with a woman?"

"It's not like that. It's loving caresses and kisses. Sometimes more. Not like with a woman. Not better. Anne. I love you. You're my wife."

"But not beautiful. Not golden and blue-eyed and entrancing. Not clever, not rich, not educated. Not a man. Not young."

"None of those things," said William, "but a pleasing woman and fiery, and my wife."

"And you are my husband. I love you and always will. Unless you wear out my love by giving your love to others. Harry is for the moment. We are bound, you and I."

"I come home to you, always."

"And with that I must be content?"

"Content? More than that. Because I come home out of love. For you. Yes, Harry's for the moment, and I cannot deny that I love him. But I love you too, and you are forever."

"Yet you thought I didn't tell you of Kit's death out of spite and jealousy."

"I know you better than that."

"I hope so. When we married we said we would always be friends and partners. Yet often I feel that if your heart, let's say your love, were, say, London, then I'd live on its outskirts. Or a hundred miles away. Or, perhaps I feel less like your wife than like a mistress you keep hidden away for the occasional visit."

"Anne, I repeat: you are my wife, my friend, my partner. I do love you. Let's be happy with that."

"Yes. It's all we have."

They lay holding each other and both wept a little for Kit Marlowe, for what couldn't be mended, for what they had, precious for all its imperfections.

Part Four

1594

24.

William was an accustomed guest at Southampton House. The servants greeted him warmly and bowed him towards the great salon. He could hear music from within, a boy singing. He stepped in quietly, standing behind a knot of men just inside the doors.

There were perhaps two-score people in the room, women as well as men for this was one of Harry's regular musical evenings. He was at the far side of the room, sitting beside Essex. They were both intent on the singer. A servant went by with a tray of wine and, taking a cup, William moved into the space left by the man's passing so he could see the singer.

Not a boy. A woman. Emphatically a woman, for the first thing he saw was a pair of splendid breasts exposed nearly to the nipples, spilling down onto the lute she played. She had an unusual voice, pure and true, husky, with the timbre you sometimes heard in a just-broken boy's. She was singing an old country air, a hackneyed, sentimental piece that would usually have made this sophisticated audience scoff, but she had set it in a minor key and changed the tempo so that it became the very distillation of heartbreak and lost youth. William saw one or two women dabbing surreptitiously at their eyes.

The song ended to cries of "Brava!" and "Encore!" The woman tuned her lute, thinking, then with a quick nod struck up another tune. William stared in disbelief, for this was the filthiest of drinking songs, witty enough with its double and triple *entendres* but certainly not the thing for *this* audience, or mixed company. But, again, the singer gave it her own treatment. She used a tinkling, sugary accompaniment and sang it with the wide-eyed innocence of a schoolgirl who had no idea of the bawdy meaning and was bewildered when people laughed. It was killingly funny, and even ladies who would normally have been shocked were

crying with laughter. The singer knew how far to take the joke –
she abandoned the song before the dirtiest bits, and went straight
into an exquisite piece of Palestrina. So she wasn't just a bundle of
party tricks. There was real musicianship here.

She finished to enthusiastic applause. Clapping until his palms
stung, William watched her rise and shake out the ribbons of her
lute. She moved gracefully, but she was nothing to look at –
gypsy-dark, her skin brown, her eyes as black as her tangle of
curling hair, her thick, straight black brows giving her a scowling
look. Her dress was tawdry, a yellow satin cut oddly with a round
neck, a laced bodice and puffed sleeves that left her forearms bare.
Her hair was caught up in a yellow ribbon, and she wore a string
of amber beads wound three times around her neck. Harry might
have found her in one of the Southwark stews or among the
motley of entertainers in Paris Garden.

"Don't finish," Harry called. "Give us more."

She didn't look at him, or bow, but sat down again. "One
more, at your lordship's request, then your consort is ready to
play." She had a strong Scotch accent: *ain muir*.

This time, to William's surprise, she sang his song from *Two
Gentlemen of Verona*: "Who is Sylvia, what is she, that all her swains
commend her." She played it simply, not guying it as he'd feared,
and it was beautiful.

They begged her for an encore, but she refused, gesturing
prettily to the sulking consort clutching their tuned instruments.
"They can do better than I. And I would be glad of a cup of wine,
my lord."

"It's yours." Harry beckoned to a servant. The woman
curtsied to him, then to her applauding audience, and for the first
time smiled. She was pretty when she smiled.

The consort took up their places and struck up a tune for
dancing. The woman singer had disappeared.

William moved across the room to Harry and the Earl of
Essex. "Good evening, my lords."

"Good evening to you. Do we see you flushed with the
success of *Lucrece*?"

"Now that," said Essex before William could answer, "is a
truly fine poem. Better than *Venus and Adonis*, in my opinion."

"Thank you, my lord." William bowed. They were on friendly enough terms, given their difference in rank, but there was no call-me-Robert about Essex.

"What did you think of that woman singer?" Harry asked.

"Interesting. She has a fine voice. Where did you find her?"

"Oh, at a party. Odd-looking little thing, isn't she. I thought she must be Italian or Spanish with that dark skin."

"Scotch," said Essex. "You can hear the heather in her voice." And you could hear the edge of violence in Essex's, William thought. He shot Harry an enquiring glance, and got a sort of facial shrug in return. Essex saw this little interplay. "I count all Scotchmen as spies for King Jamie until it's proven otherwise. That wee Scotch urchin likes to know what's going on around our Queen."

"Can you blame him, when she refuses to name him as her heir?"

"*Harry,*" William warned on a breath.

"Yes," Essex agreed, scrubbing distractedly at his red hair, "have a care what you say. We *do not* speak of the succession."

"Yet everyone knows King James must be her heir. Who else? Believe it or not, Robin, the Queen is not immortal."

"Will you tell her, or shall I? And the point is that there are others with a claim to the throne. Wise men do not discuss them. Especially while there's a Scotchwoman in the room."

"Thus speaks the head of Her Majesty's intelligence service?" snapped Harry, and in horrified unison William and Lord Essex begged him to shut up.

"Master William," said Essex, "tell us of your new plays. And the new playing company. How do you get along with Lord Hunsdon?" If this was an invitation to be indiscreet, William refused it. The Lord Chamberlain, he said, truthfully enough, was interested and considerate without being interfering, and William had two new plays on the way.

"One at least a comedy, I hope," said Essex. "Speaking of comedy, we've read Henry Willoughby's thing."

"*Willobie His Avisa*? Fame at last." Neither of them looked at Harry, who was busy sulking.

"Is it true," Essex asked, grinning, "that you spoiled his sport with the lady? Got in first pretending to be him?"

Grinning back William said, "Not a word of truth to it, my lord. There are other men with the initials W.S."

"Yes and others with the initials H.W.," snarled Harry. "I've had people winking and snickering since the bloody thing came out. That little shirt-lifter Francis Bacon had the nerve to simper up to me and call me Mr H.W. to my face."

"Cheer up," said William. "I didn't figure very charmingly in that *Edward III*. If I ever find out who wrote it…"

"The smart money's on George Peele."

"Or Henry Chettle, I've heard. Perhaps Chettle didn't like having to apologise to me and Kit Marlowe. Though I rather like him. I thought we were on good terms."

"Playwrights' jealousy." Harry got abruptly to his feet and went away. William looked at Essex.

With a sigh the Earl said, "Lord Burghley's given him an ultimatum. Marry Elizabeth de Vere, or pay such a fine he'll be begging his bread in the streets. He's twenty-one in October, remember, and God knows he'll inherit more debts than money from his father's estate. Yet Burghley's talking of a five thousand pound fine if he doesn't wed the girl."

"*Five thousand!*"

"Yes. Old Burghley's a hard man, and unforgiving. Wed or pay. Oh, Harry will have money enough, but yes, five thousand. And Burghley won't give him time to pay, it's to be a lump sum. Shakspere, look, you're probably the only person who can talk Harry into seeing sense. No, don't act that modest surprise with me, keep it for the stage. I neither know nor care whether you and Harry are more than friends, but I do know you *are* friends, and he listens to you. Tell him to stop spouting dreamy-eyed nonsense about love and marry Elizabeth before he ruins his entire future. Burghley and his crowd make bad enemies. The Queen makes a bad enemy."

"Is the Queen so interested in his marriage?"

"She dislikes him. Thinks him frivolous and volatile. She listens to Burghley. Believes in people making sensible marriages according to their rank. Of course she herself couldn't marry where she willed, and no doubt she thinks others should abide by the same rules of duty. You once told Harry you were forced into marriage, yet you've come to love your wife, you're happy. Remind him of that. He longs for children. That I know. And remind him that few of us can marry to suit ourselves. If you love him, get him to marry that girl before he comes of age. He won't listen to me."

"Although you love him?"

"Despite that. We were under Burghley's guardianship together and we're bound by great affection. Also I married the woman Burghley told me to. But Harry turns a deaf ear to me. See if you have more success."

Harry rejoined them then. He looked flushed and disgruntled and he would have burst into speech but that the woman singer came to his side and said, "I must go now. May I have my fee?" She spoke, William noted, as if she and the Earl of Southampton were equals, she could almost have been his sister reminding him of an obligation.

"Oh. Yes. Four marks, didn't we say?" He felt in his purse and handed over the coins. "Thank you. You gave us good entertainment."

"Do you do this often?" William asked her. "Is it your profession, perhaps?"

"I do it when I need to pay the rent. You are William Shakspere, are you not?"

"I am. How did you know?"

"I go often to the playhouse. I admire your plays."

"Thank you. I admired your singing of *Sylvia*. Where had you the tune you sang it to?"

"I composed it." She was attaching a cord to her lute as if to carry it over her shoulder. "I have a very small gift in that direction. You are greatly gifted." She looked up, straight into his eyes. "I had an ancestress of your name."

"What, Shakspere?"

"Well, she wasnae called William." He had been thinking how disconcerting it was to look into eyes so black there was no gradation of colour between iris and pupil. If eyes are the windows of the soul, these pitch-balls were the mirror of the observer. But now, as she laughed, he realised they were beautiful eyes, and that she was a beautiful woman.

"I'm sorry. Of course, Shakspere. Where was she from?"

"From Kent, I believe. It was a long time ago."

"Well, they say we Shaksperes are all of the one family. Perhaps we are kin, you and I, although I'm from Warwickshire.

You are a Scot?"

"Yes." The brief animation left her face. "If you liked my song, I would like to set more of your work to music. You are a fine poet. Only today I finished reading *The Rape of Lucrece*. But there are many other poems and songs in your plays. You are a clever man."

"He is," said Harry, and suddenly linked his arm through William's. "A surpassing poet. It would make a pretty evening of music, your tunes to his words."

"We could discuss it," she said indifferently. "You could come to my house. I live in Blackfriars. Ask anyone for the Scotswoman's house. I must go. Good evening, gentlemen."

William watched the salon doors close behind her. "Odd creature."

"Yes. Rather good looking, when one thinks about it."

"Harry, I must talk to you."

"Not you too! Oh yes, I saw Essex busily whispering to you." He went to pull his arm away, but William held it.

"Harry, have I ever failed to have your best interests at heart? So has Essex, I believe."

"I wonder. Very well, we'll talk. But not now, not here. I want to dance. Can you stay the night with me?"

"I can." Feeling the old sting in the flesh, he wanted to add *But I should not.* "I can. Anne's taken the children home to Stratford for the summer."

"Then stay. Please."

They shared a bed in the old way. Harry lay with his head on William's shoulder, their hands linked. They had done little more than this for nearly a year, and perhaps tonight would be no different. But the strongest vows are straw to the fire in the blood, William thought, and tonight he wanted to fuck Harry. But his lovely boy was edgy and defensive; perhaps because he was a boy no longer. He had discovered women, that William knew, although they didn't talk of it.

"Say what you have to." Harry kissed the hollow at the base of William's throat. "But first tell me what Robin Essex said to you tonight." William's actor's memory allowed him to repeat the conversation *verbatim*. Harry heard him out then said, rather amused, "Well, my dear Robin is no longer quite so deep in the Queen's favour as he was, and he knows I am taken with his cousin Elizabeth Vernon. She's one of the Queen's Maids of Honour, and Her Majesty takes a dim view of men trifling with her maids."

"So she does. Do you love this girl, Harry?"

"Oh, love. How does one tell? She's pretty."

"And have you made defeat of her maidenhead?"

"What an elegant way of asking if I've bedded her. No. But she'd be willing. She loves me, I think. She's got no money, of course."

"And marrying Oxford's daughter would bring you money and a connection with one of the oldest noble families in the land. A good match, Harry. A wise match. If Lord Essex is right and Burghley fines you five thousand pounds…"

"I'd rather pay his buggering fine than be forced into a marriage I don't want."

"And what is it you want?"

"Love. Companionship. Desire."

"Those things can come after marriage. I'm a case in point."

"But you were fond of Anne before you married her. Fond enough and kind enough not to run away. Do you love her truly, Will? Do you miss her when she is away?"

"I miss the little accustomed domestic pleasures. I miss my children. Yes, I miss Anne. But since you and I are always honest with each other: I like the peace of solitude. I can write, alone, as I never can in the midst of my family. I keep my old lodgings, so I have somewhere that is entirely for writing. But it's not the same. Marry Lady Elizabeth, Harry, or ruin your future."

"I will not. There now, you've said your piece, you've done your duty. Talk of something else. That dark lady who sang took your eye?"

"What of that? At first I thought her nothing to look at, but she's beautiful. Too dark, though."

"Splendid breasts. And ankles."

"Harry, was what you said to Essex true? That he heads the Queen's intelligence service?"

"Heads it? Perhaps not. Sir Francis Walsingham has that honour. But Essex has his finger in all those pies. If he loses the Queen's favour – and he will, if he goes on thinking he can twine her round his finger – well, I wonder what will happen then. Whatever he may say in public, he is for James of Scotland as the

Queen's successor, but of course he must dissemble. There's talk of him leading a military expedition, and if he does, I want to go too."

"And why not?" William said comfortably.

"Because if I don't marry Burghley's damned granddaughter, I'll not be allowed to do anything I want."

"Then there's your answer. Don't ruin your future."

"I won't marry Elizabeth de Vere. I'm sick of talking of it." He lifted his head and put a kiss on William's mouth. It was a tender kiss, without passion, but passion came, surprising them both. They were more demanding of each other than ever before, and William told himself, as he moved with Harry in the old dance, If I think of black eyes and two plump breasts and a Scotch voice, at least I am with Harry, whom I love so dearly.

25.

He couldn't keep that singing woman from creeping into his thoughts; even into his dreams, sometimes. All the more reason to have nothing more to do with her.

He lasted a week, then went to see her.

It was a mean little house in a bad street. He waited a long time after he knocked before he heard someone trudging down the stairs, and the door creaked open.

"Oh, it's you." She showed neither pleasure nor displeasure.

"It is. Have I called at a bad time?"

"No. Come in. You have to put your shoulder to the door, it sticks."

Half-lifting, half shoving it shut he said, "It needs planing or re-hanging." She nodded indifferently. Following her up the stairs he noted other things that needed attention; chipped and grubby plaster on the walls, loose boards in the stairs and a sagging banister, the ground-in dirt of the floor. Anne would have seen to all those things almost before they occurred. By contrast, this woman looked cleaner and tidier than the other night. She wore a blue linen dress, and the high neck of a dazzlingly white smock hid those spectacular breasts. Her hair was braided tightly back and coiled on top of her head.

The room she led him into was large, untidy and full of colour. She gestured him to a chair covered with a length of old and rather dirty brocade. "You'll take wine?"

"Thank you." While she poured the drink he looked around. The room puzzled him. One wall was covered with a truly fine tapestry, while the others had cheap painted hangings. Great bunches of fresh summer flowers were stuffed without artistry into cracked earthenware jugs, but the bowl holding white roses was of exquisite crystal. Some of the cushions were covered in gold-tasselled velvet or beautifully embroidered silk, others were of shabby woollen. A handsome carver stood at the head of the table, with two matching chairs on one side, but on the other was only a common bench, cushioned and covered with another length of brocade. The wine she gave him was of average quality and served in ordinary pewter cups, but she poured it from the finest wine-jug he had ever seen, silver-gilt, swan-necked, with a crystal stopper.

There was another, smaller table under the window, two shelves of books, a sideboard. The rest of the room was taken up by musical instruments; a virginals, two lutes, a gittern, a hautboy, two flutes.

"Do you play all those?"

"Only the virginals and the stringed instruments." Absently she reached down to what he'd thought was a bundle of cast-aside knitting. It was a dog, very ancient and seedy-looking. It had paid him no attention, but under her touch it flapped the end of its tail. "Well, the flute, a very little and very badly. I really have a very small gift for music."

"But you set my song to music, and that Palestrina you played…" Eyeing him over the rim of her cup she said something about a strict music master, anyone could do that much. "No. You played with real sensitivity and taste."

"Thank you."

He didn't quite like the mockery in her tone. "I know enough of music to know that. And I mean it. May I know your name, by the way?"

"Did you come here not knowing it? Sometimes I call myself Mara or Maria, but I was christened Marian. Well, have you brought me some of your work?"

He gave her the folio he had carried with him. Watching her slender, ringless fingers picking at the knot, he noted the way she sat, straight-backed and with her ankles together and to one side, and he realised something about her. "You're a lady, aren't you?"

Her eyes flashed up to his. "Whatever do you mean?"

"That you're gently bred. Of high birth. Perhaps even of noble birth."

She had turned rather pale, and her brows had drawn down over eyes that held a sudden spark of – anger? No. fear.

"Whatever makes you say such an odd thing? Do I seem to you to live like a lady?"

"No, but it's in the way you sit, and in the shape of your hands and the bones of your face. In the books on your shelves. And the quality of some of your things. In your voice, too, now that you've forgotten that Scotch accent."

She went on looking at him, frowning at him, her shield-shaped face taut. At last she said, on a caught breath, "You notice too much. I suppose you couldn't write as you do if you didn't. I've come down in the world, is that what you mean? That I'm on my way even further down? While you are on your way up in the world, my fine gentlemanly friend?"

Stung, he said, "I wasn't born a gentleman but I'm amending my position, if that's what you mean."

"Oh, so I gather, and amending it right fast. You have no lands or title or coat of arms, and your father is of ordinary stock, but your mother was an Arden, and I know about that family. You'll end your days rich, and a gentleman. And if you hadn't that quality of breeding, that gentleman's nature and your wit, your high-born friends wouldn't do more than tolerate you, for all your cleverness."

"You've been asking about me?" He found the idea flattering.

"A little."

"More than a little or you should hang for a witch. My father thought some years ago of applying for a coat of arms, but he lost money and put the thought away. Lately, he's been talking of it again."

"And what will your coat of arms be, Master William?"

"What is yours, Mistress Marian?" he countered. "Are you really Scotch at all?"

Slowly, sipping once more at her wine, she said, "Don't call me Marian. If you can keep a secret, I was born and raised in Scotland. I speak and read Scots and some Gaelic. But my family has lived there less than a hundred years. My ancestors were as English as you. And had a certain English battle gone another way..."

"What battle?"

"Never mind. May I look at what you've brought me or will you take your boarded folio and scuttle back to Lord Southampton?" The coarse gesture that accompanied these words made it plain she had asked about him to some purpose.

"I'll show you some of my work."

Again she stared at him then suddenly smiled. It was the sweet, engaging smile which the other night had made him realise she was beautiful. Then, ducking her head, she opened the folio and began to glance through its contents. "These are beautiful," she said at last. "Are they songs from your plays?"

"One or two are. The others may go into plays one day.

They're ideas that came to me at different times. A poem or two, also."

"I've heard of your sonnets. Your friends admire them. What's this? *When that I was but a little tiny child.* Hmm. Oh now, this is splendid. *Fear no more the heat of the sun, nor the furious winter's rages.* Yes…" She drifted over to her virginals and began to play little disconnected snatches of music, changing key, changing tempo, humming to herself. "I could make beautiful music for this. How beautifully you write." Idly he had followed her across the room. As she put down the lute they were very close together. For a moment their eyes met, and clung, then she leaned forward and kissed him on the mouth.

All his senses jumped. Her lips seemed to tingle against his. It seemed he tasted honey. His hands rose to embrace her. He dropped them, and moved away.

"I'm married."

"So am I, but you don't see me bringing my troubles to you."

Somewhere in the back of his mind was the thought, *I don't even like her.* But thought had nothing to do with it, it seemed.

On the following Sunday William went to church. This was usually something he did only often enough to set the children a good example and avoid the fine for non-attendance. Today he went eagerly, and as he followed the service he thought with guilty longing of the Papist rite of confession. What comfort must there be in telling your sins, then *Ego te absolvo* and you went away cleansed. Go and sin no more.

Sin no more. Aye, there's the rub. He could promise himself or a listening priest that he would never again visit that woman's house or be tempted into that bed, but promises are easy. After the first time, he had promised himself and God, or the gods, *never again,* only to return the next day, and the next, and to spend the nights reliving what they did in the rank sweat of that adulterous bed.

She had kissed him. So. In his mind's eye he saw himself paying her a sweet, teasing compliment and leaving her house on the instant. Taking horse to Stratford that same day, perhaps, back to Anne.

Anne.

Anne, his wife, his good wife, his loving companion. Sweet

Anne with her narrow, seemly body and her sleek dark hair. Anne with the wit and spirit concealed under her wifely manner. Anne who satisfied him in bed and held him lovingly. Anne, who didn't deserve this.

Not that she would ever know. She must not know. Harry was one thing, but she had said, "Take another woman and I will kill you." She had meant that her own jealousy would kill some of the love between them. She must never suspect this frantic, besotted need that turned him into a rutting dog with a bitch on heat. Conscienceless, careless, throwing everything to the winds for that supple little open-arse, going back time and again for the feral pleasures of her body.

The things they'd done! Things he'd never before known he wanted. *Had* not wanted. Slaps and blows and biting, restraint and constraint, no gentleness once she'd shown him what she wanted, raping each other, taking satisfaction in every possible way. Spending and spending again till he swore he could no more, and had let himself be teased into more while she was still greased with his seed. Lapping at every crevice of her body, letting her lap at him. Probing and invading, hurting each other with the pain that brings exquisite pleasure.

He'd tried to hold her after the first coupling, he had drawn her head onto his breast and held her hand and stroked her hair, calling her the sweet things of habit. And she'd drawn away, had mocked at him, had said, "This isn't love."

No, not love. Lust in action. Self-despising lust. Spending and spending, scraping his body raw to hear her scream. Vowing *never again* as he staggered away from her house, ruined. And returning the next day, and the next.

More than lust. Less than love. Not even liking. And yet, on the second day, she had taken her lute and played a perfect, lyrical setting for one of his poems, a musical beauty to call the heart out of your body. She had sung to him, and for the time he had loved her, liked her. But soon the husky voice which phrased his song so exquisitely had been demanding *More* and *Harder* and *Do it like that*, and goading him with tales of other men, and the fingers which were so nimble on the lute strings were drawing blood from his back. Physical satisfaction, oh yes, like nothing he had known before. Of sweetness, affection, mutuality – nothing.

"O God," he said aloud in the silent church, groaning the

words, and won a look of approval from his neighbour in the pew.

Was there anyone he could tell about this? Anyone he could ask for help? Kit Marlowe would have understood, William could have told him, but he was dead and turned to clay. A year dead. His fellow actors? But they were mostly married men, and if they strayed while they were on tour, well, that was nothing. This they would neither understand nor condone. Besides, most of them knew Anne, and would take her part. And in fact, there further down the church sat James Burbage with his wife and his sons, Cuthbert and Richard.

Harry? Perhaps. They never spoke of other lovers. He was a boy who longed for love, and he could be fastidious. But he was a friend, he might listen. Though what would he say? "Go home to your wife," (being practical). "Avoid the occasion of sin," (his Catholic boyhood coming out). "Suffer," (his odd streak of Puritanism speaking out). "Introduce me to this woman," (Harry being Harry).

Don't sit here putting words in Harry's mouth, William told himself. Follow your own advice. Go home. To Stratford, to Anne. Three months in the country and you'll come back cured. And if this woman Mara-Maria, if you could believe even that much of what she said, is still in London, you'll pass her by in the street without regret.

"I preach today," droned the vicar, "on the woman taken in adultery."

William lifted his head and stared at him incredulously.

He was at her house again that night.

And the next, and the one after.

At the company meeting on Wednesday everyone commented that he looked tired, and the boy players snickered at the love-bite on his neck that his ruff couldn't hide. James Burbage was distinctly cool to him.

He stayed away from Mara-Maria-Marian that night and for the next two days. He wrote his play, scene after scene pouring from his pen as the magical world grew around him. It was good, he knew that. But on the Saturday he was stalled; his characters turned stale and trite, their speech wooden. The magic had gone.

He wrote doggedly on, but what he wrote was soon scored out. A snatch of dialogue sprang to his mind, but it was from another play entirely. Still, he noted it down. Began a poem, scored that out. Re-wrote it. Ate a meal. Drank a lot of ale. Read. Tried again to write, and knew his heart wasn't in it.

At five o'clock he gave up, threw his papers together into the box, locked it, and before he could think better of it, went around to Mara's house.

The street door was unlocked. He went straight upstairs and knocked briskly. She came to the door yawning, wrapped in a sheet, her hair loose. "You again. I thought you'd sworn off me."

"So did I."

"Well, come in. I was asleep. An Italian habit, to sleep the afternoon away." She drifted back to her bedroom and lay down on the tumbled bed. The window curtains were drawn against whatever late sun could penetrate this narrow street. The room smelt of wine and her heavy slumberous scent. It was one of her days for looking beautiful, her skin like clotted cream, raspberries, honey, the angle of her cheekbones and jaw delicately defined. As she lay back on the pillows, she flung off the sheet that had covered her, and all her body was displayed to him. Rounded, narrow-waisted, the lush breasts half-veiled in her hair. Beautiful. Desirable. His for the taking.

He kissed her and her tongue was quick in his mouth, quick as her hands to undress him. He put his lips to her nipples, making her groan and twine her hands in his hair to hold him there for her pleasure. His fingers strayed over her waist and hips, under her bottom, up and around. His mouth followed his hands.

He drew away, his flesh crawling. "Asleep? In bed, perhaps. You've been with another man. You stink of it, you bitch."

"I thought you weren't coming back."

"And your bed's hardly cool from him, whoever he was. You haven't even washed him off you. Yet you'd take me too?" His fingers shook so that he could hardly fasten the buttons she'd undone.

"Some men like it that way."

"Do they? I don't. It disgusts me."

"And excites you." Fast as a rabbit she lunged forward onto her knees to touch the proof of what she said.

"No. No."

171

"Yes. Yes."

"No." But her hands closed over his, undoing all the buttons again, and he was helpless to resist, didn't know if he wanted to resist, lay back with a moan and let her do her will with hands and mouth, and she greased him with another man's cum, and he let her do it, and he stared up at her as she rode him, her tongue-tip caught in her teeth, her eyes hidden by the veined lids and furry lashes, her heavy pendent breasts pushing against his chest and his nails scoring her plump backside as she worked her pleasure out on him. His pleasure too, oh yes, like never before, and be damned to spirit and love and heart and mind.

Afterwards she curled up in the sheet again, cuddling the pillow under her head like a sleepy child. Dressing, he watched her. She might have been alone for all the notice she took of him.

"I'm going now."

She nodded.

"I leave on tour. I told you. Months."

"Then give me a kiss goodbye." She lifted her head, her hair streaming back. With distaste he put a kiss on her puckered lips. Even that touch affronted him now. "I shall miss you, William. Enjoy your tour."

"Thank you. Good bye."

"Mmm, good bye." She was turning back to snuggle into the pillow as she spoke, and he thought she was asleep before he had left the room.

At home he shouted to the maid for hot water, and standing up before the basin he washed himself all over; he wanted a bath but it would take too long. Then he dressed in clean clothes, gave those he'd been wearing to the maid to give away, packed his belongings. Every clean, ironed shirt, every darned stocking, every polished boot was a reproach, because Anne had left all these things ready for him, laying them away in the clothes chests with herbs to keep the bugs at bay. He packed the books he couldn't be without, paper, pens, his travelling ink-stand. The presents for Anne and the children. His cash. Ran downstairs, gave the maid money and instructions. Paid a neighbour's boy a penny to go to the livery stable to hire a horse. Threw on his cloak and hat and sword. Scribbled a note to James Burbage saying he would meet the company at their first stop outside London on Monday, sent the neighbour's boy, with another penny, to deliver it.

An hour after he had left his mistress he was riding out of London.

26.

By September the company was in Oxford and almost at the end of their summer's touring. It had been a good tour, profitable and successful. William was back among his fellows, his substitute family, and he was William again, the rutting animal had been left behind in London. Had it all been a dream? He was writing dreams into his play. Perhaps the play had come first, bringing the dreams. A man bewitched by a love-potion, a woman similarly beguiled and, waking, looking with horror at the man she thought she had loved. Yes, a dream. Or nightmare. He was William the player, William the theatre-owner, William the playwright, William the married man.

In Oxford they took an evening in the inn to plan the next leg of the tour. Stratford, why not, a sizeable town and hospitable to players. Then on to –

"Stratford-upon-Avon?" said a man at the next table. "You'll get no good takings there. Man, didn't you know? There's been a fire in Stratford. My auntie comes from there and she says half the town's been destroyed. Hundreds dead, she told me."

William rode flat-out, all through the dying of the day. Richard Burbage rode with him, because the players were his family and would not let him go alone.

The sun had set before they reached Stratford, but enough light was left to show the devastation. William cried out when he saw that half of Henley Street had gone. Here and there a chimney stack still stood, a roof tree or part of a wall. Some of the owners had managed to save something from the ashy rubble; a thick oak door, scorched but whole, a pile of bricks, some furniture. William saw the corpse of a dog, charred and shrivelled, in what had been a front garden. His friends the Sadlers' house had gone.

They rode on, at no more than walking pace now, afraid of what they might find. And the fire had gone almost to the Shaksperes' house – only three houses away what had been an inside wall showed where the flames had licked it. A girder, broken bricks, stood out as if a malign giant had reached out and torn half the house away.

His own house was dark and silent. No sign of life.

"Steady on, lad," said Burbage, clutching William as he tumbled down from his horse. "They're all a-bed, that's all. It's past ten, and this isn't London, Will"

"Yes. A-bed." William tried the front door. Locked. He swung dementedly on the knocker. Shouted. After what seemed an age a window opened and a night-capped head peered out.

"Who's that making all that noise?"

"Gilbert, it's me, Will. I heard of the fire. Is everyone safe?"

"*Will?* Is it really you? We didn't expect you."

"I know. Gilbert, the fire. *Are my children safe?* Is Anne safe?"

"Oh yes, quite safe. Wait and I'll let you in." His head withdrew and they saw a flare of light as he lit a candle. Gilbert fumbled the door open and lit the way into the parlour.

"Where's Anne sleeping?" William demanded. "And the children? Gil, are you sure they're safe?"

Gangling and harmless, Gilbert turned around from lighting the candles and said, "Of course they're safe. God save us, man, d'you think that if they'd been hurt we'd not've scoured all England for you? A playing troupe's not that hard to find. God save the mark! They're asleep."

The twins were cuddled up together like puppies, the fair hair and the dark mingling on the pillow. They didn't stir as William kissed them. Their breath smelt pure and milky. "I love you," William whispered. "I love you more than you will ever know." He tucked the blankets more tightly around them, disturbing the tabby cat asleep at the foot of the bed.

Susanna slept sprawled on her back, her arms flung up beside her head. They'd years ago given up trying to tuck her in or change her position. She had grown again, just in these few weeks – eleven was an age for shooting-up. She sighed in her sleep and tossed her head as if aware of William's gaze. Very gently he touched her cheek then kissed her brow. She wrinkled her nose as if about to sneeze then murmured something, but she was fast asleep.

So was Anne. The moonlight showed her lying on her side, one hand tucked between her knees. The other, thickly bandaged, lay on the pillow. Her forehead showed the red mark of a burn. Her hair was braided back in its usual night plait and shorter than usual. A herbal, winey smell hung about her. William recognised the potion his mother used when anyone was ill.

He undressed and slid silently into the bed. He turned on his side towards Anne and she opened her eyes, sat bolt upright, and screamed.

"Shh, darling, it's me." He pulled her down, cradling her against his shoulder. "It's me, it's Will. I've come home."

"You *frightened* me!"

"I didn't mean to," he said humbly. "I didn't want to wake you."

Someone rapped sharply on the door, his mother called a worried question. "It's all right," Anne said. "I didn't know Will was here, he startled me. Goodnight. Will, what *are* you doing here?"

"Heard about the fire. Came. Darling, your hand. Are you much hurt?"

"It's nothing. I've done worse on the cooking pots." Abruptly, she fell asleep.

William held her for a long time before he too could sleep. It wasn't the reunion he had pictured, not that he was sure what he had imagined. Passionate words of relief and love, whispered into Anne's ear? That would only make her suspicious. More burblings of punishment? Because that was what he had thought when he heard: he had broken his marriage vows in the worst possible way, so he had to be punished by losing his wife and children. Foolish, mawkish stuff he'd never dare put in a play, but so horribly real for those few hours it took to come here. On the verge of sleep he realised that the desperate journey was his punishment. Not an innocent woman and children horribly dead, but his fear and its offspring, the knowledge of how much he needed and loved them.

27

He could stay only that night and a day. He came back, however, when the end of summer meant the end of the players' touring season and Anne was eager to return to London.

"Perhaps by next summer we'll have our own house here," she said wistfully as she packed their last belongings.

"I hope so." It had been disconcerting to realise he was now the richest person in the family, so much had his father's income and investments dwindled. Flattering, of course, to be looked up to and relied upon, but he feared his family thought money grew on trees in London. It seemed that all he heard was, Will, we need money to repair the shop; your mother should have another maid; what about Joan's dowry; what about the boys' future?

He was thirty and head of the family in all but name. Of a family of three children of his own, of four siblings, a few ne'er-do-well cousins and uncles and a father who retreated more and more into a private world of Catholic dogma. Of Catholic practice? William could only hope, and hint, not. An edifice of responsibility built on his power to go on acting six days a week and writing plays that kept the money rolling in. If he lost his gift, or his mind, or his power to go on working, it would be the poorhouse for the lot of them.

And now, it seemed, another responsibility. His youngest brother Edmund wanted to be an actor.

"Why?" William asked when the boy came stammering and blushing to ask him.

"B-because it's all I've ever wanted. Ever since I saw that first play of yours. I see them all, Will, every time the players come to Stratford or anywhere nearby. I know all your plays by heart. It's all I've ever wanted and I'm not bookish enough for university even if Father could afford it."

"*Can* you act?" William asked.

"I'm sure I could."

"Show me."

"What, here and now?" Edmund looked pathetically at Anne. She hardened her heart and nodded. After Joan, Edmund was her favourite of William's family. He was the children's favourite uncle, being not three years older than Susanna and five more than the twins. He was growing very like William to look at, and she remembered another russet-haired boy whose hazel eyes had shone with longing as he confided his dream. But Edmund wasn't yet fifteen and it would mean their housing him in London and, doubtless, paying his way. Had he any idea what he was in for?

But when he looked so helplessly at her she said, "Yes, here and now. You said you know all Will's plays, so give us whatever speech you think best."

Twisting his bony hands before him Edmund said, "I-I can do some from *Two Gentlemen*."

"Then favour us with that," said William, and lay back on the bed with his hands behind his head. So pale all the faint freckles stood out like birthmarks, Edmund stumbled through a speech. William nodded judicially. "But you're fourteen and you'd play girls' parts. Give us a girl's speech."

"I know Lady Anne from *Richard the Third*."

"Go ahead." With a little more confidence, Edmund obeyed. He wasn't very good, but nor was he irretrievably bad.

"Yes," said William, "but remember your husband and father have just been killed. Try to seem at least a little upset. Do it again." Edmund did it again. "Not so bad. But I doubt I can simply get you into the Lord Chamberlain's Men for the asking."

"Oh no, I didn't expect that." But he clearly had. "I could start by running messages and helping and, perhaps, playing pages and soldiers, that sort of thing?"

"We've got a dogsbody boy. Called Nol. Tread warily with him, by the way. He's your age in years but centuries old in worldly vice. Do our parents know of this ambition of yours?"

"Oh yes, and they said it's up to you."

William and Anne exchanged a glance. Of course. "Well, why don't we give you a trial period, say until next summer? That's if Burbage and the others agree. You won't be paid, of course. Later, if it works, you can be apprenticed. Here." He tossed over a bundle of papers he'd been about to pack. "My new play. Lose it and you die. Learn Juliet's part by tomorrow. You won't play it for ages, if ever, but you have to learn to get a part by heart in a day or two. Tomorrow I'll hear you in it. I'll play the other parts and give you your prompts, see how you go."

"Oh thank you, Will!" Edmund rushed at his brother, caught him in a violent hug, blushed again, and raced out of the room flapping the pages. Then he raced straight back in again. "You'll tell Mother and Father? And I'll come with you when you leave tomorrow?"

"Yes. So go and pack. And learn that part." Off he flapped, and Anne and William looked at each other. "He can't go into lodgings, not a boy of fourteen who doesn't know London."

"No," Anne sighed. She liked having her little family to herself. "He must have a truckle bed in the twins' room. And it's a good time to part them and make Judith sleep with Susanna. I suppose he'll need clothes, and he eats like a horse."

"Doubtless. If you're against it, Anne..."

"Oh, no. He's a dear boy. As long as he helps me in the house a little. Will he make an actor?"

"I've seen worse, first time of asking. We've plenty of boy players already, experienced ones. But he deserves his chance if he wants it as badly as he says. But, oh, if I'd had my chance at his age..."

"You'd never have met me," Anne said curiously.

"I wouldn't. And that would have grieved me." He took her hand, turned it over and kissed the palm.

"No, for you'd never have known it." Looking down at his bent head Anne said, "You know, Will, you seem different lately. I thought so when you came home after the fire. And, again, now."

"How, different?" With a light little laugh he dropped her hand and went to put clothes into his travelling bags.

"I'm not sure. Older? Gentler? More... I can't explain it."

"Probably it's just the weight of responsibility of owning theatres and sponsoring brothers. And it's been a tiring summer."

"Perhaps that's all it is." Watching him, Anne noted, and almost said aloud, that his hair was starting to recede at the front. She knew he knew about that. She'd caught him at the looking-glass, twisting and turning and fiddling with his hair like a girl going to her first party. It wasn't the sort of thing men liked mention of. She held her tongue.

Part Five

1595

28.

William and Harry Southampton were playing chess. Expecting the *coup de grace* any moment, for he was not a good player, William sat back and watched Harry pondering his move. "You won't be going to the wedding, I daresay?"

Harry took his time with both move and reply. "Checkmate. Ah, but I will be going." The amusement in his eyes was at odds with his pious expression as he said, "How could you doubt that both bride and groom have my very best wishes for their happiness together?" They both laughed. It was a good joke, if an ironic one. Lord Burghley had at last accepted that Harry's 'No' meant 'No' and had brokered a marriage between his granddaughter, Lady Elizabeth de Vere, and the Earl of Derby. The latter was the brother of Ferdinando, who had been patron of William's old playing company. Ferdinando had died the previous year, to William's grief. He didn't much care for the new Earl, but a commission was a commission and he thought Ferdinando's shade would be pleased at his players performing for his brother's wedding.

"I never bore Lady Liz any ill-will," Harry went on, "even if it did cost me five thousand pounds not to marry her."

"That was unfair," William said hotly. "No one ever thought Burghley would insist on that fine. And as for demanding it all in a lump, not giving you time to pay, that was vindictive."

"He can be vindictive. A good man in so many ways, but mean, and unforgiving. Don't repeat this, Will, but I went to the Queen about it, asked her to intercede and get Burghley at least to let me pay the fine in yearly instalments. No luck. I am well out of favour there." Suddenly he swept William's queen from the board and held the piece in his clenched fist. "The most powerful piece on the board. So much for the queen." He dropped the piece to the side of the table.

"Oh Harry, my dear," said William, "have a care what you do, and say."

"The Queen can't live forever."

"Harry, Harry, Harry. With all your gifts, you can be such a fool. Stay out of plots. Be careful."

"I shall." Harry touched one finger to the back of William's hand. "I love your care for me, but don't worry about me."

"Can't help it. Love is like that."

"Yes." For a moment it seemed he would say something more of that, but then he leaned back in his chair and said with apparently intense interest, "Tell me of this play your company is to do for the Derby wedding. A comedy?"

"Yes, one I've had in my mind for some time and suitable for a wedding."

"About?"

"A royal wedding. Theseus of Athens and Hippolyta, as in Chaucer's *Knight's Tale*. Other lovers. A girl who loves a man who doesn't love her. People who refuse to marry where their guardians insist they do." Harry raised an eyebrow, his mouth stretching into a sweet, wry smile. "A happy ending, of course, after complications. It's Midsummer's Night. I call it *A Midsummer Night's Dream*, and the fairies are about. The King and Queen of the fairies, Oberon and Titania, are at odds. Robin Goodfellow, the puck, has a love-juice which, squeezed on the eyes of a sleeper, will make him or her fall in love with the first person he or she sees upon waking."

"And things go wrong?"

"And things go wrong. I've written some comic rustics, artisans, who put on a play for the royal wedding. They get caught up in the fairies' and lovers' action."

"It sounds enchanting." They both grinned at the pun.

"It's good. And my brother Edmund is to play one of the fairies."

"Your brother? Oh, yes, you told me of him. Is he making a success?"

"Dick Burbage isn't having any sleepless nights. No, the boy's competent enough. And keen."

"A poet, like his brother?"

"No. Odd, isn't it. Five of us, and I'm the only one to write. What's the time? So late? Harry, I must go. We're rehearsing early tomorrow, for the wedding play." He pushed his chair back and stood up. "Sorry not to have given you a better game."

"Don't be. I like winning."

"And with a more worthy opponent you should play more carefully." William slid his hand round Harry's head, kissed him. "We'll meet again soon?"

"As ever. And we will meet at the wedding festivities."

"*See* each other. You're an honoured guest and I'm merely an entertainer. *Adieu.*"

The wedding was celebrated with all due pomp of masques, dancing, feasting. And, of course, William's play. It was a wild success. Perfect for the occasion, everyone said, charming, funny, touching. The echoes of applause ringing in his ears, William accepted his author's due of praise and Lord Derby's gift of an extra twenty pounds above the agreed fee. And, out of kindness for the players who had once worn his brother's livery, Lord Derby begged them stay and take drinks, mingle for a few moments with the guests. "Keep your costumes on," he said, twinkling, "so that as at that other wedding, we may have the Fairy King and Queen and their court among us – not to mention Bottom; a splendid part, Will. Come, join us at our feast."

Free food and drink of wedding guest quality wasn't to be sneezed at. Amused and hungry, the players obediently mingled.

And, mingling, William came face to face with her.

Mara-Marian. His dark and damnéd beauty.

Clad in shell pink and gold lace, colours that became her, with her hair tidily curled, rings on her fingers and gold at her ears and throat, her bosom no more displayed than was proper. Dignified as any great lady there. Only the heady, heavy scent was the same.

"You," he said. "You, *here?*"

She gave him a heavy-lidded, bland look then her eyes slid sideways to a man standing nearby, watching her. "It's Master Shakspere, is it not? I think we met some time since. Two years, was it, or three? Are you acquainted with my husband, Master Leigh?"

The stage lost a great player in her. "I think not," said William, bowing, as she introduced him to the watching man.

"Master Shakspere? Ah yes, you wrote that excellent play we have just seen. A fine work."

"Thank you, sir."

"And how do you come to be acquainted with my wife?" Yes, there was jealousy there, and suspicion. Perhaps he knew what sort of woman he had married. He was at least twenty years her senior.

"We met at one of Lord Southampton's *musicales*."

"Ah."

Lord Derby came to speak to William then, and for a time he lost sight of the woman and her hornéd husband.

Later, however, she found him alone in a quiet corner of the garden. "William." She leaned in to him, her breasts pressing against his arm.

"My lady."

"Oh, none of that nonsense, not between us."

"There is nothing between us, Madam. As in my play, the enchantment has worn off."

The moonlight showed the flicker in her black eyes as she hit back swiftly. "What did Titania say? 'Such dreams as I have had? I dreamt I was enamour'd of an ass'?"

"Ass I may be, but you were never enamour'd."

"Say you so? I told you I should miss you, and I did."

Some hopeless, half-wit, gullible fool said wistfully, "Did you truly?" William actually looked around to see who had spoken before he realised it was himself.

"Yes I did. Well, the playhouses opened before Christmas, so you've been back in London some time, I suppose."

"Yes, since after the summer tour."

"And you managed not to come to me."

"Yes. So that's your husband. Poor man. Though I daresay he's a rich man."

"Why, William, what a pretty compliment. A rich man for having me?" Mockingly girlish, she flirted her fan. Against his will, he laughed. She wasn't what you would call a witty woman, but there was a core of self-mocking honesty under all her guises. "Well, we women must make our way as best we can. I thought I'd never see you again." She moved in front of him and slid her arms around his waist. He started to say, "No," but she put her lips on his.

And it was all there again, and his body remembered what his mind was determined to forget. All his good resolutions fled. There was a low wall beside them, and he lifted her onto it and flung her skirts up. She laced her legs around him, panting as he touched her. He was desperately, ragingly eager for her, but he was in costume as Philostrate, and the unfamiliar clothes cost him a moment's fumbling. Then he thrust into her, and her tongue was halfway down his throat, and she used his mouth to stifle her cry at the end.

She leaned her head on his shoulder, almost as a child does. "Ah, William, my Will. I've missed you."

"And I had vowed never to do that again."

"Would you order love?"

"It is not love."

"Well, you know best." She disengaged herself, hopped off the wall and shook out her skirts. With trembling hands he fastened up his clothes. "If you want to come to me again, I no longer have that house, I live now with my husband. Is there somewhere?"

"I keep my old lodgings, I go there to write. Two rooms."

"One would be enough for this kind of love. Tell me the direction."

In bitter self-hatred he did so.

"Then perhaps we will meet again."

She began to stroll back up the garden towards the house. William fell into step beside her. And, strolling thus, two mere acquaintants, they ran into Harry Southampton. He was slightly drunk.

"Well-met by moonlight, my Will. Will, Will, Will, my sweet William, my pet poet, my tame songbird, what a play you gave us tonight." He had a wine jug in his hand, and he waved it in punctuation of his words. "What – a – play! What wit, what charm, what gaiety. What a triumph of love. I liked the lion. Thyramus and Pisbe. *Pyramus.* Good old Ovid. And who are you, Madam? You look familiar."

"Mistress Leigh," said William.

"Your humble servant. But do I not know you?"

"We have met, my lord. I sang for you once."

"Oh yes, the lady with the eyebrows. I remember. Sang Will's song. You're here to make music for the wedding feasting?"

"No, my lord."

"A pity. You could have sung about the potted snakes; from the play, you know. Sssssspotted."

"Yes, my lord. Charming. May I beg your lordship to excuse me? My husband will be seeking me."

"Of course." Harry bowed, nearly falling over. William righted him. "That's a damned lovely woman, Will."

"Oh, do you think so?"

"'Course I do. Not being blind. Damned lovely. Taking." He peered owlishly at his friend. "Aha. *You* are taken with her!" Then he made one of those leaps of intuition William had thought the preserve of women. "*And* you've taken her. Last year... she was the one. When you had no time for me. Always busy, always dreaming."

"I always have time for you, Harry."

"Not last year. Different. And you are in love with her."

"No, Harry. Do guard your tongue!"

"Sick of guarding my tongue. People here, half the Court, old Burghley, Derby caught up with the Papists, Essex out of favour with the Queen, the queen's little maid of honour, Bess Vernon, making eyes at me, not that I mind that, she's very fetching, Raleigh always underfoot, Anthony Bacon and his little arse-licking brother, Francis, and I must guard my tongue. Always guard my tongue. And my back, from the daggers of my enemies. No friends. No real friends. Except you, Will."

William smothered a sigh. "I am your friend, forever. Come, Harry, I have to give my costume back to the 'tire-master, then let us have a drink together."

Harry had a poor head for drink. Another glass or two and he'd be asleep. As for William, he longed for nothing more than to be in bed, alone. The other players were staying on, to grace the wedding festivities with another play tomorrow. But out of friendship and love, he would have to keep Harry apart from anyone who could hear his ramblings and pass them on. He set a brisk pace back to the players' quarters, Harry trotting docilely after him, and handed in his costume, noting as he did so that it reeked of his mistress's perfume. The 'tire-master, in charge of the players' wardrobe, looked at him oddly, and winked. Then he sat out in the garden with Harry, drinking, until Harry's eyes drooped and William could hand him over to his valet. When at last he tumbled into bed beside his brother, he thought he would toss and turn through a sleepless night of guilt, but despite Edmund's snoring he fell asleep at once.

29.

In the days before they could afford to send their laundry out, Anne might have noticed sooner. As it was, when all she had to do was to sort and bundle the clothes sent for washing, it took her some weeks to recognise that William's shirts had not acquired some of their marks in the theatre. The players taking women's roles used lip-rouge and face powder, they wore long wigs. But usually the wigs were blond, not black. And not the most ardent actor could week after week press his lips to the same place on William's shirts. And that faint scent, which now she knew she had smelt before? But of course he met many people out of her ken. He went often to Harry's house and no doubt there were women guests. Suspicions were ignoble and she put them away with the clothes to be washed.

But the following week there was lip-rouge on the hem of a shirt, and long black hairs, too dark to be her own, caught in the lacings. The week after that, his under-linen was torn. And that scent seemed to cling to every garment. Anne stored clean clothes with rosemary, lavender and pepper to keep the fleas and lice at bay. This scent was of chypre and roses and ambergris.

After that she began to watch her husband. He came and went at the usual times. Or if he did not, always there was a reason, freely discussed. A company meeting, rehearsals, business with Lord Hunsdon their patron. Always a good reason. But he was different. Different in the way he'd been at Stratford last year after the fire. Gentle, loving, entirely himself. Yet different. Alert. Given to odd silences.

Sometimes she would catch him looking at her with sadness or even pity, but if she asked, he would say he was thinking of a new play and read her a scene as proof. In bed he turned to her less often, he would complain of being tired and fall asleep or think he heard Edmund or one of the children still awake. He brought her gifts more often, coming home with earrings, a box of sweetmeats or the fruit he knew she loved, a book, a pair of shoe buckles. Not that he'd ever been ungenerous, and certainly they now had the money for these fairings, but these presents came so often, for no reason. Presents for the children too, she noted. Hair ribbons or dolls for the girls, books and toys for

Hamnet. He acted differently with the children too, more indulgent and at the same time more demanding, less tolerant of noise or squabbles, then overcome with remorse when he snapped at them.

Anne watched him. He watched her. Often she had the feeling he was on the verge of some confession, but always held back.

And then he suggested they move house. A man called Francis Langley was building a new playhouse, to be called the Swan, on the other side of the river, near the Rose in Bankside. Why, said William, should they not move house to Southwark? So much easier, to be near the new theatre (the word was coming to be used, now, after The Theatre). The company would be based there. Surely it made sense to move.

"But Southwark is all brothels and bath-houses," Anne objected.

"Not all. There's —"

"What's a brothel?" Hamnet piped up. They had forgotten he was in the room, so silently had he been working at his school books.

"Nothing for you to know of. A bad place."

"It's a house where the whores and punks do business," Susanna told her brother with chilling authority.

"Susanna!" shouted both her parents. William added, "Where do you learn such words? You shouldn't know of such things."

"But everyone does. I'm not a little girl any more, I'm twelve."

"All the more reason," he shouted, "not to talk of such things!"

Susanna burst into tears and ran out of the room. Listening to her thudding furiously up the stairs, William and Anne exchanged a long, rueful glance.

"Twelve, aye. It's time I talked to her. She'll be a woman soon. We shouldn't have been angry with her. Children hear things, they pick up words and the knowledge to go with them."

"Knowing but innocent. The worst combination. *Twelve*. Where have the years gone, Anne?"

"I often wonder. Where have many things gone?" Their eyes met again, for a long, taut moment. William was the first to look away.

"Are you angry with me?" Hamnet asked tremulously.

"Not at all. Get back to your work, dear." With a worried glance he did so. "Well, *revenons à nos moutons*. What do you think of a move across the river?"

"I don't want to. I like this house, Will, we're settled here. And surely it will be a long time before this new playhouse is built. I dined with Mrs Burbage yesterday and she said nothing of the company moving to a new theatre."

"It will come. But perhaps you're right. It was just a thought. Very well."

Perhaps it was the unacknowledged workings of the back of her mind that took Anne to William's old lodgings. Perhaps it was an odd glance or two from the other players, conversations cut off abruptly when they knew she was near. Whatever the reason, she set out one day, six weeks after William had talked of moving across the river, to do her regular shopping, and had found her steps taking her in the other direction.

She hadn't been here for nearly a year. There was no reason to visit. William used the rooms only when he was working at white-heat and could tolerate no interruptions. But today she went, walking briskly and without a second thought up the stairs and into the familiar quarters.

The outer room was very untidy, William at his worst. Dust coated the few books on the shelves. His writing table and the floor around it were awash with papers, blank, written over, scored through, flung down in crumpled balls. Seven broken pens lay surrounded by ink splatters. A stale piece of cheese and the heel of a loaf sulked on a flyblown platter. Wine glasses showed a sticky residue. No one had been here, you would say, for days; weeks, perhaps. Certainly not the house-proud landlady.

Feeling foolish, Anne almost turned to leave. But there was the inner room, the bedchamber.

The blankets and coverlet were shoved to the foot of the bed. Stained, rumpled sheets trailed to the floor. Two pillows atop one another lay halfway down the bed. The other showed fine russet hairs and some long, coarse, curly black ones Two wine-glasses – *two* – stood together on the bedside chest. And the air smelt of that heavy, musky perfume.

Quite blankly Anne walked back to the outer room. She felt very cold, but to her surprise she wasn't shaking, she felt no desire to cry, not even any anger. Just cold, a chill that frosted her soul.

Then she went home, took a hairpin and picked the lock of the box where William kept his private papers.

She found the poems.

30.

"Mistress Shakspere, you asked to see me?" Harry Southampton came into the room with something of a rush. Anne rose and curtsied and, as usual, he brushed the courtesy aside. It had been some time since Anne had seen him, and he had grown up remarkably. He was twenty-one now and the girlish delicacy of his looks was hardening into something very attractively masculine. It was said he was in love with Elizabeth Vernon, but perhaps that was only gossip.

"Yes, my lord." With a glance toward the serving man, she lowered her voice to say, "This is going to be a very improper conversation."

"Oh? Then perhaps we should take a glass of wine." He was doing his best to seem *dégagé*, but his fair skin showed the nervous colour of embarrassment. No doubt he thought she had come to accuse him of seducing her husband.

"Thank you, yes." As soon as the wine was served, Harry dismissed the servant. Anne took a fortifying swig of her drink. "Do you know who Will's mistress is?"

Harry was sitting in the light. Anne saw his face clench as if in pain, and also with some surprise. "Why do you ask me?"

"Oh, come, boy," she snapped, "did you think I didn't know about you and William?"

"Ah. He told you?"

"I saw it in him, right from the start. He told me no details, but he never denied he loved you." His mouth opened and shut like an unperfect actor forgetting his lines. This time when he blushed it was no defensive colouring but a full, fiery reddening from collar to hairline. Anne's son blushed like that when caught out. "You're very young still, aren't you, Harry. And do *not* ask if I minded or say you're sorry."

"I was not going to." He stared at her, almost squinting in his intensity. "You are an extraordinary woman, Anne."

"No, only an ordinary woman whose husband is mad for another woman. You were never the rival this woman is. So tell me, do you know about it? Who she is?"

"I knew there was someone. He has told me nothing. But some things become obvious."

"Ah."

"Yes. It hurts me. We share that, Anne." Abruptly he shoved back his chair and stood to pace about the room. His slender, long-fingered hands twisted together. "Yes, an improper conversation indeed." He stopped pacing and leaned on the back of his chair, facing her. Impatiently he pushed back the long hair that fell forward over his shoulders. "I love your husband. And he has fallen… no, not fallen in love. Fallen. Into lust, infatuation. Against his will, I think. He's unhappy."

"I think so too. But so am I."

"Yes. Poor Anne." Harry sat down again, and took her hands. "He loves you very dearly. I have always known that. Loved you more than he knows, I truly believe."

"Maybe, maybe. That's no comfort. I bore his children, I believed in him when he was a dream-starred boy, I helped him. We've been married thirteen years and more. We are friends and companions. But he loves this woman. Unhappily, perhaps, but it is still love. Of a kind. Harry, he's written poems to her, about her."

"Has he." Harry's voice shook. "Love poems?"

"Poems *about* love. Poems of lust, love, hatred, guilt. Fine poems, but of such misery and shame. I saw his copies of all the poems he wrote you, and I can tell you he loves you far more than he does this woman."

The silence went on for some time before Harry said dully, "Does he write you poems too, Anne?"

"I'm only his wife, so no. Or only once, when we first met. To prove he could write."

"Oh, Anne. Well, to answer your question, the woman calls herself Mistress Leigh. A musician. An educated, travelled woman, a whore in all but name. She's a Scot and I suspect her of spying for King James, or perhaps on the people who are for King James as our next monarch."

"Beautiful?" One of the poems had spoken of dun skin and wiry hair. Not at all a good poem, she'd thought.

"In her way, she is beautiful sometimes."

It was like a sword through Anne's heart, but she said, "Tell me. Make me see her."

"Black eyes and black, dense, curling hair. Skin that is sallow or like honey or like clotted cream. Of middling height with a slender waist and rounded hips and a bosom to cushion a man's head. A low voice for a woman, and she sings very well, and plays. She has a mouth made for kissing, and for less proper things."

"Beautiful, then," Anne said in a dead voice. "And plainly you desire her too."

"Yes. Yes I do. Most men would."

"And she has youth, I suppose, as well as Will's heart."

"She's not so youthful. No younger than you, I would guess. I doubt she has his heart. What she has is his prick and his balls in her tender little hand. She is a bitch in heat, and if Will thinks he's her only lover he's mistaken. Anne, it won't last. He'll sicken of her."

"He hasn't yet, and he has had her for a long time, I think." Her voice broke and she struggled against tears. "What do I do, Harry?"

"Tell him you know. Put your foot down. Say you'll leave him if he doesn't give her up. He would, if it meant losing his family."

"Probably he would. But then he'd resent me, and she would be his lost love, the love of his life that he couldn't have, for duty's sake. I want to see her."

"What would that achieve?"

"I don't mean I want to confront her. Certainly I am not going to beg her to give me my husband back. I just want to *see* her. To see what she has that holds him in such thrall. Because none of his others have so held him."

Harry blinked. "He has had others?"

"Of course he has. Did you really think...? You did. What did you think, Harry? That he was a faithful husband until you made him recognise that part of himself that could love another man? Me for duty, you for love? And nothing else?"

"Well..."

Taking pity, Anne said, "I doubt any of the others were for more than convenience. But this woman I want to see. Just to *see*. Can you arrange it?" It didn't occur to her that he would think it an outrageous request or that he would take offence at her asking. He had as much malice in him as any other man. As any other thwarted lover.

"I can. I shall invite people, one evening soon. I shall hire her to sing. She has a lovely voice. It will not be a respectable evening."

"None of this is respectable."

"No. Well, I shall let you know when. I shall send someone for you. You can get away at night?"

"My husband is not likely to notice that I am not virtuously at home, is he?"

Four days later William mentioned in an off-hand way that he would be out that night, possible quite late. Theatre business. Of course, said Anne.

Just after he had taken himself off to the playhouse, a man in the clothing of an upper servant but with none of the usual livery badges to show whom he served, brought Anne a message. Tonight. Ten o'clock. Dress finely.

She asked Edmund to stay in to watch the children. A sick friend needed her, she said. Edmund was too young to wonder why she should wash her hair and put on perfume to nurse a sick friend. Nor did he notice that under her cloak she was wearing a new, very expensive and fashionable dress suitable for a party.

Prompt at ten the manservant returned. He had brought a horse, for they had to go clear across the city to Holborn Hill. Without a word he helped Anne into the pillion seat, as if escorting cloaked woman to secret assignations was all in the day's work. Perhaps it was. At Southampton House he took her to a back gate and showed her through a garden to a door and then up a stair to a room that held nothing but two chairs and a table on which stood a wine jug. From the other side of the house she could hear music, laughter, the sounds of voices.

After nearly half an hour, so close as Anne could judge, the door opened and Harry came in. "They are both here," he said without preamble. "Are you ready?"

"Yes."

"Put this on." It was a mask, a feathery bird's face. "It is that sort of party. Not everyone is masked, but many find it convenient. Take your cloak off." She did so, and he nodded approval of her dress and handed her a short satin cape. He himself was dressed very finely, more elaborately than she had ever seen, in blue and cloth of silver and velvet, with diamond buttons, a sapphire earring, two sapphire rings on his hands. It made her aware of his rank and wealth and of how thoroughly she was out of her depth in every way.

"That woman is about to begin her performance," he said. "We'll go down and mingle. Best if you stay with me, but if you need to go away, come back up to this room and ring the bell. The man who brought you will take you home."

"You are taking good care of me. Thank you."

"Somehow," he said, "it seems the least I can do."

It was not at all a respectable party. Anne recognised a few of the more raffish theatre players, and several men she had seen at Court or who were famous men of Harry Southampton's rank. Anyone in London would have known them. A lot of the women and the prettier boys were obviously prostitutes, here with clients or lovers or plying for hire. Incense and chypre hung heavy in the air, blending with the smoke from candles and torches, tobacco smoke, the smell of wine and food. A red-haired man, his arm around a louche boy whose eyes were blank with drink or some sort of drug, spoke familiarly to Harry and ran his eyes in automatic appraisal over Anne. Safe behind her mask, she eyed him boldly. Harry flung his arm about her waist and muttered something that made the other man wink and go away.

"Come through," Harry said softly and took her hand to lead her into the next room.

A woman was playing the virginals, singing to her own accompaniment. A lovely voice indeed. An odd face, not beautiful at all, too dark and scornful, all eyebrows and rouged lips. Her dress was ice-blue satin, expensively trimmed and cut very low over enormous breasts. She was not very young, not very anything.

Harry thrust a glass of wine into Anne's hand. "Look to your left."

Sipping, smiling falsely, she did so.

William was one of the twenty or so men listening to the music. He stood against a wall, leaning back, looking half-away from the woman at the virginals, beating time with his fingers and drinking wine. Just another of the crowd appreciating good music. But Anne had been married to him for so long that she knew every tiny shift of his stance, every trick of his eyes and line of his body, of his mouth. She knew desire and hope and self-disgust when she saw it in him. She was glad about the self-disgust. She wondered if he knew that the woman didn't love him.

The song ended. There was a polite patter of applause, and the woman took out a new sheet of music. She said something Anne didn't quite catch, something about a new song, written especially for tonight, and as she spoke her eyes moved around the room until she saw Harry. She smiled, for him alone, and Anne saw that she was beautiful after all. William saw that smile and stiffened. Harry gave him a cheerful wave, and after a moment he too smiled. Not very happily. His eyes moved over the dark-haired, green-clad woman in the bird mask beside Harry, and narrowed in something close to recognition, then he shook his head as if laughing at a ridiculous idea. Then he looked back to the woman at the virginals.

Halfway through the song Anne moved smoothly away. Harry followed her, back up the stair to the room she had first come to. Glad of the mask, she said, "I have seen enough. I shall go home now."

"I too have seen enough. Odd that I did not really know until now."

"Well, our clever wordsmith could explain that and, indeed, has done so. *So true a fool is love that in thy will, though you do anything, he thinks no ill.* One of his poems. I'm sorry, Harry."

He made an indeterminate sound and, before she could move away, he reached out and very gently took off her mask.

"I thought you were crying."

"No. I knew already, you see. All that's new to me is what she looks like. I can see that she has beauty but she's nothing. *Nothing.* And I still cannot compete. But I knew that. And do you know, it would be easier to bear if she were a true beauty or very young. But then, of course, he might truly love her."

"You think he doesn't?" he said, with hope springing in his voice.

"It is what you said the other day – lust, and guilt, and love of a kind, but nothing true or good."

Harry stared at her. The room was lit only by two candles and the light glittered on his eyes, making them as vivid as the jewels he wore.

"What will you do?"

"I don't know."

"Pay him back in his own coin. Settle for revenge. Take a lover."

Anne stared at him incredulously. "Oh, a fine sensible idea, exactly what I'd expect of a man. Who in the wide world would want *me*? No, I have a better idea. Harry, my lord, seduce that woman."

31.

The door was latched but unbolted. It was the usual arrangement. In went William, smelling his mistress's perfume in the air. He heard her voice in the bedroom and was pulling off his clothes as he went to her. She was sitting up in bed, naked, her back to him. She didn't turn to greet him. She often didn't. Talk was for later, in the act of love, for the lewd demands and praise of lust. He dropped his doublet and breeches on the floor and slid up behind her, admiring the lovely lines of her back, sliding his hands around to clasp her breasts.

And saw the man under her.

A man whose auburn-gold hair spread across the mattress, unpillowed, for the pillows were underneath his hips. A man whose long, slender fingers clasped the woman's hips, moving her upon his shaft. William had seen that hair spread like this so many times, had felt those elegant fingers clasping his body.

"Harry!" Standing like a fool in his shirt, his engorged prick wilting, his heart breaking.

And Marian-Maria-Mara turned her head and smiled at him and said, "There is room enough for three, Will."

"No." But he had never seen other people coupling, and he began to rise again.

"Yes," she said and reached for him. This was the nadir of lust, the expense of spirit in a waste of shame, moving onto that bed, knowing he wanted to and sliding down beside them, touching them where he could, kissing where and whom he could and taking his mistress where and how he could, and taking Harry, being taken, all in a tangle of limbs and hands and mouths. Hating it all but powerless to resist.

Afterwards he was the first to leave the bed. He dressed in silence. The woman was sleeping. Anyone else would have pretended to be, out of shame, but he knew she had simply fallen asleep like a child after play. Harry lay there, watching him.

"Was this the first time, Harry?"

"No." With something close to pity he said, "I had only to ask, Will."

"I'm sure. I loved you, Harry."

"I know it. And I love you. It's not in the past, for me. When all's said and done, she's only a woman. A jade for common hire." He stretched out his hand, and to his own surprise William took it, desperate for the warm, familiar clasp.

"I love you still," he said uncertainly and kissed the boy's lips. "But for now this is farewell."

"Make it *au revoir*. For we do love each other, my dear."

"I know. Just now I wish it were otherwise," said William, and left.

He went home. There was nowhere else to go. Home. To his wife. To Anne. To his children. To Anne. He resolved to tell her everything and beg her for forgiveness. Anne would understand. She always did.

But at home he found Edmund sitting alone in the parlour, eating bread and cheese. Seeing his brother, he stood up and strode angrily across the room.

"If you're looking for your wife, William, she is not here."

"What?"

"You *dare* ask 'what' in that mincing tone!" Edmund gripped him by the collar of his shirt. He was shaking with rage, and William noted, bemused, that the boy was now as tall as he. "You rutting swine. And you with a wife like Anne!"

"*Where is she?*"

Edmund hit him very hard across the face and dropped him contemptuously into a chair. "She's gone home. And who can blame her? She's found out, William. She knows what half London's been trying to keep from her. About your *mistress*."

"Oh Christ. Oh Christ." William sank his head in his hands, trying not to cry.

"She left a letter," Edmund said. "Which is more than I would have done in her place. You piece of shit, Will. She was crying – or no, she was trying not to cry. So as not to upset the children. *Your* children."

"Where's this letter?"

"In your room, I believe. I'm going out now. I only waited in to have the pleasure of telling you. I've nowhere else to live yet, but I daresay I can lodge with one of the other players. I think I prefer not to stay under your roof. Convenient, eh? You can bring your tart here whenever you like now. Fuck her in Anne's bed, why don't you?"

"No. No. Edmund, don't go. Come back." But he was speaking to a closed door and an empty room.

He sat there for a long time then wearily climbed the stairs, throwing off his clothes as he went. In the bedroom he poured cold water into the basin and washed. Then, naked, he went slowly across the room to the table under the window. Anne's letter lay there, folded twice and with his name written across it. Beside it were all the poems from his lock-box. Anne had laid them out in order, from the first he had ever written Harry, to the latest, the one written two days ago when he'd thought he knew was misery and self-hatred were.

At last he unfolded Anne's letter. She spelt by guess, but her message was admirably clear. She knew of his affair with that dark woman and could no longer bear to live with him. She had gone home to Stratford, taking the children, who knew and must know nothing of why she went. She would prefer not to see him while he was in thrall to that woman. Divorce was impossible, but they could live apart. She trusted him to send money for the children. If he wished to come home it must be on her terms now.

She had signed it, *Anne Shakspere.*

Part Six

1596

32.

Anne had gambled, and as spring became summer she knew she had lost. She never heard from William. He sent a gift for Susanna's thirteenth birthday in May, and money, but no letter, not even a verbal message. Night after night Anne lay awake, knowing she should have gone about things differently. William loved her as best he could, and she should have been content with that. She should have turned a blind eye to his affair with that woman. She should have stayed and waited for it to end. After all, she had swallowed his affair with Harry, so why should she choke on his loving a woman? But that was exactly the point. His love for Harry might have had its element of desire but it was outside the realm of man-woman dealings. That woman was a rival, as Harry was not. She had made Will into a stranger. All I have, Anne told herself, is my dignity and our children. But the better part of dignity might have been to ignore the whole matter. I didn't have to make enquiries about her. I didn't have to force the issue. And if it comes down to mere adultery, well, there are worse sins. Yet it seemed important to draw a line and say, "This I will not take."

And in clinging to her dignity – or was it only hurt? – she had lost her husband. Probably he was with that woman all the time now. Perhaps they shared a house as well as a bed. Perhaps he and Harry shared her. Perhaps he and Harry laughed together as Harry revealed their little plot. Perhaps, perhaps, perhaps.

She had no one to confide in. Her friends were William's friends too. And she had not quite realised until now how much she had changed in these last few years. Stratford was home, and she loved it, but it was a little, provincial country town and few of its inhabitants had ever been more than five miles away. Or wanted to. Here in Stratford, the people Anne had met and known in London were merely names, unreal people held in awe for their position and wealth. Government and politics were mystifying things that went on far away, affecting ordinary people only if a monarch died or there was war. Here, people rose at dawn and went to bed at nightfall, and if that was the life Anne had once accepted without question, now it was different. *She* was different. She was a woman of the world now.

Oh, there was fornication, adultery, drunkenness, feuding, in Stratford. London held no patents on sin. Country men raped their daughters or sisters and, in one notorious local case, their sheep. They sodomised each other. Women beat and hurt their children. But after London, even these vices lacked a certain spice. Yet spice was something Anne felt she could do without. She had surfeited on spice, and look where it had got her. Back where she started, but with the after-taste of wilder things on her tongue. And with no husband.

People gossiped about that. Walking to market, going to visit friends, Anne saw people murmuring behind their hands, looking slyly. Thought she was so grand, going off to London, and don't tell me she's back only because her husband's busy with the players. I always knew, I always said. Gives herself airs now she's got money, but what's a married woman doing home without a husband. No smoke without fire, you know. Yet these same people deferred to her because she had money and her husband was famous in London and had even met the Queen.

Yet when all was said and done Stratford was home. Probably she'd never go to London again, or anywhere else. Probably William would never come back. So, then, she had better start making something of life in Stratford.

She spoke to Hamnet's schoolmasters and, although they were unused to dealing with a woman, they knew enough of her husband's connections to go warily with her. Yes, they agreed, Hamnet was a clever boy who must go to university. He was eleven now, time to start making such plans. Money was not a difficulty? Just so. Oxford, then, in four years' time and, meanwhile, he must press on with his Greek.

The girls? Well, they might not make grand marriages here in Stratford, but dreams of their marrying above their class were just that, dreams. So long as they married good men. Preferably not actors. Judith was happier at home, she had her grandparents and cousins, her uncles and aunts and the farm, and as long as she had Hamnet she was content. That meant problems ahead, perhaps, when Hamnet went away to university, but Anne would cross that bridge when she came to it. Susanna pined for her father but she seemed not to miss London.

And as for me, Anne thought, I have my friends, I have my family. And now I will have a house.

She was careful not to ask around too openly on her own behalf. Women ran households and farms and businesses – a woman ran the country – but a woman doing business of this kind, no. So, discreetly, she asked a few questions, she kept her ears and eyes open. And one evening, when she'd been home two months, Joan knocked on her bedroom door and came in with a sparkle in her eyes.

"News! Maybe only gossip, but you should ask around. Anne, they say New Place is to be sold."

Anne sat up and put her book aside. "What have you heard?"

"Only that, that it's a chance. People were talking in the market today. You always liked New Place, didn't you." Perching on the bed, she sat on Anne's book. "Sorry," she said vaguely, turning it over and losing Anne's place. Then looking at in curiosity, she said, "This is Will's?" She could read a little, enough for everyday life, but the idea of sitting down and reading a book bewildered her. "*The Rape of... of...*"

"*Of Lucrece.* A classical tale. Yes, Will wrote it."

"Oh. I thought it was Venus he wrote of."

"That was his first long poem, the one that made his name. This one came the next year and many people think it the finer."

"Do you?"

"I'm not sure. I don't even know why I was reading it, Joan. New Place? Yes, I always liked it." Anne clasped her hands around her knees, thinking. The largest house in Stratford. The grandest house. But, "I'd heard it's in a bad way?"

"Aye, so they say. It's been neglected. But perhaps that means Will would get it cheap?"

"Perhaps. But if it needs a great deal of work it'd be a poor bargain. And there have been murders there. Still…" She had always shared the management of their money. It was her thrift and careful budgeting, as much as William's determination never to go the way of his father, that saw them with money in hand. She had a hundred pounds free and clear of coming expenses. William was making money hand over fist these days and, together or apart, he would never see his wife and children need for anything. And she deserved a house. Yes. The best house possible. William, too, had talked longingly of New Place.

"Do you think we could go and see it? New Place. Let's not tell anyone just yet, but we could look."

"Let's." Joan gave her a companionable grin. "After all, there's nothing says we can't *look*. And Anne." Her smile faded into a look of mild discomfort. "I wondered... say no, of course, be frank with me... but I wondered... if you and Will had a house of your own, could I live with you?"

Afraid of a blunt rejection, afraid she'd gone too far, she wouldn't meet Anne's eyes. But Anne was thinking, Why not? She loved Joan. They were friends. The children adored her. And, the only girl in that family of boys, Joan had never had much of a life. She'd known little interest or affection from her mother, who frankly preferred her sons.

"Of course," she said roundly. "I'd like it if you did. It would please me to have another woman in the house, a companion."

"You wouldn't mind? You wouldn't find me dull?"

"Never." Anne took Joan's hand. "I've never found you dull, how can you say it?"

"Well, you're different now. You're... you're..."

"Lonely," Anne said, the word bursting out before she realised.

"Ah. I have wondered. Things aren't right between you and Will, are they?"

"No. That is, I'm not sure." She would have given anything to spill out the whole story, but Joan was William's sister, and too innocent to hear this story.

"I've seen Will's plays performed," Joan said tentatively. "And sometimes I've wondered how much is made up out of his head and how much is, well, experience."

"Oh, some of each, Joan, some of each."

Blushing, Joan stretched her own imagination to the limits. "He's had another woman? Sorry, that is not something I should ask, is it. I know things are different in London, but..."

"I really can't tell you about it, Joan. Let's say you're not far off the mark. I think he fell in love."

"Men do that, I suppose. Even when they're married." Joan fiddled with the ends of her hair. "No wonder you're unhappy. Is that why you left London this time?"

"It is. Perhaps I'm making too much of what happened. Perhaps it was nothing but a passing temptation."

"Perhaps," Joan agreed, clearly relieved. "He loves you, Anne, I know that."

"Yes he does, in his way. And why did you say that just now, 'Men do that, even when they're married'? Why did you say it like that? Joan?" For her sister-in-law had bent her face down against her knees, her shoulders shaking. "Joan? Is there a man? Someone's hurt you? Let you down? Ah, come here, love, tell me." She pulled the younger woman against her shoulder, stroking her hair and wiping away the miserable tears.

"Yes," Joan said. "There's a man."

"Oh God, he's not married, is he?"

"No. No, he's… You won't tell Mother?"

"Of course not," said Anne, by now really worried. "Joan, are you pregnant? Is there real trouble?"

"Nothing like that. We've never... I would not. It's just that I love him and he's gone away."

"Forever? He doesn't care for you?"

"I don't know. No, not forever. Probably not forever. I don't know if he cares for me. But I love him, Anne."

"Who is he?"

"William." She stopped to blow her nose. Anne stared at her. William? Well, the world was full of Williams. Too full.

"You don't mean my brother?" She nearly added "Or yours?" but stopped herself in time. Things like that went on in the country, but they decidedly did not happen to people like the Shaksperes.

"Willie Hart." Joan blew her nose again then seemed to see Anne's complete incomprehension. "I forgot you hadn't met him. He was here last year. He was here through the winter. He's a hatter."

"And?"

"And he has fair hair and blue eyes and he's the handsomest man I ever saw."

Shying away from the thought of handsome men with blue eyes and fair hair, Anne asked for more information. Through Joan's alternating tears and rhapsodies she gathered that Master Hart had drifted to Stratford a year or so ago looking for work, had found it, lost it, drifted off again. Leaving Joan broken-hearted behind him. No, they'd never talked of marriage – of anything to the point, so far as Anne could discover – but there had been *something*. He had said he would come back. He was off to London to look for work. (London again, thought Anne.) But he would rather live in the country. He had said he would come back. He sounded a good-natured, likeable, useless fellow, and Anne looked down an uncomfortably clear vista of years of supporting Joan and this handsome drifter, and the no doubt enormous horde of children they would have.

"I can see why you love him," she lied. "But you can make a good marriage, Joan. You're a handsome girl, your parents have position, Will has money and he's well-known. Is this passing hatter suitable for you?"

"I'm twenty-seven this year and no one's ever offered to marry me. And I love Willie Hart. Though Mother and Father would say what you said. They'd say he's not good enough for me. But he's the only man I've ever wanted to marry. Oh, Anne, what am I to do?"

"Wait and see if he comes back. If he does, well, we'll see. If he doesn't, then face it, Joan, he doesn't care for you."

"I suppose so," Joan said sadly. "But he said he'd come back at the end of summer or write to me. Mother met him, you know, and she was spiteful about him. Called him a wastrel. He's not, Anne, she only said that because she knew I want him. So I thought if I told you… I thought, when Will comes home next, if I told him…"

Oh yes, thought Anne, he's going to be enchanted at the thought of his pretty, carefully reared sister throwing herself away on some itinerant hatter with, no doubt, not a penny to his name. And at the thought of finding a dowry for Joan to marry this fellow. But, tactfully, she told Joan that talking to William about it was certainly the thing to do, but to put it carefully. "Not that I know when he'll next come home," she couldn't keep from adding.

"Anne, I'm sorry, I'd forgotten, talking of myself. Anne, is it really that bad? He might not come back?"

"Oh, he'll be back, to see the children, see his family. Back as my husband? Well, let us wait and see. Both of us, Joan, waiting on men called William. But meanwhile, let us see about a house. Tomorrow you'll come with me. We'll try to see New Place."

"Yes," said Joan, and managed a smile.

Brisk talking having failed to persuade the New Place housekeeper to let them in, Anne tried the London method: bribery. A shilling changed hands and they were in. Joan was scandalised. A whole shilling! But Anne thought it money well spent. For she had fallen in love with New Place the moment she stepped inside its iron gates.

A courtyard at the front. A deep porch. Room for a garden. Ten chimneys twisting up from the slate-tiled roof. Large, glassed windows at the front, more above.

Inside, however, things were less good. Plenty of rooms, yes, almost too many for their needs, but what a state they were in. Peeling plaster, damp, worm-ridden timber, a kitchen Anne honestly mistook for a pigsty. Filth of every kind wherever one looked. And the tax on ten chimneys would be enormous. And yet... and yet... Clean the whole place, scrub out that kitchen, sweep the chimneys, mend the stairs and the floor-boards, fix the roof. A parlour, a dining room, a servants' hall, a buttery and dairy, a wash-house, a still-room, a pantry, two more rooms. Upstairs, a room running the width of the house and holding an immense, elaborately carved bed with tattered crimson hangings; what a guest chamber it would make. And at the other end, another large, airy room which Anne's fancy immediately furnished with a carpet, tapestries, the green silk coverlet she had been embroidering for two years, their faithful bed, the clothes presses they had bought in London, the silver, the looking-glass. She curbed her imagination. All very fine, for a woman living alone. But why not, after all those years of one room in his mother's house?

A room for Hamnet, one each for Judith and Susanna. That was grandeur for you, a room for each child. And one for Joan, with or without the famous Master Hart, and other guest chambers, servants' bedrooms, a storeroom, a room for sewing, a room William could use for books. A family house at last. A gentleman's house. A house for guests, a house from which to marry one's daughters.

And in the garden, mulberry trees, apple trees, walnut and almond trees, a well, peaches growing against a wall, a kitchen garden and a herb garden, a struggling grape vine. Add some brick paths, clear away the undergrowth and cut the grass. Stables and outbuildings. Repair that tumbled wall. Roses...

"It needs a great deal of work," Anne said as she and Joan walked home.

"More than I'd imagined. I'm sorry, Anne. Not such a good idea of mine after all."

"Oh but it was, Joan. Indeed it was. I am going to buy that house."

"But Anne..."

"A hundred pounds should cover it. I wonder if they'd take less."

"A *hundred?*"

"We shall offer sixty and see what they say."

"But Anne..."

"I'll... *we* will go up to a hundred, but hope to get it for less considering all the work it needs."

"But Anne, what's Will going to say?"

"Do you know, Joan, love, I don't care."

Anne confided in her friends the Sadlers about New Place, and although they warned her of the expenses in buying a run-down house, Hamnet Sadler opened negotiations for her with the owner. Nothing was settled as yet, it was all in the manner of vague enquiries, for Anne didn't want to drive the price up by seeming too eager, but the owner grudgingly agreed to give Master Shakspere first refusal if the house was actually to be sold.

The first step, Anne thought in satisfaction.

33.

After two months at home, Anne moved out to Hewlands Farm
with the children. Nothing had yet happened about buying New
Place, and she had had enough of people called Shakspere.
Besides, she discovered, when your life is falling apart you want
the old certainties, the reminders of more innocent times. It was
good for the children, too; fresh air after London, healthy
exercise, Bartholomew's four children for company, Bartholomew
and his wife as well, out from Stratford where they now lived, to
lend a hand. Also good for Anne. As summer wore on and
harvest time approached, she worked out in the sun with the rest
of her family, and twelve hours a day of hard physical work meant
that she fell into bed tired enough to sleep.

Her family knew something was wrong. They never asked, for
they were not people much given to talk, but as summer wore on
Anne felt them closing around her, forming a protective rank. She
was their daughter, sister, aunt. She belonged to them. They liked
William, but if he had done her wrong he would not find her
defenceless.

The day-labourers hired for the harvest took their noontime meal
and, with luck, an hour's snooze under a shady tree, or wandered
into the Forest of Arden. The Hathaways and their employees ate
indoors. When the bell rang Anne rounded up her children and
trudged back to the house with her brothers. The men stopped to
sluice themselves under the pump, as much because Mrs
Hathaway was fastidious as because they were keen to wash off
the sweat-stuck chaff dust. Hamnet joined them, for at eleven he
was old enough to want the male camaraderie of work and
physicality. Had she married a farmer, Anne reflected, an eleven-
year-old son would probably be a fully-fledged farm worker.
Missing some school didn't matter. This summer with his uncles
and cousins was doing Hamnet good. He had filled out, he was as
brown as a nut and he was healthy. They were all brown. Hot,
Anne wished she and the girls could shuck off their clothes and
leap under the pump's cool gush. A wash, in decency, at the basin,

would have to do. But tonight, she thought, perhaps we'll go to the river.

The meal was ready. In his Puritan way Bartholomew made much of the blessing, until at last everyone could fall to, niceties of service reduced to "Mustard," or "Pass the salt." Anne was wondering why her children had to eat as if they were gardening, when the door opened and her husband came in.

He appeared so unexpectedly and was so outlandish in that setting that he could have been some cunning artificer's apparition from a play. They all jumped and Bartholomew dropped the pipe he had begun to fill with tobacco.

"Marry come up, it's Will!" said Mrs Hathaway.

"Yes, Mother, and good day to you all. Anne, my dear." He bowed. Hemmed in at the end of the table, Anne couldn't rise to greet him. But to be cool would look too odd. She smiled rather stiffly, and to her annoyance he blew her a jaunty kiss. Then the children were all over him and Mrs Hathaway was telling the maid to bring fresh plates and more food and everyone was talking at once and no one noticed she didn't return the kiss.

How like him, she thought. How very like him to turn up without warning, so sure of his welcome. With a rush of good solid anger she looked him over. He had dressed plainly to come into the country, but next to the other men in their homespun and russet, his sober dark blue suit with its edging of satin was a gorgeous as a courtier's. He was neat, sleek and expensive. Master Shakspere the playwright and theatre-owner. Master William the adulterer and sodomite.

She had not until now seen the theatre's boy, Nol, hovering by the door, still clutching Will's bags.

"Nol, how good to see you. Are you well? You look hot. Come, a mug of ale."

"Good to see you, Mrs S. But I'll take me ale in the kitchen, I reckon. Master Will, 'ere's your gear."

"Thanks, Nol. Did someone mention ale? But I must wash first."

"Yes indeed," said Mrs Hathaway. "Hamnet, love, take your father... well, you know where everything is, Will. As for you, boy – Nol, is it? – you are very welcome to my house and you shall have a good dinner, but first we'll have you out under the pump, thank you very much. Fleas, in *my* house! Come along."

"Weren't expecting him, eh?" Bartholomew murmured to Anne as they went out.

"No."

"And not too pleased to see him?"

"Yes and no. We parted on rather bad terms, Bart."

"Aye, he looked a bit shifty. Though he looked at you like he'd come home and hadn't known it till now." His big hand closed over hers, clenched on the edge of the table. "Cheer up, Annie. Remember the children."

"I do. And I'm full of cheer. Though I won't be if you call me Annie again."

"Made you smile, though. Have some more ale."

She had another cup, noting glumly how her daughters had brightened up. How she herself felt, she hardly knew.

Mrs Hathaway and William came back in, both a little damp around the edges. William smelt of Mrs Hathaway's yellow soap. He was in his shirtsleeves and breeches, and Anne noticed that the shirt was one she had made; Holland cloth, snowy white, so fine it was almost transparent, with a smart gored collar and black-work bands at the wrists and neck. It made Anne very conscious of her shabby working dress, of her greasy hair knotted under a practical but unflattering cap, of the fact that in months she'd no more than washed her hands and face, her pits and parts, in the cold water of a bedroom basin.

"I got that boy under the pump," Mrs Hathaway reported, as one who had fought the good fight. "I've never *seen* such dirt. And don't tell me London dirt isn't worse than country dirt. Fleas all over him. Farm or no farm, fleas and lice and filth do not cross my threshold. Hamnet's burning the boy's clothes. He can have a suit that Thomas has grown out of."

"Dick Burbage and I got him into the bath-tub back at Christmas," William said, spearing slices of beef. "How he squealed. He thinks washing isn't natural."

"Papa, have you come to stay?" Susanna asked, piling salad onto his plate. Recently she had decided that 'daddy' was babyish.

"That depends. Excellent beef, Mother Hathaway. The theatres are closed because there is plague in London again, so we've sent a reduced company on tour. The Burbages have stopped on in London and Augustine Phillips heads the tour. I should join them, but I made no promises." Under his lashes he shot a look down the table to Anne. She drank some more wine. "You all look very healthy. You've been in the sun, I see."

"Too much in the sun, perhaps. But of course, you like a brown skin, don't you, husband." She had timed that as neatly as any actor.

His mouth full, William shot her another look, then, having swallowed, said, "The sun's kiss on a fair woman's skin is better adornment than any face-paint. I wrote a poem on the subject a while ago. Do you not remember?"

"I do, but you write so many poems."

"Aye, too many. Or not enough."

"It looks as if they pay well," said Bartholomew, enjoying himself.

"Those for the right audience do. My two long poems have gone into several printings. They make money for the printer, but not for me. It's the plays that pay."

"It don't seem the wolf's at the door, though. How much would you get for a play?"

"Oh, usually some ten pounds." Smiling at Susanna and Judith as they filled his plate again, William didn't see the effect of this.

"*Ten pounds!*" Bartholomew lowered his pipe. His wife Isobel stared at William as if he'd announced he had been crowned Queen. "Ten pounds for words on paper for men to act?"

"Oh yes," said Anne, "Will makes good money. And," she added, "good plays."

"They'd want to be good. *Ten pounds.* Well, I enjoyed that one of yours the players did last time they came to Stratford. The one about the king. Laugh? I thought I'd crack my sides." William gave him a sickly smile. "The bit with the clown... he had a little dog, and it was the funniest thing I've ever seen." Anne smiled. William hated the clowns extemporising, she had seen him near come to blows with Will Kemp once over the latter's inserting his act with his dog into a tragedy. "Yes, that was a good one. So tell me," Bartholomew went on with an irritatingly man-to-man air, "you own part of a playhouse, Anne was telling us. What sort of income would that bring in?"

"We each get a share of the profits," mused William, now cutting a great slice of quince tart, "so, six plays a week, and twelve of us share. Call it four or five pounds a week on average, plus commissions for private performances."

212

"God's wounds," breathed Bartholomew. "And I've been telling my boys to stick to the farm or plain trades here. Will, that's two hundred pounds a year. And plays; how many would you write in a year?"

"Usually two." William glanced up at Bartholomew, smiling. "I usually write a comedy and a tragedy – the latter have the dog scenes – each year. Three, some years. I made over three hundred pounds last year."

"Well, I'll be! All that from the playhouse and writing. What do you do with it all, eh?"

"Will spends a lot on music," said Anne. "He's very fond of music. He has a particular liking for Scotch music."

"What, the bagpipes?" asked Mrs Hathaway.

"And other instruments, played most sweetly."

"But you are out of date, wife," said William. "I had a passing liking for certain things from Scotland, but I find I prefer the sweeter music of the south."

"Ah yes, South –"

"I mean England," he swiftly interposed. "Give me English music."

"Amen to that," said Bartholomew, draining his cup and standing up. "And if you stop with us, as I hope you will for a time at least, we'll have music in the evenings. But for now I must be back to work. Come on, boys. We'll see you at supper, Will?"

"Indeed. I would like to stay, if I may." He glanced at Anne.

"You may. But what of your family? Have you visited them?"

"Of course. They told me you were here. Edmund is at home, our mother cossetting and cramming him. She thinks we don't have food in London. Now where's Hamnet? Not still washing Nol?"

"In the kitchen, eating."

"Then let's find him," said William, standing and putting his arms around his daughters. "And perhaps we will take a walk to digest our dinner. Anne, you will come?"

With her family all looking at her, Anne could not refuse.

They walked in the forest. The sun shone, dappling through the trees, alternately casting William into shadow and making fire of his hair. Susanna's head, resting sometimes on his shoulder, shone with the same ruddy light. Judith held his hand, while

Hamnet walked jauntily in front of them, backwards so he could talk to his father.

Strolling behind them, Anne thought, I gave him handsome children, children he adores. And I told him to come home on my terms or not at all. We women are powerless. Our husbands can beat us, betray us, use us how they like, and we can do little. Quiet domestic revenge and little else, unless we turn to murder. He knows I would never take his children from him, not that the law would allow it. Yet he has come home.

"It's quite pretty 'ere," Nol's voice broke in on her thoughts. "Not enough 'ouses, though. I'd rather London. Do you get wolves in these woods?"

"No wolves. Or not four-legged ones."

"Master Will's been that miserable since you come 'ome, Mrs S."

She had never thought this boy stupid. "Oh?"

"Yes. Looks like someone who's lost a shillin' and found a groat. Finished 'is new play, 'e did, and 'e was that snappy takin' the players through it you wouldn't believe. I reckon he was lonely."

Anne knew a hint when she heard one. "Lonely?"

"Aye. Not so fick with Lord Sarfampton since his lordship took up with that Scotch tart, and now 'e reckons 'imself in love with that lady at Court. Sarfampton does, I mean. An' there was a story goin' round that you'd walked out on him, like, and someone twitted 'im on losin' his wife, jokin' like, and he fair 'it the roof."

"Really," said Anne with great satisfaction.

"Yeh, really. Said 'e wouldn't 'ave his wife talked about, like, when she was the cleverest, most truest woman in the world. The players give 'im a round of applause. 'e's been workin' 'ard, too 'E's near finished another play. Lonely, like, and workin' to take 'is mind off of it."

"Nol," said Anne, looking at him with love, "what would you like most in the world?"

"To learn to read so I can be a player," he said promptly.

"I didn't know. Well, we can have you taught to read, nothing simpler."

"Isn't it 'ard, though, to learn? Y'see, Mrs S, I thought, like, if I could read and the players took me on, I'd 'ave a trade, like, and

I'd 'ave summat to offer a girl."

Amused, Anne glanced at him, and made two discoveries. He was blushing, and his eyes were fixed on Susanna.

On Susanna. On my *daughter, who will not marry a common Cockney street boy. Who is a* child!

But no, Susanna was not a child. Thirteen, and her menses had begun just before her birthday. A woman, as the world counted it, and marriageable. And lovely. She too had grown this summer, and Anne had had to let out her bodices for the new fullness of her bosom. Her russet hair framed a delicate, heart-shaped face full of lively charm. Mothers are partial, but yes, Susanna was a lovely girl. And too good for Nol. Poor Nol.

"How old are you?" Anne asked him.

"Dunno. I fink I might be seventeen."

"No family?"

"Nah. Well, I must of 'ad, but I never knew 'em. You don't miss what you ain't never 'ad, they say, but sometimes I think I'd like to 'ave people what belonged to me, like."

"Yes, there is nothing like it. Well, why not think of learning to read and see if a playing company will take you on. You must know a good deal about the stage by now. And when you're older, with a trade, as you say, you'll find a girl and have family of your own. But I don't think very young marriages are always a good idea."

"Nah, p'r'aps not." He shivered suddenly, sneezing. "I don't mind washing sometimes, Mrs S, but that old lady 'ad me in me drawers under that pump. 'Tain't natural, all this scrubbing. I reckon I've been and gone and caught a cold."

"You'll survive," Anne said heartlessly. "The Queen takes a bath every month, they say, and she's still hale."

"P'r'aps." Nol giggled. "Master Will 'ad a bath last night. Cor, 'e was like a girl at it, Mrs S, scrubbin' away and puttin' sweet 'erbs in the water an' cuttin' 'is toenails."

"Indeed," said Anne. "And Mother had him under the pump too."

"She's fussy, ain't she? But it's fine to be in a grand 'ome like yours, Mrs S, with everything clean, like. Like yours was in London. I missed you when you went away. You reckon girls'd like me if I washed a bit more? Master Will said last night, when 'e was washing 'imself, women like that sort of fing. And I could learn to speak more gentlemanly, I fink."

"Aye, we do like those things." Anne felt suddenly light-hearted. "Learn to be a player, Nol, and have a bath from time to time, and anything is possible."

"And what are you two talking about so intently?"

Anne looked up at William. The children had scampered on ahead, while he stopped and waited for her and Nol. "Bathing, and what women like."

"They say Cleopatra bathed in asses' milk. Nol, the children are going down to the river, why don't you join them?"

"Why not?" said Nol, and with a wink at Anne raced after the others. Anne noticed that Susanna waited for him.

"Bathing, eh?" said William.

"Yes. I hear you had a bath last night."

"I did, madam. I washed off the dust of the roads and the dirt of London to come home."

"And have you come home, Will?"

"If indeed I have a home."

Walking slowly on, Anne said, "You may well have a house, if you agree my plan. You have children, who love you. That is a home, always."

"And a wife?"

"Have I a husband?"

"You have a fool for a husband."

"A fool, who enjoys fooling?"

"No, a fool who fooled against his will. Your will. Your Will."

They had stopped, standing together under a tree, sheltered from sight. Distantly their children's shouts came to them. Slowly, as if he thought to be rebuffed, William put his hand on Anne's cheek.

"I have come home to my wife. To you. Because I did not know how deeply I had hurt you until I knew about Harry and that woman."

"How very like a man," Anne remarked. "You break my heart, and you don't even know you've hurt me."

"And how very like a woman of think of precisely *that* revenge. For it was your idea, was it not?" Anne said nothing. Which was an answer of sorts. "Clever of you. A neat revenge. But you always were a clever woman. You know me too well."

"And what of your Scotchwoman?"

"She's with Harry, so far as I know. Or Essex. She casts her net wide."

"You would have her again if she returned?"

"No."

"Be sure, for I will not share you."

"Then you shall not." When she still stared up at him, unresponsive, he cried, "I can spin words out of air but not make my wife believe I love her."

"Don't love your *wife*," Anne cried back. "Love *me*! Love *Anne*. Love the woman who fell in love with you fourteen years ago and who loves you still. *Love me*."

"I do. Anne, I do. All that passionate love, infatuation, pining... that's for boys and girls, not for us. We are married, and we love each other in the only way that matters. Forever, forgivingly. Anne, I wrote you a poem. Do you want to hear it?"

"Yes," she said warily, and, holding her hands in his he began to recite.

> *When in disgrace with Fortune and men's eyes*
> *I all alone beweep my outcast state,*
> *And trouble deaf heaven with my bootless cries,*
> *And look upon myself and curse my fate,*
> *Wishing myself like to one more rich in hope,*
> *Featur'd like him, like him of friends possess'd,*
> *Desiring this man's art and that man's scope,*
> *With what I most enjoy contented least;*
> *Yet, in these thoughts myself almost despising,*
> *Haply I think on thee and then my state,*
> *Like to the lark at break of day arising*
> *From sullen earth sings hymns at heaven's gate;*
> *For thy sweet love remembered such wealth brings,*
> *That then I scorn to change my state with kings.*"

Anne had an excellent memory. That poem had not been among the ones she had found locked away. "So, after fourteen years, I get a second poem."

"A poem of love, my dear. A poem of need and belonging and knowing. Love me, Anne, love your fool husband who loves you. Forgive me if you can, and love me." He held out his arms. Slowly, sighing, needful, Anne went to his embrace. She rested her head against his shoulder, felt his lips caressing her hair, her brow, her cheek. "Don't cry, love," he said softly. "Don't cry."

"I didn't know I was."

"Yes. Tears, idle tears." He kissed her then, claiming her mouth so sweetly that she put her arms around his neck and clung to him. "Forgive me, darling, and let us start again."

"But when something is broken..."

"It can be mended, and the mend makes it stronger."

"But the mended place still shows and takes the wear until the unmended part tears, or breaks."

"But if the mend is done well, no one else need know the thing was broken, and you are all the more careful in handling the mended thing." His voice hardened. "Or shall I go away again, Anne, after this short visit? Shall we live apart, pretending, for appearances sake, for the children's sake, that it's merely that you prefer the country while I must be in London? Shall we never meet again as husband and wife?"

"I *do* prefer the country. But never meet again? No, Will. We'll swallow pride and hurt and carry on."

"With love. Yes, with love. And, wife, I told you I stopped at home before coming here, and I talked with Joan. She told me –"

"Of her hatter?"

"Her *what?*"

"She's in love with some wandering hatter."

"Mad! What's his name?"

"Willie Hart. And she's breaking her heart."

William shook his head, flummoxed. "Who and if she marries is up to my father, though I expect I'll have to put up a dowry for her. But Anne, forget that. I have something for you. A proof I'm in earnest." From inside his doublet he produced a paper, folded lengthwise. He gave it to Anne. "See?"

But of course she didn't see. This had the look of some important thing, a legal paper perhaps. She saw William's signature at the bottom and a stamped seal, but she was used only to William's writing and to print. These small and tightly written words were beyond her. She thought she made out 'contract' and ... "New Place?"

"Yes." William was watching her very intently. "Joan told me how much you wanted it, so I have bought it for you. I hope, for us. That is the contract to purchase and I have put twenty pounds down to seal the bargain. How much have we in the bed-head, Anne?"

"Over a hundred pounds, I think. Will, *New Place*!"

"It's in bad condition so I shall insist on some repairs before we pay the balance of the price and we may not get clear title to the place for some time, but it's ours. We could be living in New Place on our wedding anniversary. How like you that?"

"You need to *ask*?"

"And is it proof enough that I need your forgiveness and will amend my ways and be a faithful husband?"

For a moment Anne still hung back. "Dare you promise that? *Can* you promise that? What of Harry?"

"A part of me will always be his. In memory. Nothing else. I dare and do promise you. And that's the proof in your hand. A house of our own at last. A different life. I must still be often in London, but from now I'm excused from the summer touring. I shall use that time to write, here, at home. You shall join me in London if and when you wish, but I think a new life in a New Place?"

"Yes," said Anne, and once again the words were spoken between them. "Come, clap hands and a bargain."

Hands clasped, they began to move toward each other for a kiss, but: "Here are the children."

"You look hot, Mama," said Susanna.

"Do I? Well, it's amazing how hot one can grow here in the Forest. And you, Hamnet, look cold. Been in the river, I see."

"Yes. Fell in."

"We were paddling," Judith said anxiously, "that's all. And Nol and Hamnet went in too deep."

"So I see. Well, never mind. But walk briskly home, get in the sun and warm yourself. You too, Nol." For he was shivering quite violently in his wet clothes, and sneezing.

"It's all that washing," he grumbled. "'Tain't natural. I told you that."

"That boy Nol is ill," Mrs Hathaway said that night after supper. "I think he's taken a chill. God forbid it's the sweating sickness. I've put him to bed with a mug of hot ale and my goose-grease liniment on his chest."

William looked up from reading to the twins. "I wanted him to ride on to Coventry, to tell the players I'll not be joining them."

"Give him a night's rest. I'll see to him before I go to bed."
She settled down with her knitting. "Now read on, Will, I love to
hear you read."

But when she looked in on Nol, Mrs Hathaway came back
looking like her own ghost. "It *is* the sweating sickness. He'll be
dead by morning."

He was, but by the time he died the twins had it too.

34.

The sweating sickness. The sweat. Unknown in England until Henry Tudor's ragbag army of French mercenaries and freed prisoners came to wrest the crown from King Richard. No one knew what caused it. There was no cure. If you lived a day with it, probably you would survive. Most people did not. Usually, children did not.

Hamnet had it badly, worse than Judith. The fever burned the flesh from his body, and nothing could slake his thirst or ease the pain in his chest. Once Anne thought the fever was breaking when Hamnet's skull-face broke into a weakly smile and he knew her and called her "Mama" and drank some watered wine. But it was only a moment's respite, cruel for the fleeting hope it brought, and soon his sweat was soaking her gown again as she cradled him against her breast. He was so hot, so very hot, and screaming out with pain. Bartholomew's wife Isobel tended to Judith, for she, like Anne, had survived the sweat as a child. They told each other as they worked over the children, Two of us had it and lived. A good omen, and the twins had survived a day...

The light thickened towards the close of the second day. Sponging Hamnet over with cold water, for a moment Anne almost slept from sheer exhaustion and looked down terrified at Hamnet as some noise aroused her.

Arms closed around her and her son.

"Will."

"Aye. God help us, Anne. Is this my punishment?"

He moved away. Desolate, her tears dripping onto her son's ghastly face, Anne wondered why she had thought he could help.

"My son is dying. I do not need talk of punishment."

She thought she had said the words aloud, throwing them at him like weapons, and realised she had spoken only inside her mind. Judith had been asleep after all, for like Anne she jerked awake and looked in terror at Hamnet, then saw her father. She neither spoke nor reached for him, but gravely she smiled then turned back to her twin.

Anne heard William open and close the door. Heard him murmur to someone. Heard his boots hitting the floor, then the rustle of garments. His hand touched her brow, stroking the dirty, damp hair back from her face. "I can no longer leave this to you alone. You will go with Mother Hathaway to wash and eat a meal then lie down upon your bed. I will care for the twins. Isobel will tell me what to do. Go, my dear. It's all I can do for you. All I can do to help." Very gently he lifted their son away from her.

She stood up, so unsteady she had to lean against him. For the first time she looked at him. He was tired, of course he was. He looked older. Exhaustion in his eyes, and fear. Pain in every lineament, pain and grief and hopeless love. A mark on his neck that could have been a love-bite from small, greedy teeth, but was only dirt. A new, pale line at the top of his brow. Her poor, vain, darling William was going bald at the front. He was thirty-two. Not one-and-twenty when their son was born. The son who would not live to see his twelfth birthday.

"Oh, Will," said Anne, and in his arms Hamnet stirred, tried to wet his lips, looked up at his father and knew him. "Give him the wine-and-water in that cup. I'll bring some more."

"The maid can bring it." William eased down on the tumbled bed so Hamnet lay against his shoulder. "You must rest and eat, Anne. Go, do as I bid."

He must have told her stepmother of his orders because a bowl of hot water awaited Anne in her bedchamber. With the heavy, slow movements of a swimmer about to drown, she stripped naked and washed herself all over. She broke a comb trying to drag it through her damp and tangled hair, so ran handfuls of water through it and brushed it out properly. In a clean smock and gown she went downstairs and surprised herself by being able to eat some bread and baked chicken. Bartholomew was there, similarly cramming down the cold food. She had thought he too had gone away with their brothers.

"No," he said, "I've had the sweating too, Mother told me. And you need your family with you. I've been doing what I can for Will." His big hand fumbled out across the table and took Anne's. "It's worst for the mothers, perhaps, but dammit, it's hard for us fathers too. Will's breaking his heart. His only son."

Anne let him give her two cups of wine, drinking them with her head on her hand. This is needful, she told herself, I need the food, the wine, this little respite. Will is here, he is with our son. I will need my strength. Her stepmother came in and silently pushed the platter of meat and bread towards her again. She shook her head and Mrs Hathaway sat down in the chair beside the empty hearth. Bartholomew took her hand.

After a moment Anne stepped out into the garden, gratefully breathing the clean night air. What time was it? She hadn't seen a clock since morning. Then suddenly she turned, hitched up her skirts and ran back inside and up the stairs to the twins' room.

William nodded as if she came in answer to his call. She scrambled across the bed and slid her arms around her son. "Send for Susanna and your family. The Sadlers too."

William left the room in silence. He was soon back, and from downstairs Anne heard Bartholomew leading the horse from the stables.

Hamnet's breathing had changed, it was slow and sterterous. A fingernail of white showed under his eyelids. *Oh my son, my little boy, my heart's delight, my child.* She kissed him, rocking him as she had done the first time he lay against her breast. *Hamnet my dear, my boy, my love.* William was holding Judith. The girl was alive and better, but still unconscious. How long passed? An hour? Two?

They heard the noise of arrivals, and then the family were all in the room. Susanna leaned against her father, her hand on Hamnet's. John Shakspere knelt at the foot of the bed, his rosary openly in his hand, his lips moving in prayer. If the Queen's men burst in now, thought Anne, would an old man's grief for his only grandson excuse this treason? There is but one God, and He is taking my only son from me. The Blessed Virgin to whom my father-in-law prays lost her only Son. *Will no one take away this cup? Hamnet, my son, my dear, my clever boy, my loving boy. Sir Hamnet Shakspere. Lord Shakspere. The Earl of Stratford. Lord Chancellor. My little boy who talks with his mouth full and scuffs his shoes and watches his father's plays with such delight, who tried to write a poem for my birthday and wept because it wouldn't come out right, who wanted to go to university, who kisses me at bedtime. Never again. Never. Never. Never.*

The Sadlers came into the room, Hamnet's godparents who had given their names to the twins. Judith Sadler was weeping softly, her husband clearing his throat and dashing at his eyes. Joan knelt by her father, Gilbert's arm around her. Richard and Edmund stood against the wall, tears falling unheeded down their faces. Mrs Hathaway held Mary Shakspere, their eyes never leaving the dying child.

The dead child. Suddenly, between one breath and another, Hamnet Shakspere had ceased to be. Anne felt it. She saw and felt him die and felt his soul depart. *My son is dead. Dead. Never again. My son is dead.*

– Anne, my dear, come away now.

– So young, not twelve, so young.

– Susanna, love, I'm sorry, but it is over.

– Lay him down, my dear.

– He is with God.

– My son, my darling dear.

– William, take her away.

– Someone take Will away.

Anne heard a clear, calm voice – her own – saying, "Someone see to Judith. Lift her up, give her to me." But she herself was being lifted, carried in warm and loving arms, and her husband's tears were falling onto her face. "Judith," she repeated and saw Bartholomew carrying the little girl from the room. So it's both of them, she thought. Both gone.

But her brother said, "I'll take her to the next room. I think she is better. Go, Anne."

Then there was a soft bed and wine with a gritty, herbal taste, and the pain of *my son is dead* became a muted, distant knowledge. Susanna snuggled in her arms, and William beside them, crying silently into the drenched pillow, and *my daughters are still alive, my darling girls*, and an old man weeping, and more wine, then peace and oblivion.

They went alone to Hamnet's room. Their mothers had done what was needful. Their son lay silent, pale, on linen sheets, candles burning, white flowers clasped in his hands. Anne bent and kissed his cold brow.

"Hell is empty," William said, "and all the devils are here." He knelt beside the bed, his fingers lightly touching Hamnet's lips. "My son is dead."

"I've no comfort for you," Anne said. "I cannot give you another son. I cannot share my grief, not even with you."

"I know it. I've no comfort for you. Not yet. Except that I shall tell Judith, when she's well enough to know."

"Thank you. I could not bear to do it." She turned away, no more able to bear the sight of William's face than of her son's. She was crying, and it was the first time, and she knew she must not let herself or her howls would bring the heavens down. "Bartholomew brought the flowers."

"I know. A little thing, a kind and loving thing. Anne," he said in simple curiosity, "how *do* we bear it?"

"I have no idea. We just go on." Then she said, "Will, had things happened differently, had I stayed in London or you come home with us, Hamnet might still have died. Nol brought the sickness with him, but Hamnet could have taken it in London, had I stayed. Or caught it here. Stratford is no magic place where illness doesn't strike. You were born in a plague year when half the townsfolk died."

He was silent for a long time before he said, "So you have comfort for me after all. I thought if I hadn't stayed, if I hadn't done what I did so that you had to leave... And I brought Nol and brought with him the disease that killed my son. My punishment."

"God takes the children of virtuous parents too. So many children die. It is not punishment. Or if it is, we share it. My son is to be buried tomorrow." She kissed Hamnet's lips and went away to tend her daughter.

Two funerals. One for Nol, who must lie nameless, for no one knew his surname, under a cross saying only "Oliver". Bearable, that one, almost. One for Hamnet Shakspere, aged eleven. Buried in Holy Trinity's graveyard, Stratford-upon-Avon, on the eighth day of August 1596. A little grave.

35.

"Judith still never speaks."

"No. Leave her, let her work her grief out if that's her way."

"But it is two months since Hamnet died."

"She will speak in time. I think it must be worse for a twin. Worst for a twin who shared the womb and the mother whose womb it was." Lightly William touched Anne's hair.

"Or for a father, to lose his only son, his posterity and future? His name." Something sparked in the back of Anne's mind, a dim memory of someone saying *Your name will live forever.* Not now. There would be no descendants named Shakspere, and who would remember the Hathaways?

William moved sharply away, turning back to the window. The autumn sun caught the chestnut in his hair and struck points of light from the angles of his face and the silver threads in his ruff. His son's death had aged him in so many ways, and he had become punctilious about his clothes, no longer the untidy, ink-stained William of London and carefree times. Perhaps it helped him to honour his son with the perfection of his mourning clothes. Or perhaps this was just the Stratford Master Shakspere. But, come to that, Anne too was finely dressed, her gown and cap of black silk with a velvet trim. Rich people, the aristocracy, erected lavish tombs to their dead children, they commissioned music and poetry or endowed churches in their memory. People of the Shaksperes' position could do naught but show their mourning in the expense of their clothes.

Another point of light sparkled from the ring on William's hand as he lifted a paper from the table and seemed to read it through. "This came today."

"I saw the messenger, but you said nothing so I didn't ask."

"Oh, it's nothing private. Just meaningless, now." He put the paper, opened, into Anne's hand. "The College of Heralds has granted my coat of arms. I am Mister Shakspere, gentleman, now."

It was the first thing that had interested her since Hamnet's death. "William Shakspere, gentleman!" She squinted at the French words under the drawing. "What is this motto here?"

"*Non Sans Droit.* Not without right." He watched her, the corner of his mouth twitching.

"A very proper motto. Right – write. A pun, Will?"

"Not on my part, though it occurred to me too. No, just a suitable motto. Remember that my father applied for a coat of arms some years ago? He was keen to do so again, the matter's been in hand for some time. He – I – we thought it would be for Hamnet, that he would go to university and into his profession a gentleman's son. These things matter."

"Yes. But it will matter to the girls, Will. A gentleman's daughters can look for good marriages, they will have standing now. But Judith?"

"Doesn't speak. I know." With a sign he sat down facing Anne. "Leave her be. She grieves in silence, I with words." He made a long arm to take another paper from the table. "I still have to work. The Company send their condolences, their sympathy, their gifts and their love, but still they need a new play."

"Did you write nothing in London all spring and summer?"

"I wrote. Poems. Sonnets. A play, yes, but another is needed soon." He leaned forward, looking into Anne's eyes. "I found that woman with Harry, as you knew I would. I know you and he planned it. Well, it worked. But still I went back to her. I shared her with Harry for a week or two. Then I sickened of her. I never saw her again, or not alone. I saw her twice, in the distance. She came to the playhouse, she applauded my plays. She is with Harry, now. Or was. She caught him as she did me. Held him in the same way."

"That hurt you?"

"I suppose it did. Odd, isn't it? I can hardly remember now. She, and all those things, are in the past. I frittered away my son's life in that woman's bed. I wasted time when I could have been with my son."

With a little shrug Anne said, "It's past praying for. Hamnet loved you."

"And missed me? Wanted me here with him, when I was in London, with that woman?"

"He missed you, yes, but all his life that was the pattern, that you were in London, acting and making plays. He would not have had it differently, my dear. He was proud of you. He liked to read your plays, he loved to see them acted, you were *glorious* to him."

"And I suppose that is something. Anne, see what I wrote, here. This is the new play about King John. A mother grieving for her son ..."

Anne took the paper from him, held it up to the light.

Grief fills the room up of my absent child,
Lies in his bed, walks up and down with me,
Puts on his pretty looks, repeats his words,
Remembers me of all his gracious parts,
Stuffs out his vacant garments with his form:
Then have I reason to be fond of grief...

Her voice cracked. "Yes, Will. Yes, yes, yes! That is what it is like, yet I must not be fond of grief." All at once the tears came, the storm of weeping she had longed for and denied herself. She wrenched forward, the paper caught between her knees and chest as she huddled herself, crying for her son.

William closed his arms around her and together they slipped to the floor, clutching each other, weeping, talking through their tears of Hamnet, blaming themselves and each other, blaming God and chance, remembering the living child.

After moments or hours they perched shoulder to shoulder on the floor, hugging their knees, sharing a handkerchief.

"And what do we do now?" Anne asked at last,

"We go on, my dear. We look to our daughters, I look to my playing company and my writing, which I think from now on will be only plays, I make money. Do you still want New Place?"

She nodded. "More than ever. I don't want to live again in a place where Hamnet lived. I don't care if the house is falling down, I'd sooner move in with all its dirt."

"Then we shall."

"That poem you spoke to me that day in the Forest; did you truly write that for me?"

"I truly did. Because I'd learnt by then what I had, and nearly lost. I do love you, Anne, and without you there's no comfort in the world."

She looked assessingly at him for a while, then said with a brisk nod, "I know you love me. And I know I can never be everything to you. But I won't take away what completes you. So we'll go on as we did. Stratford is home, you'll come when you can, and sometimes I will come to London, when our daughters want to come."

"Judith will never want to. She must stay where Hamnet is."

"Later she will. I won't let grief fill her life. Or mine. Or yours. But if you go to London, Will..."

"I will share my lodgings with Edmund, I will work, I will see my friends, including Harry, but you need fear no... attachments. That is in the past. All of it is in the past." They looked at each other again in silence. "Remember we said, clap hands and a bargain? Never again will I renege on a contract. I broke my wedding vows, but that's my past. Stratford now is my future."

"A bargain," she said, and they clasped each other's hand. The first time they'd met they had touched hands and William had beguiled her with words. As he always would do, no doubt.

"Come," she said, "let's take the girls and go look at our new house, our *gentleman's* house, and start our plans. That side garden wall must come down and we should rebuild the outhouses."

"There'll be a lot to do," he agreed, and followed her down the stairs. "And years in which to do it. But Anne, is there a writing room for me there? A library? There'll be no more poetry, but I must write my plays, every year, even when I'm home."

Anne glanced back over her shoulder, half-smiling. "Yes, Will, there's a library. It was the first thing I thought of when I saw the house."

"Good. And I think we'll plant roses. And mulberry trees. We could play with our grandchildren in the shade of a mulberry tree. And a grape-vine?"

"Not warm enough for grapes."

"We could try... Go and fetch the girls, and we will see."

Epilogue

1603

"The grapes flourished. The roses, too. And things changed, of course. I went home less and less, yet when I was there it was more real than London, I loved it more, and I wrote more there. Here..." William turned away and went to the window, staring down into the swirling fog that misted Tower Green. On his first visit to London, he had come here to see the Tower, that epitome of English history. Never had he thought he would be here like this, bribing the guard to let him in to visit a prisoner, waiting through an icy night that could spell the end of a reign or of his lover's life. Harry's little black and white cat, Deborah, sprang up onto the window seat and rubbed her head against his arm. Absently he stroked her, as once he had stroked her master. "Here," William went on as the cat purred, "here in London, it was all business. Running a playhouse. Building the Globe. I was back to clerking and keeping accounts, just as I did for my father twenty years ago. And acting, of course. All the usual routine of a show a day, six days a week, and fretting over the management of the whole thing, and going on the road. Never writing, it seems."

Harry had said nothing for almost an hour. He was watching the clock. "But you did write. All those plays."

"Oh yes, of course I did. But at home, in Stratford, in our beautiful house. Not here in London. And when I am at home, I am William Shakspere the glover's son, the landowner and wool dealer and malt dealer, not William Shakspere the playwright and poet. Stop a man in the street in Stratford and ask what I do for a living and he wouldn't know, except that he'd probably say I must make a fair amount out of wool and malt. Pushed, that man might say he's heard I own shares in a playhouse or some such thing. Meaningless, at home."

"Except to your wife and daughters?"

"My daughters spend my money and don't care where it comes from. But Anne cares in her way. Now she's come under her brother's influence and turned Puritan. So has Susanna. Odd,

I never thought Anne cared much for religion. Susanna is interested in a doctor – calls himself a physician – called John Hall, and he's rabidly Puritan and does not approve of me. Of my money, yes, but not of me or my work."

"Does Anne ever come to London? I've been away so much…"

"She comes sometimes. When we built the Globe, for instance, she came to the opening performances. She brought Susanna and Judith. Susanna liked the plays and the visit to London, but Judith was bored."

"She doesn't understand how famous you are? Your reputation?"

"She has no idea, and couldn't care if she did. She's a country girl and keen on men. She blames me for her brother's death."

"Surely not."

"Oh yes."

Harry came to join him at the window. "You note they have given me a room with a view of Tower Green. Of the beheading ground. Where Essex died. And so many others. And," he laughed wryly, "they charge extra for a room with a view. I pay nine pounds a week for this."

"They make you *pay*?"

"The final refinement. Yes." His fingers closed on William's arm. "If the old bitch doesn't die, she'll put me to death after all."

"Even now? After two years?"

"She never did like me."

"Well, you did join Essex's rebellion against her. You were neck-deep in treason, Harry."

"Oh, can no one resist the temptation to say 'I told you so'?"

"I haven't said that."

"You mean it, though."

William sighed. They sat down, turning their backs on the window. The cat jumped into Harry's lap. Cuddling her, he said, "For a while she was my only friend, my only visitor. D'you know, she made her way here from Southampton House to be with me?"

"A touching story."

"True."

"You mean, why did I never come to visit you before tonight."

"Well, why didn't you?"

"Because what we had was over years ago. Because these past seven years I have been busy being a good, conscientious father and husband – as have you – and playhouse owner. Keeping out of trouble. It is not wise to visit prisoners in the Tower of London. Or at least not wise for ordinary people like me, people without power and influence."

"I have no power or influence now," said Harry. "Nor title. They stripped me of everything. I'm plain Mr Wriothesley. We're equal. Middle-aged married men. You've probably more money than I now. We're equals."

"Unless the queen dies and Scotch James becomes king."

"Unless."

"Why did you do it, Harry? Why did you join in that brainless, hopeless rebellion of Essex's? Because he was your lover? Because you loved him?"

Harry put the cat into William's lap and stood up. He poured two glasses of wine. Fine, expensive crystal glasses, William noted, despite his pleas of poverty. "He was my lover but I never loved him. A few times, when we were young together, and again in Ireland, on military service there. But there was loyalty, of a kind. I knew how badly the Queen treated him over his command of the Irish campaign, I thought he had reason.

"Although now, two years later, I suppose a lot of it was vanity and spite. He thought he had made the Queen love him beyond reason. But Elizabeth Tudor loves no one beyond reason. So I joined him in his stupid, petty, badly planned rebellion, and he was beheaded down there." He pointed over his shoulder to Tower Green. "And for some reason I was not put to death. Just indeterminate imprisonment; not for the first time, of course – remember when I married Bess Vernon she popped us both into prison till her temper cooled.

"And if the Queen rallies, lives, comes back to health, she'll have my head."

"They say she's past that, they say she's dying."

"'They' have been saying that for days, for weeks, for years. She uses it, Will, she plays at ill-health. She takes to her bed and swears it's her death-bed. She's been doing that for forty-five years."

William shook his head. "This time it is sure. I asked."

"Oh, before you dared visit me?"

"Don't reproach me too far, Harry. I would have tried to talk you out of that rebellion, had you asked me, or told me of it. I would have done anything to stop you taking part. Don't forget that when you and your friends asked my playing company to stage *Richard the Second* for you, with its dangerous, dangerous theme of regicide and rebellion, I did so. That nearly had the lot of us in here with you. But we talked our way out of it. We said we did it for the money."

"And did you not do it for the money? Or did you believe, just a little, in our rebellion?"

"I never believed in it. The Scotch king will be the Queen's heir, without silly plots in his favour. But I put that play on for you. Out of the memory of our love. I did love you, Harry, very much."

Harry leaned his head against William's shoulder. "And I you. It seems so very long ago."

"Nearly ten years."

"And I am married now, and a father. Just as you advised in all those poems. Like your Anne when you married her, Bess was with child and loved me. And it was worth it for my child, my daughter."

A little time went by in silence. They drank their wine, petted the cat, let their hands meet on the animal's fur.

"So why did you come tonight?" Harry asked again.

"Because it is sure the Queen cannot live the night out. She will die, James will be king of England and you will be free. Earl of Southampton again. Because it is the end of a reign, and of the only monarch you and I have ever known. And because it seemed a good time to ask you something."

"What?" Harry sounded very tired.

"That woman. That Scotchwoman. That dark woman. Marian something."

"What of her?"

"Was she a spy? For Scotland?"

Laughing, Harry said, "Oh yes, all the time. That is, she was spying on who was *not* for King James. Burghley, Essex, me – we were all in it, all for James. If the Queen dies and James of Scotland becomes King, you'll see her riding in his coronation procession. A hundred years ago her parents were for York, you see, and fled to Scotland after King Richard died at Bosworth

Field. Her father's an earl, and an intimate of the King's. So yes, you'll see the Lady Marian Robsart, meek as butter, her husband conveniently dead, no hint of the whoring spy, riding with King James's courtiers. She did quite a lot of spying, I think. She was after Essex, and didn't get him. But me she got, and had, for a while."

"And you told her secrets?"

"Oh, Will, what secrets did I ever know? I was never in favour at court, never given any duties, never in the Queen's confidence, never part of the spying service like Essex or poor Christopher Marlowe. Ten years since he died, Will, ten years in May. So no, I had no secrets to sell. I didn't betray my country. Unless you count sending letters to that Scotch sodomite James, assuring him of my support and utter loyalty at need."

"Was that what the rebellion was about?" William asked.

"Yes. Essex thought he would overthrow the Queen and invite James down from Scotland to take her place. Glory and rich rewards for Essex and Southampton *et alia*. A stupid plot."

"One put up to you by that Scotchwoman and her friends?"

"Not to me. Perhaps she did get to Essex. Not in bed, though. She bedded you and me for fun, I think."

"Fun that nearly cost me my wife, and did cost me my son's life. And cost me you."

"Never. Everything has changed, but nothing can take away the memories." With a change of tone he went on, "You remember that hundred pounds I gave you ten years ago?"

"Why, do you want it back? I could afford to pay it now."

"Of course I don't want it back. I just meant, I gave you that money because I was in love with you and wanted to give you a gift. And now, because I still love you, if in a different way, I can give you another gift. If I live. If the Queen dies. If James becomes king."

"What gift, Harry?"

"King James of Scotland likes plays, likes your plays. They perform them at his court in Scotland. He admires you. For me, and for his admiration of your plays, and perhaps a little for that dark-haired woman who spied for him, on you as much as on the Queen, James will make your playing company his royal one. The King's Men, William. Royal servants. Courtiers. You will be the King's playwright. You will have his royal protection forever. And money. Position, status. You are already famous, you need no one, king or commoner, to give you fame, but it is not nothing to be the King's playwright and his favourite."

"I know it." William lifted Harry's hand and kissed it. "Thank you. Odd, isn't it? I wanted to be known as a poet. All I wrote was three long poems and a clutch of sonnets, and it's my plays people clamour for. But they'll go out of fashion, you know. Already it's all these new men, Jonson, Fletcher, Beaumont. New men. I'm going out of fashion."

"Not yet. You'll write great plays for King James."

"Perhaps."

"You will. And if that bell rings, the Westminster passing bell, to say the Queen is dead, then you can start buying your scarlet livery, for you'll be established forever, you and your fellow players. Not any other players, not for the King. You, and yours. He'll commission plays from you, Will."

"I'll have to dance to his tune, you mean."

"You won't dare write anything he doesn't approve, but what's new about that? You barely got away with *Richard the Second*. Will you ever write a play about the Queen? *Elizabeth the First*, by William Shakspere? *Queen Elizabeth*? *Gloriana*, perhaps?"

"I doubt it. About her father, perhaps. Although I've little enough interest in history plays any more."

"I enjoyed your *Hamlet*," Harry said. "And *Henry the Fifth*. I've been little enough to the theatre in these past few years, but those I did see."

"You did all the things I longed to as a boy; you've been a soldier, you've been to sea, you've fought on campaign."

"Ireland," Harry said on a grunt of contempt.

"Yes, Ireland. I used to want all those things."

"You've written about them, you've made them real to other people."

"I suppose so."

"Will you," Harry said, "ever write about me?"

"Oh my dear, I have. Every golden youth I've ever written was you."

"And every woman was Anne?"

"No. But some of them were her, at least in part. The loving, steadfast wives were all Anne. No doubt more will be, too. Or my daughters. The rest are, as usual, imagination. And one day soon people will lose interest in my plays and laugh at my poetry. I'll be out of fashion and forgotten. And then I shall retire permanently to Stratford and marry off my daughters and sit by the fireside with my wife and fret about repairing my house and saving my money."

"Or go on to even greater fortune as the King's pet playwright. Perhaps he'll knight you. Give you a pension."

"I'd like it, but I doubt it."

"It's possible. Anything is possible."

"Trite but true."

They were holding hands now and William could feel the pulse in Harry's wrist racing. "Whatever happens," he said awkwardly, "she won't put you to death. Not now."

"She might." Harry's blue eyes had dilated with fear and tension so that they looked entirely black. Black as that woman's. "She might give the order as the last thing she does, to show that traitors are not to be forgiven. Even as she dies, so might I, by her order. Or someone may try to seize the crown before James can do so. Think of Lady Jane Grey. There are always ambitious people, always people plotting. If I am to live, James must become king. Elizabeth killed his mother and he has never forgotten or forgiven that. Her enemies are his friends. His friends are her enemies, and she may be vengeful even after death." Feverish colour burning in his face, he turned to William again. "If I die, write something for me. Something on my death. So that I shan't be altogether forgotten. Promise me, Will."

"I promise."

"And that song of yours, the one that woman set to music, *fear no more the heat o' the sun*, make that mine, say it at my funeral or over my grave. Make my grave renownéd."

"I promise. But there is no need, Harry, the Queen will die, you will live. And when we meet again, you as the new King's Counsellor, perhaps, me as one of his tame players, we'll bow and perhaps talk. You'll tell me of your children and your wife, I'll speak of mine, and then I will retire to Stratford and be forgotten, and sometimes I will hear news of the Earl of Southampton's latest glories. I promise."

Muffled at first by the fog, a sound began to come clearly to this room. Outside, the passing bell was ringing, to say the Queen was dead.

The End

Of the people in this novel:

Elizabeth I died on 24 March 1603 and was succeeded by James VI of Scotland. In April 1603 the new king issued Letters Patent making the Shakespeare's company The King's Men. Shakespeare wrote some of his greatest plays after Queen Elizabeth's death, and retired, rich and famous, to Stratford not long before he died in April 1616.

Anne Shakespeare died in August 1623. Famously, or notoriously, Shakespeare left her only his 'second-best bed' in his will, which may mean anything or nothing. Probably her husband assumed she was automatically entitled to the widow's share of one third of his estate, although some biographers say there was no such entitlement in Warwickshire. If not, unless she had some private settlement of money, Anne was left to the tender mercies of her elder daughter and son-in-law.

Susanna Shakespeare married John Hall, a Puritan and quack physician without any medical training, on 5 June 1607. Although in his will Shakespeare was pathetically anxious to settle his estate on Susanna's male heirs, she and Hall had only one child, a girl, Elizabeth, born in February 1608. She married Thomas Nash, son of one of her grandfather's friends, in 1626, and after his death married John Barnard, who later received or bought a baronetcy. Lady Barnard died without issue, and the Shakespeare estate went to her Hart cousins. Susanna Hall died in July 1649, her husband in 1625. The Halls received the bulk of Shakespeare's estate in his will. (In 1637 creditors chasing a debt against Hall's estate broke into New Place and stole "divers books...and other goods of greater value", probably including all of Shakespeare's books and other papers.)

Judith Shakespeare was thirty-one when she married Thomas Quiney, son of a prominent Stratford family, in February 1616. The following month her husband was found to have impregnated one Margaret Wheeler, who with her baby died in childbirth. It must have been a juicy Stratford scandal, and may have accounted for Shakespeare's reducing Judith's portion of his estate and making sure Quiney couldn't get his hands on her inheritance. None of Judith's children survived her. She died in 1662.

Shakespeare's **father** died in 1601, his **mother** in 1608. None of his brothers married. **Gilbert** died in February 1612, **Richard** in February 1613, and **Edmund** in December 1607, five months after the death of his illegitimate son. He is buried in Southwark Cathedral, and it can be assumed that William paid for his funeral with the expensive tolling of the passing bell.

Joan Shakespeare married William **Hart**, who died a few days before his famous brother-in-law and presumably of the same disease. Joan died in 1646, and it was the descendants of her several children who eventually inherited what was left of Shakespeare's estate.

The **Earl of Southampton** was released from prison by King James on 5 April 1603, and restored to his titles and properties. (True or not, the story that his cat followed him to the Tower is recorded.) He had married Elizabeth Vernon in 1598, only just before the birth of their first child, Penelope. They had four other children, and their marriage seems to have been happy and affectionate. In 1624 Southampton, like Shakespeare, suffered the anguish of watching his son die, then himself died the next day, presumably of whatever killed his son. By his daughter Penelope's marriage to a Spencer of Althorp, Southampton was the ancestor on their mother's side of Their Royal Highnesses The Princes William and Harry of Wales.

I have always read a lot of and about Shakespeare. In the 1990s, when I was stuck between a contemporary novel and what would become my first published novel, *Treason,* I became very irritated with so many (mostly male) authors' insistence that the tortured genius fled a carping, illiterate farmer's daughter who, thoroughly on the shelf at twenty-six (in fact exactly the average age for Tudor women to marry), trapped him into a shotgun marriage and saddled him with three children before he was twenty-one. We all have our own 'vision' of Shakespeare, and mine did not include the unhappy marriage or horrible wife that is so readily assumed. So I started writing a novel about a happily married but unfaithful, bisexual Shakespeare. And then the film *Shakespeare in Love* came along, and suddenly there was a new novel about Shakespeare almost every week. So this book went on being my 'security blanket' when I was stuck with other writing – until one day I realised I'd finished it and had nothing more to say. So far.

Hard, provable facts about William Shakespeare and his wife are scarce, although as research and scholarship march on, one would now need not the back of a stamp but perhaps a postcard to fill with what is known. We know the date of his baptism (26 April 1564) and the date of his death (23 April 1616) but not the date he was born. We know he married Anne Hathaway in November 1582 and that their first child, Susanna, was born six months later. We know the baptismal dates and names of his three children, the date of publication of his long narrative poems, and when, but not why, his son Hamnet died.

There are records of his land and house purchases and of his endearing refusal to pay taxes, and of his (evidently reluctant) involvement in legal disputes. There is nothing provably in his handwriting. There are six extant signatures, all different, three of them (possibly forged or "assisted") on that curious document, his will, clearly made when he was too ill to know what he was doing, and in which he almost forgot to leave his wife anything.

There is little agreement about when most of his plays were written except where there is an extant record of someone seeing one of the plays. The few other facts give us no real picture of Shakespeare.

No one knows whether the Sonnets tell the story of two real and passionate love affairs (as they do in this novel) or if they were simply sophisticated literary exercises. Certainly it seems Shakespeare made no attempt to publish them, but nor did he attempt to publish his play scripts, yet he took great care with the publication of his two long poems. That the plays still exist at all is due to the dedicated work of two of his fellow actors.

So most biographies are about five percent fact and (except for Bill Bryson's recent book) the rest wishful thinking, imagination or some very strange assumptions. Really we know nothing about the private Shakespeare.

Might as well write fiction, then, and have some fun.

Meredith Whitford. 2010, 2018

Select Bibliography

Ackroyd, Peter	Shakespeare: The Biography. Chatto & Windus, London, 2005
Akrigg, G P V	*Shakespeare and the Earl of Southampton.* Hamish Hamilton, London, 1968
Auden, W H	*The Dyer's Hand and other essays.* Vintage Books, 1968 edition
Bate, Jonathon	The Genius of Shakespeare. Picador, London, 1997
Bryson, Bill	*Shakespeare.* (For the Eminent Lives Series) Faber & Faber, 2007
Cook, Judith	*Shakespeare's Players.* Harrap, 1983
Duff Cooper, Alfred	*Sergeant Shakespeare,* Viking Press, New York, 1950
Duncan-Jones, Katherine	*Ungentle Shakespeare: Scenes from his life.* The Arden Shakespeare, 2001.
Greenblatt, Stephen	*Will in the World: How Shakespeare Became Shakespeare.* Jonathon Cape, 2004.
Greenblatt et al (eds.)	*The Norton Shakespeare,* 2nd ed. WW Norton and Company, 2008
Greer, Germaine	*Shakespeare's Wife.* Bloomsbury Publishing Plc, London, 2007
Honan, Park	*Shakespeare: A Life.* OUP, 1998
Kermode, Frank	*The Age of Shakespeare.* New York Modern Library
Kernan, Alvin	*Shakespeare, the King's Playwright.* Yale University, 1995
Kerrigan, John (ed)	*William Shakespeare: The Sonnets and A Lover's Complaint.* Penguin Classics, 1986.
Nolan, Stephanie	*Shakespeare's Face.* Text Publishing, 2002.
Nuttall, A D	*Shakespeare the Thinker.* Yale University Press, 2007
Plowden, Alison	*Tudor Women: queens and commoners.* Sutton, London, 2002

Schoenbaum, S

Shakespeare's Lives. Clarendon Press, Oxford, 1991
William Shakespeare: a compact documentary life. OUP, 1987

Sim, Alison

The Tudor Housewife. Sutton Publishing, 2001

Stone, Lawrence

The Family, Sex and Marriage in England 1500-1800. Weidenfeld & Nicholson, London, 1977

Wells, Stanley

Shakespeare for all time. Macmillan, 2002

About the author

Meredith Whitford lives in Adelaide, South Australia. Educated entirely after leaving school, she finally went to university as a mature-age student. In her BA she majored in history, with English and Classics minors. In 2011 she graduated Master of Creative Arts (Creative Writing) from Flinders University, Adelaide.

A professional editor, she has been Director of *Between Us* Manuscript Assessment Service (www.betweenusmanuscripts.com) since 1998.

Her first novel, *Treason,* won the 2002 international Eppie Award for historical fiction. *Shakespeare's Will* has been sold into China, for publication in translation. Her other published books are the biography *Churchill's Rebels: Jessica Mitford & Esmond Romilly* (which won a Wishing Shelf Readers' Award), and the modern novel *Missing Christina.*

When she is not writing or reading (and she usually is) her hobbies are history, cryptic crosswords and sleeping.

She suffers from Chronic Fatigue Syndrome (ME/CFS). On the up side, she has the great good luck to be a synaesthete.

She can be contacted at:
meredithwh@yahoo.com
meredithjwhitford@gmail
T: meredith_wh
F: Meredith Whitford Author
http://meredithwh.wixsite.com/home